Jokers Club

By
Gregory Bastianelli

JournalStone
San Francisco

JournalStone books may be ordered through booksellers or by contacting:

JournalStone
199 State Street
San Mateo, CA 94401
www.journalstone.com

The views expressed in this work are solely those of the authors and do not necessarily reflect the views of the publisher, and the publisher hereby disclaims any responsibility for them.

ISBN: 978-1-936564-30-9 (sc)
ISBN: 978-1-936564-31-6 (dj)
ISBN: 978-1-936564-32-3 (ebook)

Library of Congress Control Number: 2011938190

Printed in the United States of America
JournalStone rev. date: November 4, 2011

Cover Design: Denise Daniel
Cover Art: Philip Renne
Author Photo: John Huff

Edited By: Elizabeth Reuter

Acknowledgements

I would like to thank the staff at JournalStone for providing me with this opportunity and for the enthusiasm they have shown for this manuscript. I also want to thank my parents for their support; my children, Casey and Jenna, for providing me such life fulfillment; and my Aunt Agnes for encouraging my writing.

Several people previously read this manuscript and provided helpful insight, especially Richard Krawiec and Jim Spilios, and my many friends who always believed in me. I also owe gratitude to my writing instructors at the University of New Hampshire: Mark Smith, Thomas Williams and Theodore Weisner.

Of course, none of this would have been possible if my imagination had not been sparked by the likes of Ray Bradbury, Richard Matheson, Robert Bloch, Stephen King and Peter Straub. And a special thanks to Cherrie Nesman and her children, Andrew and Emma, for bringing a bright light into my life.

To my sister Deanna, for her encouragement, criticism, advice and concern that stretches back many years.

Check out these titles from JournalStone:

Shaman's Blood
Anne C. Petty

The Traiteur's Ring
Jeffrey Wilson

Duncan's Diary, Birth of a Serial Killer
Christopher C. Payne

Ghosts of Coronado Bay
J.G. Faherty

Imperial Hostage, Book 1 of the Destruction Series
Phil Cantrill

That Which Should Not Be
Brett J. Talley

Reign of the Nightmare Prince
Mike Phillips

Available through your local and online bookseller or at
www.journalstone.com

CHAPTER ONE

I had only typed a single line on the page:

"Jason Nightingale had no idea when he joined the Jokers Club of the horrible events that would follow."

Sitting in my rental car on the side of the highway after having driven all night, I felt inside my shirt pocket for that piece of paper. The rest of the page was blank, and I had stared at it many times trying to fill its emptiness. I took it out, unfolded it and looked at it again on that backwoods road -- a long runway through a gauntlet of pines and maples: tall trees whose branches stretched across the pavement, almost touching. The sun had risen moments ago and light splintered through the limbs. I had pulled over for just a moment, to rest and shake the sleepiness from my eyes. I had inadvertently dozed for a few minutes.

It was early October, and most of the leaves had turned a pumpkin shade, with splashes of red and yellow here and there. Leaves lay discarded along the embankment. Some departed their limbs and drifted down silently, settling on the hood of the car. If I stayed here long enough, the entire automobile would be buried.

The road reminded me of a dream I had about a week before. I was traveling on the very same route, but on foot. It was early morning, and a light mist hugged the asphalt surface. I was walking down the center yellow lines, toward town. It was quiet.

Up ahead in the darkness was a figure shuffling toward town, its movements slow and stiff and its body hunched over. I was gaining on him.

Tattered clothes hung on his thin body, lending him the appearance of a walking scarecrow. I wanted to catch up to him, find out who he was and where he was going.

As the road veered upward, his movements slowed. I didn't think he would make it up the hill, and I stopped to watch. Each progression was a slow, jerking movement. I could sense pain in those steps. When he reached the top, he stopped and, without turning, languidly motioned with one arm for me to follow. With caution, I ascended the hill, wary of the figure at the top whose back was still to me. My body shook with a chill as I came alongside him.

"Why did you come back?" he asked, staring straight ahead. I gazed at what lay below us, the town of Malton. It cuddled along the perimeter of the lake like a sleeping lover too early to awaken. I turned back to the man beside me. I had recognized the strained voice asking the question.

The face turned toward me. It was long and thin, skin drawn tight on the cheek-and-jawbones like dried leather, stubble poking through the flesh. There were dark bags beneath bloodshot eyes swallowed up in their sockets. His unkempt hair looked gritty.

I know this man, I thought. It's Paul Woodman. *My God he's so thin.* I didn't like thinking about the last time I had seen him.

"Woody," I said. "It's good to see you."

His gaze shifted back to the town. "You shouldn't be here."

"I had to come back. I needed to."

"None of us should be here." His brow furrowed, and his eyes squinted, as if he were concentrating on something or remembering something. "Not after what happened."

"That wasn't our fault, Woody."

He looked at me. "Do you really believe that?"

I do. Yes, I really do. I couldn't answer him.

There was a stump I hadn't noticed before, right in the middle of the road where we stood. Woody sat on it slowly, carefully, like a constipated man settling his buttocks on a toilet seat. He winced with pain.

"God, my muscles ache," he said.

I looked down at the pathetic creature he had become.

"Why have you punished yourself, Woody?" It was a question I had asked before, at that other time, at that other place that also seemed like a dreamland.

"It's too late for me. But not for you."

"What are you talking about?"

"Let the past lie."

"I can't." I looked back at the flickering lights from the buildings below. "It's all I have left."

He stood up and turned away. "I have to go now."

I watched him as he proceeded back down the hill, feeling the pain in his shuffling steps. "Will I be seeing you, Woody?"

He stopped and for a moment, I didn't think he was going to answer. Then he turned and looked up at me.

"Don't open it."

"Huh?" Open what? What the heck was he talking about? Did he mean the past?

He walked off and was enveloped in the mist. I stared after him for a while and then realized I was awake. I felt cold and alone. Unlike most dreams, the memory of this one lingered for quite some time.

When I looked out the windshield, I saw the leaves, brightly colored like burning embers, had nearly covered the hood of the car. I realized how long I had been sitting by the side of the road lost in thought. I started the engine and pulled away, the leaves bouncing off the windshield, scattering in the vehicle's wake.

As the car began its ascent of the hill I had frequented recently in the dream, I took in the town I had not seen in years. The descent onto Main Street brought forth colonial brick and wood-framed houses soon giving way to small shops and businesses: Mr. Pepper's Five and Ten; the Malton Lake Loom Shop; Nick's Barbershop; The Cobbler Shop; The Used Office Supply Store; The Book Bazaar; Mr. Under's Lakeside Memorials; Town Hall; St. Charles Church; the First National Bank.

A grassy, pie-shaped island wedged into the end of Main Street just before the lake split the road in two, its tributaries becoming Lakeview Boulevard which ran along the perimeter of the downtown side of the lake. A granite fountain stood at the tip of the island. Its water dried up in the fall like the rest of the town. The gazebo directly behind the fountain held folk singers and jazz quartets in the summer but cobwebs and shadows in colder months. The little boutiques and galleries that lined the boulevard across from the lakefront were closed and boarded up against the winter winds that sweep across the lake. Parking meters along the boulevard were decapitated after Labor Day, leaving headless poles lined like grave markers. The boardwalk that separated the boulevard from the public beach lay still like an empty railroad bed, its wooden planks warped and scuffed from the wear and tear of summer crowds. To the left of the beach, the marina slips held only a few boats, wrapped in canvas tarps. Summer cottages poking out through the woods on the other side of the lake were lonely beacons, their occupants gone back to Massachusetts or wherever they had migrated from for the summer.

That side of the lake seemed another world away, accessible as the moon from this side.

An old woman walked her dog along the boardwalk, their feet clicking on the planks, and a car drifted by on the boulevard. Other than that there was no one around. I rolled down the car window and felt the cool air blowing over from the lake.

I pulled into a parking space in front of the Book Bazaar. Something in the window caught my eye. I got out of the car and approached the store. My eyes widened, and I smiled. There on the display shelf were copies of three horror novels, all with the name of the same author: Geoffrey Thorn. That was my name, my book titles. It felt good to know my success reached all the way home, where the stories had really begun. It made it all worthwhile. Not just the money, but to know I had succeeded. It felt so unreal, as if I could blink and it would all be gone.

I did blink.

It was gone.

The window display held some faded gardening books, long past their timeliness for this season. I looked around.

My homecoming wouldn't be what it should have been -- what it could have been. I had no books published; I had given up writing years earlier. The rejection slips had swamped me, pulled me down like a fierce undertow, drowning my hopes and my confidence. My success lived only in my fantasies. I touched my shirt pocket. All I held was a piece of paper with one line printed on it, one line that led nowhere. I hoped that here in Malton I could find the rest of the story that came after that sentence. Then I could come away from here with a resolution to the decision that was also a part of my return. Only then could I go back to New York City and my mundane job at the textbook publishing company. I had fled to the city with a fury that was going to drive me to the top. Instead, I had clawed out of the pit with my inspiration shattered.

I laughed. It occurred to me in my rush to get here, I forgot to pack my laptop. Some writer I was. Even if I was inspired, I had nothing to write with.

I looked down the block. It was too early for most of the businesses to be open, but I spied the used office supply store and noticed it was busily occupied. I passed the other empty shops and walked in, a bell ringing on the door as I entered. A bespectacled old man with a feather duster was cleaning a shelf of adding machines. He glanced at me with barely a twitch of his facial muscles.

"Hi," I said, looking around and feeling awkward with the lack of response. The left side of the store contained rows of several types of wooden and metal office desks. Filing cabinets of different heights lined the back wall; shelves of adding machines and typewriters clung to the wall on my right. Everything looked antiquated. "Any used laptops for rent?"

"Ha," he said. "Have you looked around the place?"

I had and realized it was a foolish question.

"I've got some 'lectric typewriters, best I can do."

Figures, I thought. I hadn't used one since I was a kid. I remembered my mother bringing me in here to purchase my first typewriter. It was a junior high school graduation present. I marveled at the bright shiny machines and imagined all the stories I could write on them, instead of the spiral notebook and pencil I regularly used. I could write so much more with one of these, I had thought at the time.

This same old man had been the proprietor then. I looked over the rows of antiques, running my fingers along dusty keys. At least the letters were the same. I walked out of there with a small case and a ream of paper. Blank paper I was hoping to fill. And if I couldn't, this whole trip might be a waste.

I got in the car and pulled onto the boulevard, driving along the right side of the lake. The beach was empty, like most of the town. To the east of the pooling water, the sun had cleared the tops of the pine trees. Soon the town would be awakening: businessmen sifting in to open their shops, kids waiting at street corner bus stops for their escorts to school.

As I rounded the lake, past the public beach, away from the stores and shops, I could see the old Victorian mansion looming ahead of me on the right. I pulled in front of it and stopped.

The iconic structure had been empty when I moved away. It had been owned by a trio of aged spinster sisters by the name of Peas who collected stray cats by the dozens. After two of the Peas sisters died, the lone survivor became a recluse. The house deteriorated, becoming nothing more than a pile of weathered, graying clapboards. Finally, after a strange odor began exuding from the walls, the police broke in and found the sole remaining sister had died. They didn't know how long she had been dead, but they surmised it must have been a while. The cats had gone hungry and picked her flesh nearly clean to the bone.

After several years of desertion, the mansion had been renovated into the Tower House Inn. Its walls were painted a light, glossy blue that, when struck by the dawn light, resembled the lake water it overlooked. A cylindrical turret loomed large in the center of the mansion, looking much like the tower of the inn's name. A wide porch, with a hanging swing, clung to the front frame of the house. On both sides of the stone walkway that led to the front steps was a black wrought iron fence with pointed spikes. It was four-feet high and ran the length of the walkway and along the perimeter of the front lawn. A set of white-painted metal patio furniture chairs lay scattered on the neat trim lawn. A flower bed encased in a rim of stones occupied the landscaping. Rising from its center was a post with a wooden sign that read: Tower House Inn – Bed & Breakfast.

Underneath it: Strangers Welcomed.

It was too early to check in. I continued driving along the boulevard which soon gave way to Autumn Avenue. I realized I was heading toward my old neighborhood so I turned quickly down a dirt lane that led through the woods by the east side of the lake. I knew where it would take me.

I parked the car and got out, walking along the familiar path. It was still worn from recent use and I wound my way along it, past evergreens and birches. There was a chill in the air. A breeze from the water was weaving its way through the trees. I heard the slight lapping of waves and came to the clearing.

This was a spot I had been to many times while growing up. The oak tree still stood at the edge of the banking, the rope swing hanging from a limb that stretched out over the water. Though the rope had been replaced many times over the years, it was still all the same to me. Voices from the past hung in the air around me. I remembered wrapping my hands firmly around the fraying rope, just above the knot, running forward and, with a holler, lifting my legs and sailing out. I remember the feeling when the rope reached its peak and you hung there in mid air for just a fraction of a second, but it seemed long enough that you could look across the lake at the town and wave to the people on the boardwalk. You would let go of the rope and gravity would reach up and grab you by the ankles, yanking you down, the air whooshing by, the water parting at the touch of your toes, swallowing you up. The world shut off from your senses. Your feet would touch the soft, sandy bottom and your knees would bend and propel yourself upwards, the screams of the others filling your ears as you broke the surface.

Yes, I remembered.

I turned and, as if finding an old friend, I spotted the other oak. I didn't know if it was the chill in the air, but I shivered. I wasn't sure if I expected it to be there or not. Maybe I figured it would have died and fallen by now. But it was there.

I walked over to it, stood in front of it, and scanned the bark. They were still there. It didn't seem possible, after all these years. I had been nineteen when I carved them and didn't realize they would last this long.

But there they were, at eye level: G.T. & M.R.

There were other initials and obscenities carved in the bark around it, but mine had been first. They stood out strong and clear after all this time. It's too bad the relationship hadn't lasted as long.

Meg Rand.

I ran my fingers along the furrows of our initials.

Then the headache struck.

They had started a few months ago. The first of the symptoms Dr. Cutler said I would experience, followed by blurred vision, blackouts, maybe even hallucinations. It felt like a claw had ripped its way through my scalp and grabbed my brain in a vise-like grip – and squeezed. Pain burst through the left side of my skull. My feet became wobbly as everything blurred around me. I grabbed hold of the oak, nails biting into the bark, to steady myself and stood there, head hung down, waiting for the roaring pain inside to subside.

As it started to dissipate, I opened my eyes and looked up. As my vision cleared and I began to focus, I noticed the words carved just above my initials on the tree. I didn't remember seeing them before.

It said: R. U. Next?

I wondered what it meant, who it was meant for. It almost seemed like a message speaking to me. (Next? Next for what?) Even though it was a question, it felt more like a warning, or a threat.

I don't know how long I stood there, staring at some silly words that surely weren't meant for me. I left the tree and headed back to my car.

There was no getting around it. My car knew where to go, and I let it lead me, feeling the steering wheel move in my hands as I turned onto Maple Street. I drove slowly, the houses coasting past me, anticipation building. I could catch a glimpse of it up ahead. Just a glimpse, but my throat dried up and my heartbeat hesitated. It came into full view, and I stopped in front of it and got out of the car.

My house.

This was where it all began. This was where it all happened. This was my neighborhood. Ten, fifteen, twenty years ago. The years drifted backwards like pages in a book. (But I haven't written it. Can't get past that first line.) Nothing changed; it was all still the same.

This was my playground, where my stories began, the tales grew. There in the ravine of trees between the rows of houses on Maple and Elm streets. There in the Pines on the hill beyond. There down the end of Shadow Drive where the Tin Man's house stood.

I shuddered.

I stared at my house.

Paul Woodman's house stood on one side, Dale Carpenter's on Elm Street behind the ravine. Oliver Rench lived across the street from me, Lonny Mudge beside him. Martin Peek's house was over on Autumn Avenue. And down Maple Street, on the corner of Shadow Drive, was Jason Nightingale's house.

I could feel it in the air. We were all here. This is where I wanted to be, where I really wanted to be. I could feel it now. A group of boys, maybe eleven years old, maybe twelve are running toward the ravine.

It's Martin, Woody and Dale. Oliver and Lonny. And my god, it's Jason too. They stop and look at me, waving their arms for me to follow.

Come on, Geoff, Jason calls out, waving his arm frantically,

My body tries to move, but my feet are embedded in the cement of the sidewalk. How I want to go with them.

Hurry up, Geoff, Jason calls again. *We're gonna play the game.*

No, I thought. Don't play the game. "No!" I screamed out loud. *(Don't open it)*, I thought. *(Don't open it)* and nothing bad will happen.

I turned around and looked across the street at the dead, burnt maple tree in Oliver's back yard with its scorched bark and amputated limbs.

Why did they leave it up? Someone should have cut it down.

"We can't play the game anymore," I said to no one, because no one was there.

I left the neighborhood and drove to the inn to see if it was okay to check in yet. I parked in the gravel lot and stepped out of the car. The typewriter and ream of paper were in one hand and my hurriedly packed suitcase in the other. I walked up the wooden steps which creaked under my weight like an old man's aching bones and imagined as I reached for the doorknob that if I opened the heavy oak door I would see dozens of cats running around the interior of the lobby, licking their chops.

I grabbed hold of the cold brass handle and turned it, pushing open the door but not taking a step inside. There were no cats of course, and after leaning my head inside and looking around, I stepped onto the wooden floorboards and approached the counter. I did not see anyone and set my belongings down while examining the lobby.

On the wall behind the counter loomed a deer head, antlers branching outwards, glass eyes staring straight ahead. Looking around the room, I immediately detected a theme. Hanging on the wall beneath the deer head were various photographs of a middle-aged man in camouflage clothing standing or kneeling besides various animal carcasses: deer, rabbits, boars, wild turkeys and pheasants. On the counter before me, next to the guest book, was a wooden duck decoy painted with great detail to represent a mallard with its green head and neck. The detail was so exquisite I half expected the bird to get up and waddle along the slick surface. Beside the decoy was a small woven basket of apples.

Across the counter was a doorway that led to another room. On the wall on one side of the door stood a grandfather clock and beside it on the wall hung a pair of criss-crossed snowshoes. On the other side of the doorway hung a painting of a doe at a stream, its head bent, about to taste the cool-looking water, its white tail raised. The picture had a calming hypnotic effect on me as I stared at it. I became lost in the tranquility of its setting. It was only after a minute of admiring it that I noticed on the right edge of the painting a figure in the bushes alongside the stream. It was a hunter, rifle raised as he drew bead on the doe.

I heard the clearing of a throat before I was aware there was someone behind me.

When I turned around, I came face to face with the man in the photographs. He was balding with a round cheeks and tough skin. He smiled and extended a hand.

"I'm Bob Wolfe, the proprietor."

I shook his calloused hand and told him my name. My fingers were relieved when he relinquished his tight grip.

"One of the club, right?" he asked, one eyebrow raised.

"Yes," I answered. "Am I too early to check in?"

"A little bit. But that's okay. Your room is all set." He picked up a pen and began writing in the guestbook, glancing once at the grandfather clock.

"It's amazing what you've done with this place. I remember what it was like when the Peas sisters owned it."

"It was a lot of hard work," he said, turning the book around and offering me the pen. "It was my wife's idea. She got me to retire early so we could run this place together."

"Just the two of you here?" I asked, signing my name slowly and carefully, like when I used to practice my signature for when I became a famous author.

"My wife died before we got to open."

I looked up in time to catch his smile fading and felt myself blush. "I'm sorry."

"My niece works with me, she's been a great help."

Looking for a way to change the subject, I picked up the wooden mallard off the counter. "This is beautiful," I said, noticing something sifting inside, like it was filled with sand. Without a word, his hands reached out, gently took the decoy from me and placed it back on the counter.

"Those are my wife's ashes," he said, not looking up from the duck. "I had that specially made, so she can be here with me at the inn. I even take it hunting with me sometimes." He came around the counter and picked up my suitcase. "Let's show you your room."

As I reached for the typewriter case, I noticed a curious look on his face.

"Quiet time is after 10 o'clock," he said.

I told him that wouldn't be a problem. I didn't think there'd be much noise coming from those keys. He led the way up the stairs, and I followed, running my hand along the smooth varnished wood of the railing.

"Place full?" I asked.

"Two others besides your gang. Young woman and the professor."

"Professor?"

"Professor Bonz. A crypto-zoologist. Spends most of his time floating around on the lake." We had reached the second-floor landing. He turned and gave me the raised eyebrow. "Says he's looking for dinosaurs in the lake." He shook his head and laughed.

On the wall at the top of the landing hung a large moose head, just like in a lot of corny old scary movies. It was the kind of stuffed head whose eyeballs would follow your movements around the house. It reminded me of a story I had written when I was young, about a moose head on a wall that torments a hunter in a cabin and ends up biting off his face.

We began the ascent to the third floor. There were three rooms on each floor, plus the tower room. Wolfe told me my room was on the top floor, along with Lonny Mudge and Dale Carpenter. Paul Woodman's room was on the second floor, which was where the young woman and the professor were staying. Oliver Rench would be staying in the tower room. He had specifically requested it.

When Wolfe opened the door, we stepped into a simple bedroom. A four-post king-sized bed stood against one wall with a nightstand beside it. Across from the bed was a bureau with a large mirror on top. The only other piece of furniture was a cherry desk up against the wall beside the window that looked onto the lake.

It was on this desk that I set the typewriter case down. Wolfe placed my suitcase beside the bureau while explaining each floor had a community bathroom. I stared out the window at the peaceful water while he gave me the rest of the rundown.

"My niece's name is Sandy. Cleans the rooms between eleven and one. There are no locks to the bedroom doors, but I have a safe in my office if you need any valuables locked up. Dining room only serves breakfast, from 6:30 till 10, though there's usually a pot of coffee on earlier. Your club's allowed use of it after hours for your, uh, meetings. Guests are allowed full use of the den. Just don't disturb them." He turned to go. "Not that you could disturb the professor. He seems already a little out of sorts." He smiled, winking, and then left, shutting the door.

Here I am, I thought, looking again at the lake. Back where it all began. Now what?

I looked at the typewriter case. I didn't lug this antique all the way up here for nothing, did I? I opened it and set the typewriter up, wondering if it would even work. I grabbed the ream of paper from my suitcase and placed it beside the typewriter. I quickly thumbed the pages. Did I actually think I could fill them?

I removed the piece of paper from my pocket and placed it beside the typewriter. My eyes went back and forth from the typewriter to the page with my one line on it while I stood unmoving beside the desk. I didn't want to sit down. I didn't want to place my fingertips on those cold keys. Keys so frigid my fingers would grow numb and be unable to move. I was afraid that once I typed that one line again, I wouldn't be able to go any further.

I thought of Jason Nightingale. And of Paul Woodman. I stared at the piece of paper by the machine. Something was missing. I let out a sigh and turned away from the desk.

Rest was what I needed right now. It was an excuse, like the hundreds I had come up with over the years, but I had driven all night from the city without stopping. The excitement and anticipation of getting here had kept me going, but now weariness had set in. I had plenty of time to kill. The others wouldn't be driving in until later. We had mostly spread throughout the east coast. Martin still lived here though, working in the tax office at the Town Hall. Last I heard, he still lived with his crippled mother taking care of her. They had moved out of the old neighborhood to somewhere on the west side of town.

And of course, Jason was still here.

I looked at a closed door I assumed must be a closet and thought about hanging my jacket in it. (*Don't open it,* Woody had said.) Instead, I just tossed it over the back of the desk chair. I kicked off my shoes and reclined on the soft green plaid comforter covering the bed. I stared up at the painted white tin ceiling for a while, my eyes following its mazelike pattern, and then closed my eyes. Sleep beckoned and I succumbed. It felt nice.

Geoffrey! A voice called. *You're late.*

I did not stir.

Wake up, it called again. *Dale and the others are here. Hurry up, you'll be late for school.*

"Mother," I said as I sat up in bed.

I looked at the clock on the night stand. It didn't appear to be working. *I should get up*, I thought, spend more time seeing the town. Besides, I was feeling really hungry.

I left the inn and walked to town, strolling along the boardwalk. The cool air from the lake brushed against me. The town was still quiet, though businesses were open. A few cars drifted by on the streets, but I had the boardwalk to myself. Not even Carrothead, a local fixture on the boardwalk, was around. My footsteps on the wood planks echoed beneath me. It sounded as if someone was walking along behind me. It even *felt* as if someone was there. I stopped – the steps stopped. I stood absolutely still. I held my breath and listened, concentrating as hard as I could to feel if someone was actually there.

Carrothead? Meg? Jason?

I turned.

It was none of them. It was no one.

I continued along the boardwalk until I came to the marina and saw an old man loading some equipment into a small motorboat.

"Howdy, Professor Bonz," I said, hoping I guessed right. He looked up at me from the boat, a cracked face squinting in the sunlight.

"Do I know you?"

"No," I said, introducing myself. "Mr. Wolfe told me about you. I'm staying at the inn too."

"Oh, you must be one of them from the Jackass Club?"

"No," I laughed. "It's Jokers Club."

"Yeah, that's what I meant." He loaded the last piece of equipment into the boat and then followed himself. "No doubt Mr. Wolfe told you what an eccentric fool I am."

"Said you were looking for dinosaurs."

He grunted, shaking his head. "Not dinosaurs. A fish. Thought to be extinct, dating back to the Mesozoic era." He pointed out toward the center of the lake and my eyes followed. "This lake was formed by glaciers. Its depth is unrecorded. It's virtually bottomless. No one knows what could be down there. The possibilities are unfathomable." He looked at me and winked.

"It's funny," I said, looking out over the rippling water. "I wrote a story about a prehistoric fish in this lake. It attacked some fishermen in a rowboat."

"Oh, are you a writer?"

I hesitated, laughed a little. It was a question I had wanted to answer for such a long time. I just wasn't sure of the answer.

"Yes," I said, before I realized it.

"What have you written? Maybe I've read you."

At least a dozen book titles ran through my head; books that were supposed to be; books that should have been; books that I just never got around to writing. What had happened? I had such high hopes for myself, such ambitions. I was going to make it big. I had fled to New York City ready to ignite my imagination. But the stories never came. There was nothing there. I was in the biggest city in the country, full of millions of people, full of stories. It was there that books were born. But I had lost it. I couldn't find the stories that had driven me since I was a boy. Somewhere along the line, in the process of growing up, I had lost them.

"No," I said. "You haven't read me. I don't have anything published." Yet, I wanted to add, yet.

"Oh," the old professor acknowledged. He seemed to understand.

"I haven't tried too hard."

"Then why write?"

I smiled. "For the fun of it."

He was quiet for a moment, and then dismissed himself, starting his motor. I wished him luck and watched him head out to the middle of the lake. I stayed on the dock, keeping my eyes on him in his boat, playing with all the knobs on his sonar detecting machines. It reminded me of the scientists in old B-movies I used to love watching on Saturday afternoons. As I turned to go, I could almost imagine a prehistoric fish leaping out of the water and eating him.

I smiled.

As I walked downtown, I decided I needed a bite to eat and something to drink. I found a new place, the Loon Tavern, and stepped inside.

The bar was dark and it took my eyes a moment to adjust from the bright outdoors. During that fraction of a second of sightlessness, a combination of broiling beef and stale beer provided a mental snapshot of the place. When my gaze focused, I saw a scattering of tables before me and a long bar against the back wall. An arched doorway to the right led to a dining room, but I ignored it and walked straight to the bar.

There were a couple of tables occupied, but the rest was empty. I settled on a stool, placing my feet on the brass rail that ran along the bottom of the sticky surface. The bartender, a bald burly man with a handlebar mustache, came over and wiped the countertop in front of me with a rag.

That stained damp-looking rag reminded me of the many years I tended bar. It was the only job I had when I got out of college. It was a way to make good money while giving me time to write. A lot of friends, and even Meg, used to ask when I was going to get a real job. Didn't they understand writing was a job, that it was hard work? At least Meg should have understood.

I ordered a beer and asked for a menu.

I was on my third drink when my meal was set down in front of me. In the city I'd had many meals served to me on a bar countertop. When you're alone, there's no need to occupy an entire table.

After eating, I ordered another beer and glanced at a pay phone I noticed earlier in the corner. I pondered doing something I had thought about many times on the ride up here, but didn't quite know if I should. Unsure, I left my stool, went over and picked up the phone book with sweaty hands. I began thumbing through it slowly, hands shaky. When I got to the R's, I ran my index finger down along the names.

I was holding my breath, heart pausing in its beats, but I let it out when I saw there was no Rand, Meg.

I stared at the space on the page where the name should have been. Either she was married now, or she didn't live around here anymore. I didn't know what I would have done if her name had been there. I doubted I would have had the nerve to call. I wanted so much to see her, talk to her. But I didn't know what to say.

I wondered what time it was and headed outside. I didn't want this weekend to go too quickly. I needed time. Walking along the storefronts, I stopped in front of one and glanced at the sign.

LAKESIDE MEMORIALS

And beneath that: Mr. Under, proprietor.

I stood in front of the store staring through the display window at all the headstones. I tried to imagine my name on one of them. I tried to envision it in my mind. What would it say?

There was another sign that read: Distinctive Quality in Granite, Marble, Bronze and Fieldstone.

Another read: Plan for the Future.

Plan for the future? For what kind of future? What was there beyond to plan for?

A door opened and Mr. Under himself stepped out, took in a deep breath and then fixed his gaze on me. I couldn't help but look back at his narrow eyes and long, thin nose that pointed at me. He looked younger than he ever did before, his hair so jet-black from dye it looked like it would melt and run down his face like hot chocolate syrup.

I had written a story about him, about how in the middle of the night people could hear him carving a name into a tombstone with his hammer and chisel. But he would carve the name before someone died and everyone would wonder who was next.

"Looking for something special?" he asked, not removing his gaze from mine as he lit a cigarette.

"No, just window shopping." He looked me up and down. "How's business?"

"Slow." His eyes stuck to mine. "For now. But, it'll pick up."

"How can you be sure?"

"It's fall. Fall is the season of death. Everything dies in the fall. The leaves die and fall off the trees, the flowers die, the grass dies, gardens die. Everything prepares for its winter coffin. Death is in the air. Death is everywhere." He studied my face for reaction, blowing out a puff of smoke. "People die."

I pulled my gaze from his. I had to get away from those eyes. Across the street, Nick stood in front of his barbershop, arms folded across his chest, looking up and down the road.

"Looks like you're not the only one looking for customers," I said.

"Everyone's looking for something. What are you looking for?"

I returned my gaze to him. I could remember my story. When the town was quiet, in the middle of the night you could hear Mr. Under in his shop. You could hear the *ping, ping, ping* of his hammer and chisel as he carved out the name of some poor soul's headstone. It was like a death toll ringing throughout the town.

"I think I know," I said, and moved away from Mr. Under, down the sidewalk.

I crossed Main Street, to the gazebo, and climbed the steps that led into it. Standing in the middle, I surveyed my surroundings. Answers came to me.

It was here all the time. I had been looking, but I was looking in the wrong place. It was here in this town, this quiet New England town that I had always perceived as dull when growing up. But beneath its surface there were hundreds of stories to tell, right here. This is where the stories had begun. This is where they were all the time. Right here, on these streets. Back in New York, I had stared at that blank page and had not been able to find my way. Right here in the past was where there were countless tales hiding. I could create, just like I used to when I was young. I could find my book here.

I ran from the gazebo as fast as I can ever remember running in my life except for that night long ago, running down the road toward the inn, the wind pushing at my face, shoving the breath back down my throat. I was ten again and running from someone during a game of Relievo. But no one could catch me.

As I approached the inn, I noticed in a second floor window the face of a woman, whom I presumed to be the guest Mr. Wolfe mentioned. There was something familiar about the way her face peered out through the glass, but it was lost in my thoughts. There was so much to do.

When I got to my room, nearly breathless, I sat at the desk and rolled a blank piece of paper into my typewriter. When I retyped that first line, I automatically expected my fingers to stop. But they kept on going, and I didn't know if I could control them.

Ever since my June visit to Paul Woodman at that awful place, I had wanted to write a story of what happened to him. But I knew it had to begin with what happened to Jason Nightingale.

THE LEGEND OF REBEL JIM

Jason Nightingale didn't realize that horrible events would follow once he joined the Jokers Club.

He was excited the boys in his new neighborhood had asked him along that Halloween night. He hated moving to a strange new town and was mad at his parents for putting him through this. His dad said it couldn't be helped; it was a career move. *His stupid job always came first*, Jason thought.

Now he had to try to make a new set of friends – again. He had seen the numerous boys in the neighborhood after his family settled in that summer, but they kept their distance. He could tell they were checking him out, sizing him up. He knew what that was like. It wasn't until school started that he got to meet them.

And now, on this late October day, he stood at the base of the huge maple tree in Oliver Rench's back yard with Geoffrey Thorn, Dale Carpenter, Lonny Mudge, Paul Woodman and Martin Peak and looked up.

The trap door in the bottom of the clubhouse sprung open and an impatient face spotted them.

"Hurry up," Oliver said. "Get the hell up here."

Dale started climbing the pieces of wood nailed to the side of the tree that formed a ladder. Geoff, Lonny and Martin followed. Jason was going to let Paul Woodman go next, but he signaled Jason to go.

"I have to go last," Woody said. "It's a rule."

Confused, Jason headed up, hearing the straining creak of the wooden rungs and Woody's labored breath behind him. As he hoisted himself into the clubhouse, Oliver explained that Woody had to go last because he was so fat, and one day he would eat one candy bar too many and would not be able to fit through the clubhouse door. No one else wanted to take the chance of getting stuck behind him, so Oliver came up with the rule that Woody always was the last one in or out.

Jason looked around.

Geoff had told him they had built the clubhouse a couple summers back. Most of the lumber had come from the Little League field when the old dugouts were torn down to make way for new ones. The boards were weathered with cracked green paint. Windows had been cut into each of the four walls and they stapled pieces of screen over them that they had found behind the Tin Man's house. Inside the clubhouse was a menagerie of mismatched furnishings. A telephone cable spool served as a table in the middle of the floor. Surrounding the table were a wooden folding chair, a couple of overturned milk crates, a torn vinyl hassock with its stuffing poking out and a couple of other unmatched chairs, including a director's chair. Geoff had told Jason that was Oliver's and only he was allowed to sit in it.

The rest of the clubhouse was mostly barren, except for piles of comic books and magazines stacked on a bench in one corner. A drawing was thumb-tacked to one wall of the clubhouse. It was a court jester's grinning face, with a black and white striped cap with little bells on the ends. Dale Carpenter told him his older sister drew it, copying it from the deck of cards they used to play blackjack in the clubhouse, one of the many things they gathered here to do. Other times they read comic books, scaled baseball cards or listened to Geoff read one of the scary stories he had written.

But other times they would gather to plot ... a prank.

"Take a look at this," Oliver Rench said, pointing to something on the middle of the table.

Jason and the others peered closely at the contents of an old pickle jar with air holes punched in the cover. There were two praying mantises in the jar. There was nothing else in there with them, just the two of them by themselves. One was twitching its front legs together, an almost applauding motion. The other held the classic praying pose that gave it its name. But there was nothing it could pray for. Its head was gone.

Oliver's face lit up. He drank the excitement of the scene into his rugged body. Dark brows narrowed with concentration beneath the bangs of his straight black hair. "It eats one of its own to survive." His grin broadened.

Jason looked at the headless insect, then back at Oliver. "Sweet."

Jason sat on the clubhouse floor because there were only enough seats for the others. All attention focused on Oliver whose eyes moved patiently amongst them.

"It's Halloween," Dale said. "And we've got nothing going on."

"Yeah," Lonny agreed, brushing his long bangs away from his eyes, "this bites."

"You guys don't go trick-or-treating?" Jason asked, and instantly regretted it, wishing he could suck the words back into his mouth when he saw the look on Oliver's face.

"Why don't you put on your nurse's outfit and go trick-or-treating, Florence Nightingale," Oliver said through gritted teeth, and then laughed.

There it was, Jason thought as everyone else joined in. The first shot.

He hated being called that and had been before in some of the other towns he lived in. It made him hate his last name – such a stupid-sounding name – so easy to make fun of.

Was this what it was going to be like? He pretended to chuckle along, to show them it didn't bother him. He wanted this to work. He wanted to be accepted by these kids. He didn't want to blow it.

Oliver stopped laughing and leaned back in his director's chair and took a deep breath.

"Don't worry about Halloween night boys," he said. "Have I got a trick for us."

"It better be good," Geoff said. "Last year's prank sucked."

"Oh, it's good all right." Oliver paused, reveling in the moment. "This will be a Halloween trick *and* treat."

"Well, what is it?" Dale asked.

"We're going to party with the Colonel."

Nobody said a word.

Jason looked at the faces of the others. He could see something registering on them, thoughts clicking, but he was in the dark.

Lonny hopped to his feet, his long stringy hair bouncing off his shoulders.

"This'll be awesome," he said.

"I'm not sure about this."

Oliver looked at Martin with contempt for saying this.

"What exactly did you have in mind?" Geoff asked.

"Yeah," spoke Dale. "What are we going to do there?"

"Can someone tell me what's going on?" Jason asked. Geoff filled him in on the legend.

Colonel James Fox was a member of a prominent family in town back in the 19th century. They had a farm out beyond the local cemetery. Colonel Fox was stationed in Virginia when the Civil War broke out, and he sided with the Confederacy. He was killed in a battle, and his body was shipped back to New Hampshire for burial in the family tomb. The Fox family had a mausoleum by the woods in a back lot of their farm. It was here that Colonel Fox was first mummified, and then laid to rest in the family crypt with his ancestors. The Fox family and farm were long gone, but the tomb still stood in that back lot by the woods, which had now begun to overtake the tomb with its undergrowth, concealing it.

But many people in town knew of the burial site. In the past, pranksters had broken into it and college kids sometimes used it for fraternity initiations. Oliver told him once of how his two older brothers and some friends from school had broken into the mausoleum and partied there. They had propped the Colonel up in his casket, tied a bandana around his head and put a can of beer in his hand.

"Now it's our turn to have some fun." Oliver grinned.

"It sounds kinda risky," Jason said.

Oliver stared at him. "Listen. We don't like chicken-shits in our club."

Jason shut up.

Oliver looked around at the rest of them. "Well, what's everybody think?" His eyes caught Lonny's. "Mudge?"

"I'm with you, you know that."

"How about you, Carpenter?"

"This'll be cool."

Oliver turned to Geoff. "Thorn, you write all the scary stories, this should be right up your alley."

"I don't know why we haven't thought of this before."

"Woody?"

Paul had just shoved the last piece of a candy bar in his mouth, so he was only able to nod.

"Peak?"

"I'll go along with everybody else."

Oliver turned back to Jason. "See, that's why we're a club. We always stick together."

"I guess so."

"No guessing."

"Okay."

"When do we go?" asked Lonny.

Oliver looked out one of the screened windows. "When the sun goes down."

* * *

At nighttime, the figures of seven young boys raced through the shadows of the tree-cluttered ravine. They came out the other end and shot through the yard between a pair of houses and out onto Elm Street, crossing it and racing up the hill to the Pines. They hesitated for only a brief moment amongst the pine trees, looking down the hill at the Little League field, the cemetery beyond it and what they knew lay even further beyond: The Fox Mausoleum.

They descended the slope and ran along the perimeter of the ball field, one behind the other. Oliver led the pack, with Lonny right behind, then Dale, Geoff, Jason, Martin and Woody bringing up the rear, a generous gap between him and Martin.

Their pace slowed to a walk when they reached the thick field of wild grass, goldenrod and milkweed out beyond the cemetery. They had to pick their way carefully through the tangle of undergrowth which seemed to grab at their limbs and clothes. Oliver, leading the way like a safari guide, almost missed the two marble pillars covered with growth.

"Here," he cried as the others gathered around him. He could now make out the slightly trampled path that ran between the pillars.

"Follow me, boys."

It was just beyond the pillars that they came to the gray stone mausoleum. The front was about eight feet in height and descended sharply toward the back into the earth, the back barely a foot above the ground.

"Wow," Geoff said.

"It's so old," Woody puffed out between breaths.

There was a white marble crest above the crypt which held some weathered and time-worn words about the Fox family that were no longer decipherable. Beneath that, Jason read the etching: Erected in 1759.

"You sure we should go in there?" Jason asked.

"We've come this far, Florence," Oliver said without even looking at him. "Flashlight." Lonny thrust it into his extended hand.

There was a heavy marble block that had been removed recently and a steel door that had been welded across the entrance in an unsuccessful attempt to keep vandals out. It was broken open. Oliver led the way in. Jason watched the others disappear through the dark entrance and then followed. Woody, who waited to go last as usual, had trouble getting through the small opening, but squeezed past by sucking in his breath and emitting a groan.

The darkness was broken only slightly by the flashlight beam. The air was thick with dust and mold.

"I can't hardly breathe," a voice gasped. It was Woody's.

The brick walls were gray with age and frosted with cobwebs. Dust hung in the air and filled Jason's lungs with every breath. Oliver played his flashlight around until it landed on a group of rotted caskets.

"This is spooky," Dale said.

Jason looked at the coffins and all around the crypt.

"Boy, I could write a wicked story about this place," Geoff said.

"Let's find the Colonel," Oliver said.

Jason was all for that so they could get the heck out of this place. He didn't like it in here.

They approached the first casket slowly, huddled around Oliver and his illuminating light. The tops of the caskets were caved in from rot and the boys peered inside the first one.

"Nothing but dust," Lonny said.

"Maybe," Jason said, "there's no such thing as the Colonel."

"Oh yes there is," Oliver responded, moving to the next casket and the next. These too were empty.

"Yikes!" yelled Martin as the flashlight pounced on the fourth casket. There were bones and the tattered remnants of clothes in this one.

"That's not him," Oliver deduced.

They moved to the next one, more bones and dust.

It was the sixth casket where the beam of light fell upon a body.

"Oh, Jesus," someone whispered.

The Colonel was well-preserved, lying in his gray army uniform with its wooden buttons. His skin had a dark yellow tint, his chin dotted with thin gray whiskers. The thread could be seen that sewed his eyelids shut. His gray hair was matted to his head. His lips held no color.

Jason bit his lip. Nobody moved or spoke.

It was Oliver who broke the silence. "Jackpot."

"He don't look too good," Martin whispered.

"He's dead, moron, how do you expect him to look? And what are you whispering for? Afraid you might wake him up?"

"I don't want nobody hearing us, that's all."

"Nobody's gonna hear us," Geoff said. "Nobody living that is."

"Don't talk like that," Woody said, still panting.

"What do we do now?" Jason asked.

Dale cleared the dust from his throat. "Shouldn't somebody touch him?"

"Right," Oliver said, "go ahead."

"I'm not gonna touch him, you touch him."

"You're not afraid, are you?"

"No. Are you?"

"Course not."

"Then you go first. This was your idea."

Oliver looked around at everyone. Jason tried not to meet his gaze, was afraid he'd make him touch the corpse. "Okay. I don't know what the big deal is."

The flashlight was handed to Lonny and the beam quivered a bit as Oliver's hand reached out toward the taut dried skin.

"Careful it don't bite."

Oliver looked at Geoff then slowly stroked the corpse's cheek.

"What's it like?" Dale asked.

"Feels like my old baseball mitt." He looked at Dale. "Your turn."

Dale reached out, grabbed onto the Colonel's hand and slowly lifted it a bit.

"It's like he's made out of papier-mâché."

"So, now what?" Jason asked, hoping it was over and they could get out of here.

"We leave," Oliver answered.

"That's good."

"And take him with us."

"What?"

"Are you nuts?" Woody asked. "We can't steal a dead body."

"Listen. This is Halloween. We have the chance to pull off the biggest prank this town has ever seen."

"It could be the talk of the town," Dale said. "We could become living legends."

Martin turned to face him. "Or dead ones if we get caught."

"We won't get caught," Oliver stressed. "Not as long as you all do what I say and don't screw up. Besides, what could they do to us? We're just kids."

"So what'd you have in mind?" Geoff asked.

"We bring him to Heifer's house. Lean him up against the door and ring the doorbell. When he opens that door, the Colonel will scare him so bad he'll crap his pants."

"Who's Heifer?" Jason asked.

"Police chief. Thinks he's such a big shot. His name's Hooper, but he looks more like a Heifer."

"He's huge," Lonny clarified.

"Like what Woody's going to look like if he doesn't stop eating," Oliver laughed. Only Lonny joined in.

Oliver told Jason about the last prank the Jokers Club had pulled, when they poured bubble bath powder into the town fountain the night before Memorial Day weekend. When the fountain was started up the next morning, the bubbles overflowed onto Main Street creating a traffic mess on the opening of the summer tourist season. Heifer had accused the club of the prank and tried to scare them into confessing, but they held strong. He said he had been looking forward to a chance to get back at the chief.

"I love it," Dale said.

Oliver scanned everyone's faces. No one else said a word, so Jason remained silent, though he had a gnawing feeling inside that this was just so wrong and nothing good would come of it.

"Then let's go," Oliver said. "Lonny, you get the lower half, I'll get the upper."

"Careful you don't wreck him," Geoff said.

"How much worse could he get?"

"He's wicked light," Lonny snorted as they lifted the body out of the casket.

"That's because they take out all the insides before they mummify someone," Geoff scoffed.

Woody turned away. "I think I'm gonna be sick."

"Let's go," Oliver commanded.

* * *

They were seven shadowy figures racing through the moonlit cemetery, and if anyone had spotted them and the body they carried, they would have thought ghouls had come out for a night of Halloween mischief. When they climbed to the top of the Pines, they stopped and looked down the hill at the chief's house on Elm Street.

"Let's think a minute," Oliver gasped, setting the Colonel down and propping him up against a tree. They sat down around it in silence, Lonny pointing out the chief's small ranch-style house to Jason.

Geoff broke the silence. "There are too many trick-or-treaters around. They'll see us."

"I know," Oliver agreed. "We have to get down to the ravine behind the house and launch our attack from the rear when the coast is clear."

"But what if we get spotted bringing him across the street?" Jason asked.

Oliver thought for a moment, and Jason hoped that maybe they would change their minds about the whole thing.

"I've got it. We'll just walk right across the street."

"We can't do that," Woody said. "We can't just walk across the street carrying a corpse."

"We won't be carrying him. He'll be walking with us."

"You lost me."

"One of us gets on each side of him and holds him upright by the arms. The rest bunch up around us, and we just march across the street."

"Sounds okay," Dale said.

Oliver handed Woody the flashlight. "You're gonna stay here and be the lookout, Woody."

"Why me?"

"Because you're the slowest. And what we're doing calls for speed. Now what you're gonna do is sit right here and keep an eye on the street, make sure the coast is clear. Whenever the street is clear of people, you turn the flashlight on. If there's anyone on the street, then turn the light off. We'll lay low. As long as we see that light's on, we'll know it's okay to move. You got it?"

"I got it."

"You sure?"

"I'm sure."

"Want me to repeat any of it?"

"I said I got it."

"Let's go then."

"I'll stay with Woody," Martin offered. "Help him keep lookout."

There were a few trick-or-treaters down the street by Shadow Drive, but they paid no attention to the group of boys that crossed the street and the taller, strange figure in the middle of them. They disappeared between two houses and into the cover of the ravine directly behind the chief's house. The Colonel lay on the ground beside them. Oliver crept over to Jason.

"Nightingale, you keep an eye on Woody's light, okay?"

"Got ya."

"I'm gonna take a peek in the back window," he said to the others. "See what Heifer's up to."

A few leaves crinkled beneath his sneakers as he slowly crossed the back yard toward the house and the lit window in front of him. He gripped the window ledge with his fingers and lifted himself up on his tiptoes till his eyes peered into the living room.

Jason lay there watching him, part of him nervous about getting caught, but part of him excited about being out here in the dark with no adults around to tell him what to do. He felt free. He had never been the daring type, but this was exciting.

Oliver turned, scrunched down, and scurried back to the ravine.

"He's just sitting there watching TV," he told them. "Stuffing his fat face with Halloween candy."

"Probably won't be able to get out of the chair to answer the door," Geoff said.

Jason looked up to the Pines, to the beacon there. "Light's on," he softly called out.

"Then let's move. Mudge, you get to the second side window. You'll be right behind Heifer's chair. Let us know if he moves."

When Lonny was in position, he peered in the window, and then waved them on. Oliver led the way with Geoff and Dale carrying the Colonel. Jason took up the rear as they crept alongside the house, low and around Lonny to the front corner by a shrub. Looking over the green barrier, Jason could still see the flashlight beam. He glanced over his shoulder at Lonny who gave them the okay sign. They crept around to the front of the house, keeping beneath the windows till they reached the front door.

Jason glanced up into the dark Pines. ...Wait, the dark Pines? The Pines were dark! "The light's out," he cried.

Oliver looked up.

"There," Dale exclaimed, pointing.

A group of kids just turned the corner onto Elm from Autumn Avenue.

"We gotta move fast," Oliver said.

They stood the Colonel up on the front stoop.

"Lean him against the door," Oliver said, "so he'll fall forward when it's opened."

They did and Oliver rang the doorbell.

"Let's book it!"

The five boys sprinted across the street and up the hill into the Pines. When they reached Woody and Martin they stopped and turned to watch. They saw the door swing open and the Colonel fall forward. That was followed by a loud scream.

Their laughter was interrupted by Oliver: "Let's get the hell outta here."

They followed Oliver down the west bank of the Pines and onto Autumn Avenue. When they reached the street, they assumed a casual, but quick-paced walk toward town.

"We'll hang out down on the boardwalk," Oliver said. "Make believe we been there all night. Harass Carrothead a bit if he's there."

"That was awesome," Dale said when they reached the boardwalk.

"We will be remembered for this one," Woody spurted out between gasps and laughs. "Even though nobody will know we did it."

"Well, Florence," Oliver said. "What do you think?"

Jason looked from face to face.

"I think I'm going to like being in this club."

CHAPTER TWO

When I finally stopped typing, my fingertips felt as if they had been resting on a hot stove. I leaned back in the chair and looked at the filled pages. It felt good. I had gotten past that first line, the line I had written back in July when I got the letter from Martin Peak.

The letter surprised me because I hadn't heard from Martin in a few years, hadn't even realized he had my New York address. When I opened the letter, I first noticed there was no salutation, just my name at the top in bold, striking letters. The letter was to the point, no questions of how I'd been and what was new. It just matter-of-factly stated Woody had been placed in a mental institution in upstate New Hampshire. The whole letter was very impersonal, except for the last sentence: *And you know why.*

I stared at that sentence for days before understanding what bothered me most about it: It seemed like an accusation.

It was then I decided to visit Woody.

Paul Woodman had always been a fat kid. We kidded him about it a lot, but his weight didn't really bother any of us, except maybe Oliver who always seemed particular about the people he let hang around him. The bigger Woody grew, the less Oliver seemed to notice him. Maybe it was just that, since it was Oliver's tree house, he was afraid Woody's mass would send it crashing to the ground. Oliver might have even kicked him out of the club except for the fact that Woody was a darn good baseball player. He was a catcher on the same Little League team as me, and his meaty arms enabled him to knock a lot of balls over the centerfield fence. Oliver admired anyone with athletic ability.

Fat certainly ran in Woody's family. I remember the first time I was invited over to his house for dinner. They served chicken, potatoes and corn on the cob. It looked like they cooked three or four whole chickens. Everyone in the family got at least three baked potatoes apiece. The plates were so full the corn hung off the edge, dripping butter onto the tablecloth. I looked at the heaping mounds of food in front of me, and then glanced at Woody. He had cut open his baked potatoes and mashed them into a massive blob, then took a half a stick of butter and plopped it on top. Watching the family eat in a frenzy of flashing teeth jack-hammering through the corn, stripping chicken from the bones and gobbling down potatoes, skin and all, I thought I was going to vomit.

Woody seemed like he wasn't ever going to stop getting bigger. But he did. After the Jokers Club broke up, we all kind of grew apart. Nothing was ever the same. Woody became introverted. Maybe it was the adjustment to high school, I'm not sure, but I noticed he was starting to lose weight. It was gradual at first. I don't even think anyone else noticed. But then Woody started wearing fewer oversized sweatshirts than normal. One day in school, it occurred to me he didn't bounce as much in the halls. By the time it became noticeable, the weight seemed to melt off him. When graduation rolled around, he had trimmed down to our size. It was then I realized all that fat had distorted how tall he was.

After graduation, Woody moved somewhere up north, and I never saw him again until I got the letter from Martin.

The place was called Acorn Estates, a brick building crawling with ivy and sunk in a pine-tree bog. What better place to hide away the lunatics of New Hampshire. I drove up there in a rented car.

I was greeted in the waiting room by Woody's doctor and led down a long white corridor. The walls were white, the ceiling was white, the floor was white and the doors were white. I thought I'd go snow blind. As we passed various doors, I noticed each had a little rectangular window in them, barely big enough to look into or out of. I wondered what the inhabitants were like behind those doors. Passing one door, a face popped up to fill the frame of the window. It was a woman; her eyes, like those of a frightened animal, watched me as I continued along my way.

We took a few rights and a handful of lefts as the labyrinthine hallway led me deeper into the bowels of the asylum. As we continued, a thought crept into my mind. What if this wasn't a doctor beside me, but a patient? What if I'd been tricked? I had no idea where he was taking me; the place had become a maze and if the inmates' doors were to suddenly spring open, I wouldn't be able to find my way back. I felt warm and sweaty and had the sudden urge to scream, but was afraid to stir the crazies lurking all around me, like being in the midst of a bees' nest. The doctor only looked at me and smiled. Why was he smiling?

We finally came to the end of a hallway, to a door labeled: Recreation Room. Once inside, I saw about a dozen patients all wearing the same light-blue garments resembling hospital scrubs. There was a group of four playing ping pong, an old man playing checkers alone, and some others milling about. The doctor directed me to a lone individual sitting on a couch by a window, and I was not prepared for what I saw.

Though his shirt and pants were loose and baggy, his face and arms gave me the clue I needed to his condition. He wasn't just skinny. He was like a set of bones that decided to throw on a layer of flesh at the last minute. He could have been made of wax held too close to a flame, causing his skin to melt and adhere to its frame. I could almost hear the sideshow barker: *See the Skeleton Man!*

"Woody?"

His gaze turned from the window and the patients playing croquet on the lawn beyond and fell on me. There appeared to be no recognition in it. This isn't Paul Woodman, I thought. They've brought me to the wrong man. Then his head nodded, ever so slowly, as it dawned on him whom I was. His attention returned to the activity outside. I almost turned and left right then.

"Not checking in are you?" he said, his voice soft.

I laughed but then it occurred to me he might not be joking. I shook my head but realized he wasn't looking at me, though I wasn't sure he was even interested in my answer.

"You know, they're really lousy croquet players." He continued staring out the window. "They don't even know the rules."

I wanted to sit down on the couch next to him, but was afraid to. He looked so fragile, as if he would crumble in my arms if I touched him. "What the hell happened to you?" I wished I could have chosen my words better.

He looked at me and stared into my eyes for the longest time. "Nobody plays by the rules anymore," he finally said. He looked back at the croquet game. "You know, there are some people here so crazy they shouldn't let them have those mallets." He looked at me. "I'm not nuts."

"I know." I didn't sound convincing.

"I have problems, that's for sure. But I'm quite sane." His eyes wandered around the room. "A lot of the people in here are freaking nuts."

I did sit down beside him, carefully. "Do you want to tell me what happened?"

He looked at me. "I almost died, you know. Died from not being able to eat. Pretty fucking stupid, huh?"

"But I don't understand."

He looked at me, puzzled. "You really don't get it, do you?"

I shook my head.

He looked straight ahead, his eyes narrowing, as if he were conjuring up an image. "It's not that I don't want to eat. It's not like I don't get hungry." His voice rose as his body trembled. "Food disgusted me. The thought of eating. The thought of opening a refrigerator door horrified me. I just couldn't eat."

"Is that what this is? Are you punishing yourself?"

He returned his gaze to me. "I thought at least you would understand."

"It's been over with the club for a long time."

"Not for me. It's never ended for me."

"So you're going to destroy yourself? Is that the answer?"

"I've gotten some help here. I'm starting to eat normally again." He chuckled a bit. "Though I doubt I'll ever reach the proportions of my younger days."

"Well, that's one good thing about this," I laughed.

"There's nothing funny about any of this." His upper lip curled in a sneer. "Nothing at all."

I suddenly felt uncomfortable. "I should probably be going now." I stood up from the couch.

"You can come and go at will. You should be glad to have such control of your life. But they said I'll be out of here in a few weeks. Then I'll be in control again. You'll see."

I turned to face him. "You just got to get it in your head that it wasn't our fault."

"We'll all pay for what we did."

* * *

As the doctor led me back out through that maze of halls, I noticed that same woman's face in the cell door window I had seen on the way in. Her eyes had an utterly mad look. A look that seemed to appear in Woody's eyes with those last words he had spoken. I began to wonder if he truly was sane.

Every time I thought about the last time I saw Woody, it gave me the willies. I tried very hard to forget that visit, but it's no use. Just like I couldn't forget the last time I saw Jason Nightingale.

As I leaned back in the chair, I smelled a faint odor of peanut butter, probably drifting up through the heating ducts from some deep recess of the inn. I closed my eyes and thought back to one warm summer day when Dale

Carpenter took a brand new jar of chunky peanut butter from his house and the two of us, spoons clasped in tight fists, raced up to the Pines. There we sat with our backs against the warm, smooth surface of the boulder, the jar between us. There was a hiss of air as Dale opened the jar and the scent of peanuts roasting in the hot sun floated up to our nostrils. We admired the smooth surface of the peanut butter, interrupted only by the speckled bits of crushed peanuts, like a thick wave settling on a coral bed.

We hesitated, each waiting for the other to make the first move. Then Dale broke that perfect surface with the tip of his spoon, scooping a long trench as the peanut butter curled up onto the spoon. Soon our utensils dug furiously into the jar and before long we leaned back against the rock, our bellies full, our mouths and throats clogged, the jar half empty. It wasn't long before we raced back down the hill in search of a beverage to scrape the coating from the roofs of our mouths.

Many times we would steal away a jar of peanut butter from either of our houses, our mothers never suspecting why they had to replenish the supply so frequently.

A soft tapping of my door returned me to the present and I stared at the source of intrusion for a moment, (*Don't open it. Don't.*) anticipating who it might be. I wanted it to be Woody. I wanted to see he was all right.

"Come in," I finally said, and the door creaked open slowly revealing the grownup version of my peanut-butter partner.

"I heard some typing earlier, so I didn't want to intrude," he said.

I strode across the room and wrapped my arms around Dale, holding him tight, not wanting to let go. It was so good to see him. It had been so long.

When I released him, he was grinning. "The Big Apple hasn't made you feminine has it?"

"I guess kissing you would be out of the question right now, huh?" We laughed. I looked into his face, at the lines and creases around his eyes and mouth. He was aging, and I hadn't expected it. He had been the best looking one of us, handsome, even pretty, if guys could be pretty. Now he was no longer the young kid eating peanut butter. Was this what was happening to me? To all of us? "How the hell are you?"

"Doing okay," he answered, nodding. "Things are pretty routine. You know how married life is."

"No, I don't."

"Well, it's nothing to brag about."

"How is the wife?" I sat down on the end of my bed.

"She's um ... well ... She's good. She's good."

"Now I'm supposed to ask you about your job, isn't that how the routine goes?"

"God, it's been so long. You look terrific."

How deceiving looks can be, I thought. "I've really missed you."

He paused for a moment, and I wondered if maybe I was being a bit too maudlin. He meandered over near the desk, and I felt an urge to rush past him, to snatch the papers away. I didn't want him to see what I was writing about. I wasn't sure why.

"We've really been strangers," he finally said.

"That's what we get for growing up. We have to go our separate ways and lead mature, adult lives."

"Well, we can forget all about that this weekend. We're the Jokers Club once again."

"Maybe that isn't such a great idea."

His expression soured. "We had some great times for a while there. That's what we're here to celebrate."

My mind wandered back to the days of the club, to the simple, fun times. I remembered summer nights, running through the warm crisp air, the whole quiet town our playground, nothing to fear. The night was ours to do as we pleased.

"You're right."

He looked down at the typewriter. "Where'd you dig up this relic?"

"Don't ask."

"I didn't know you were still writing. What are you working on?"

I jumped up and gathered the papers. "No fair peeking," I said, trying to make light of it. "It's nothing, really. Just fooling around."

He stepped over to the window and looked out. "Great view you got. Mine looks out the back. Have you seen anyone else?"

"No," I answered. "I was really anxious to see Woody, see how he's doing."

Dale didn't answer.

"Let's go downstairs," I finally said. "See if anyone's around."

When we walked through the door that led to the den, we saw Lonny Mudge. He stood in front of the fireplace of the paneled room, beneath another deer head that hung over the mantle. He was dressed in a nice suit and tie, but his clothes looked rumpled, as if he had slept in them. Though his tie was knotted up firmly beneath his collar, it hung askew, revealing his shirt buttons. One was either missing or unbuttoned, exposing a small spot of hairy flesh. He face was unshaven and his hair, much shorter than his younger days, looked ... funny.

Beside him was a portable bar filled with all kinds of liquor bottles, mixers and an ice bucket. He held a drink in one hand and used the back of the other to wipe drops of liquid from the bottom of his thick mustache.

"Hey guys, look at this," he waved at the drinks, a grin on his face. "All this booze has been set out for us. And it's free."

"It's nice to see you too, Lonny," Dale said, extending his hand as he approached.

"It's great seeing you guys too," Lonny said, pumping our hands.

If I thought it had been quite a while since I'd seen Dale, it had been longer since I'd last seen Lonny. Even though Dale and I remained close in high school, neither of us hung out much with Lonny, Oliver or the others. Lonny had gone to college in Maine, but dropped out when he got his girlfriend pregnant. They had gotten married and I was surprised I got an invitation. I think that had been the last time I saw him. I had heard he had three or four kids now and was selling life insurance."

"How's the insurance world?" I asked him.

"History. I sell cars now. Didn't happen to notice my vehicle out front?"

"No."

"Well this setup looks pretty nice," Dale said, admiring the selection at the bar like a kid trying to decide what he wants at a candy counter. He hesitated and then fixed himself a drink.

That was what I needed, what I really wanted at this point. Once in hand, I plopped myself down in a big stuffed chair. The drink felt good going down. There was a moment of silence, as if no one knew what to say.

Lonny finally broke the stalemate. "What a great idea this was, to get together like this."

"Yeah," I said. "Just great."

"So how's things going?" Dale asked Lonny.

"Great. Top of the world. Everything's clicking." He paced around as he spoke, his arms and hands jittering, but he didn't spill a drop of his drink. He moved near the windows that looked out onto the front porch. "You know, if you look out just right you can see my car."

"Later," Dale said.

"Yeah, sure." He moved from the window.

"Seen Woody or anyone else?"

"You guys are the first I've seen," Lonny said, moving to the bar and fixing another drink.

"I hope Woody shows up," I said, then got up and fixed a new drink for me and one for Dale also. I handed Dale his icy glass, and as his left hand reached for it I noticed his wedding band was gone. I hesitated as he grasped the drink, almost not letting go, till his eyes met mine and I released it, feeling the cold beverage slide through my fingers. I looked away.

"How are things in Maine?" Dale asked Lonny.

"Great. Booming. The whole state's booming. I'm selling cars left and right. I'm so damn busy, I'm up to my ass in alligators. You guys need new cars? I could fix you up with some beauties. You'll look like big shots."

"Maybe we already are big shots."

"Yeah, of course. You guys must be doing great. What do you drive?"

"I'm in the middle of New York City, Lonny. Nothing but cabs and subways for me."

"That must suck."

"You get used to it."

Lonny fixed himself another drink. "So, how's your job down in Virginia?" he asked Dale.

Dale chuckled. "Well, actually, I'm between jobs right now, mulling over my next move."

"Hmmn," Lonny said, nodding, as if he understood. Damned if I knew what he meant.

I was about to say something when I felt a presence nearby and turned to the doorway. There stood a small man with a deeply receding hairline exposing a shiny scalp surrounded by wispy graying hairs. He wore circular, wire-rimmed glasses. It took me a moment to realize it was Martin Peak, but he reminded me of someone else, someone older. He stood there silent. His eyes were the only part of him that moved, shifting from one of us to the other.

"Martin," I said, and didn't know what else to say.

"You came," he replied. I wasn't sure whether it was directed to all of us, or someone in particular. He stepped into the room, hesitantly. "I wasn't sure any of you would really come."

"Wouldn't miss this for anything," Dale said with sarcasm.

Handshakes were exchanged. Martin's was effortless.

More drinks were made. Martin only had soda water. Talk ensued, mostly about what everyone had been doing and, as it turned out, we found we did not lead the most exciting lives. I had a feeling this night was not going to get much better, that it was a mistake trying to recapture something that was so long ago. It was opening a door to the past that was probably best left closed.

When Oliver Rench strode into the room, his aura took hold of the place. The handshaking began again. When he got to me, his grip was firm. "Thorn, haven't seen your name on the best-sellers list yet."

"No, but it's nice you're keeping an eye out." In that one line that he spoke ever-so-smugly, I was reminded of how unpleasant this man truly was and wondered how I ever could have considered him a friend. He was certainly the person I least wanted to see here today, if at all.

"Let me fix you a drink," Lonny said and bounded off to the portable bar.

"Nice place I picked out," Oliver said, scanning the surroundings. "They did a good job fixing this old dump up."

Lonny came back with a drink for Oliver and a fresh one for himself.

"It's amazing that anything in this town could change," he continued.

"Not everybody cares for change," Martin said, a surprising edge to his voice.

Oliver grinned. "That's right. You're the only one who stayed behind. You seem to be content here. I'm sure you'll die in Malton, but not me. I made sure I got out. I've got more ambitious plans for my life. I was glad to leave this place behind."

I noticed we had all formed a sort of circle around Oliver as he talked about how wonderful things were in Boston and in the world of commercial real estate. It felt as if he had completely taken over.

I broke from the pack and made myself another round, then hung back against the fringe to observe. There was a lightness in my head. As I looked at the others, I felt I didn't belong here. Maybe I shouldn't have come, but there were some things I wanted to accomplish. I needed to accomplish.

Lonny began asking Oliver about the kind of car he drove and, as expected, it was quite impressive. Without breaking stride, Lonny continued on about his own car.

"I saw it," Oliver said. Lonny beamed. "It had dealer plates."

Lonny shrugged. "So?"

"So, you don't actually own the car. You just get to use it, to display it."

"Well, yeah, but, that …" His drink came to his lips and the rest of his worlds were muddled in the slurps.

Dale gave me a smirk and walked to my side.

"You okay?"

I nodded. "Just seems weird. Us being all together again."

"Not quite all."

Yes, there was a noticeable absence.

"Any word on Woody?" I asked.

"Hasn't checked in," Oliver said, gulping his drink.

"They won't give his room away, will they?" Lonny asked.

"There can't be much demand this time of year," Dale responded.

"Mostly leaf peepers," Oliver said, "coming to see the foliage. But I paid for his room just in case."

"Well, that was good of you," Lonny muttered.

"Just a drop in the bucket, Mudge."

I hoped Woody was just delayed. One of the things I wanted most out of this trip was to see how he was doing.

"He's not the only one not here," I said.

Silence filled the room. Nobody made eye contact. Then Lonny broke the silence.

"Hey, come on guys," he said between sips. "We're here to remember the good times of the Jokers Club. Not the bad."

"He's right," Dale said.

Oliver smiled. "That's why we're here."

"Now, aren't we supposed to get something to eat?"

* * *

It was during dinner at the Loon Tavern downtown that I realized how far removed the Jokers Club was from our adult lives. The talk at the table centered around jobs and each of our lives. Oliver was extremely successful in real estate and pulling in all kinds of money. Lonny babbled on and on about selling cars. Wives were mentioned briefly. Lonny, the only one with kids, rambled on about how wonderful they were.

But the more I listened to everybody, the more I began to think this wasn't really the Jokers Club. The Jokers Club was a group of kids who laughed and played and could take the world in their hands, spin it like a top and hop on. Not that I expected us to act like we were twelve again, but I at least hoped we would be able to respond and interact with each other with that bond of friendship that burned inside us so brightly as children. Those were magic times for me. But maybe, like an old magician, we'd lost our spells with time. Maybe Jason Nightingale ruined that for us all.

On the way back to the Tower House Inn, I knew what was really important to me. This trip had become a quest of many things, but I had resolved myself to accomplish one task. The past held the secret for me. I had felt it all day today, and I felt it in seeing my old friends. The Jokers Club was the key.

I wanted to get my book written. I wanted to recapture the imagination that I left behind when I left this town. It was definitely here. I could feel it in everything I saw. It was buried beneath layers of the past, but not too deep that I couldn't unearth it.

The Jokers Club would be the focal point. It would have to be. There were tales and dreams that we lived. I could almost taste the moments, savor them. Sip them from a bottle and cork it to save some for later. There was a tale to tell. A tale that was not yet complete. Jason Nightingale would be a big part of it.

But I needed something more to weave my tapestry. I wasn't sure quite what it was, but I knew I could find it buried in this place.

We gathered around a table in the closed dining room of the inn, grown-up versions of the kids who used to gather in the smaller confines of the clubhouse to play blackjack. Oliver produced a deck of cards, waving it around in the air for all our eyes to take in. He swore it was the same deck we used in our clubhouse games. I doubted it, though it was the same brand, and the cards looked worn and faded, seemingly soft to the touch. They did not snap as he shuffled, like a fresh pack would. I could not believe he held onto them all these years, even as possessive as he was. I was sure the original pack had been lost in the fire.

As he shuffled, I reached out and grabbed hold of the cardboard box, extracting, with the lightest touch of my fingertips, the jokers from within. I stared at a joker's face. There was the muse of my youth who guided my imagination. That's what was missing. That's what I left behind when I moved to New York City: The attic room in my mind where the Joker lurked had gotten shut down, locked up. The Joker wasn't around to feed my mind the horror he collected in that dark place. The city was full of real horror, overshadowing the fangs and claws my imagination tried to conjure. Maybe I would have to unlock that attic door. Maybe I needed him to help me weave this tale.

We played blackjack just like we had in the old days, though the pots now were a little more bountiful than before. Oliver won most of the money, just like he always did. We had moved the portable bar into the room and many of the bottles were nearly empty. Lonny kept the ice bucket replenished from the freezer in the kitchen. He was slamming down the liquor at a pretty rapid pace. Something was gnawing at him. He seemed agitated. Outside the tavern earlier in the evening he had some words with Oliver in private, and his mood had been sullen since.

The inn was very quiet. No sign of the professor or the girl I had briefly glimpsed or of Mr. Wolfe or Sandy the chambermaid. It was as if we had the whole place to ourselves -- as if we were in our own private world, just like it was when we were in the clubhouse, without any outside interference in our domain. Yet, it didn't feel exactly like it did back then. I thought our conversations would revolve around the times we had as the

Jokers Club, but the talk continued to be stuck in the present gear. There was no down-shifting, no backpedalling.

After Oliver dealt the cards and Dale reached with his left hand to gather his up, I noticed Oliver glance at Dale's hand, and my gaze followed his to the white strip of skin on his ring finger.

"So how's the wife?" Oliver asked, wearing a smirk.

Dale met my gaze over the top of his cards and I could tell he realized his hand was exposed. There was no way he could bluff.

"Well," he said, lowering his eyes. "Actually, we've called it quits."

"No?" Lonny said, sounding surprisingly concerned. Oliver had trouble maintaining his smirk.

"I'm sorry to hear that," I said. "Truly."

"It's really for the best," Dale answered. "For both of us. Things just weren't going well."

"Real tough luck," Oliver said. "I thought for sure you two would make it."

"So did I," was all Dale could respond.

"Well, now you can join Thorn in the singles market," Oliver said, looking at me over his cards. "Is that right, Thorn?"

"Martin's still single," I said, gesturing.

"Peak doesn't count," Oliver responded, "he's practically married to his mother."

Lonny burst out laughing. Martin just looked down at his cards, not bothering to rebut.

"Don't plan too long a time mourning," Oliver said to Dale. "The pickings out there could be pretty slim."

"Not even on my radar yet."

"Well, if you wait too long, all that'll be left are divorcees and widows." Oliver smiled, amused with himself. "And they both come with lots of baggage."

"I think I'd rather be with a divorcee than a widow," Dale responded.

"How do you figure?" Lonny asked.

"Yeah," Oliver said. "At least with a widow, you don't have to worry about an ex being in the picture. And they are always going to be around for her kids. Forever. You've got birthdays, graduations, weddings, grandkids … It'll go on and on."

"And that would really suck," Lonny added, "especially if the ex is a real asshole."

"That's very true," I chimed in. "But with a widow, you have to worry about replacing someone that she probably still loves. That would be tough to deal with."

"Yeah," Dale agreed. "And the only reason she is with you is because she can't be with him."

"And you'd know that if she could have things her way, she'd rather be with him." Lonny said. "So you'll always be in his shadow."

At the word *shadow* everyone stopped talking. Lonny had been stupid enough to use the phrase. The word brought back memories of us all taking turns being the shadow (except for Oliver). Jason Nightingale was the last one to be the shadow, and nothing was ever the same after that.

I got up from the table and went to the bar to fix a new drink.

Oliver was the one to finally change the subject.

"Well, my life is about to experience a big change as well," Oliver said, beaming at us. "Just before coming up here, I found out I'm going to be a father."

"Wow!" Lonny exclaimed. "That's awesome."

Oliver grinned as others around the table congratulated him, and we raised our glasses in a toast.

"I meant to bring some cigars," he said.

Everyone became quiet.

I couldn't believe he'd said that, and didn't even seem to realize it as he showed little reaction. Had he forgotten? Was it that long ago?

"Welcome to the club," Lonny said, breaking the silence. "You're going to love kids. Nothing like it."

"Well," Dale said, "that will certainly be life-changing."

"Mostly for Janet," he smirked. "I don't expect much to change for me."

"You'll just have to get used to the adjustments Janet's body goes through," Lonny said chuckling. "The vomiting, the bad breath, the farting."

Everyone laughed, even Oliver.

"And the bigger she gets," Lonny said, still laughing, "the less sex you'll be having."

"Oh, I'm not worried about that. There's plenty of places I can find that."

"You wouldn't," Dale looked stunned.

Oliver glared at him seriously. "Wouldn't stop, if you know what I mean."

Dale raised an eyebrow. "Does your wife know?"

"Maybe. Doesn't matter if she does. She has it too good to ever leave me."

I rejoined the table. "Why would you do that?"

"I like the challenge. It's a sport. I never deny myself something. If I want it, then I'm going to get it."

"I've sure been tempted plenty of times," Dale looked around. "But I could never go through with it."

"That's because you're weak."

"I don't need to debate my masculinity with you. I'm not Lonny." He got up and went to the bar.

Lonny was jolted alert. "What's that supposed to mean?"

"Nothing." He poured a shot straight up and downed it."

I closed my eyes. My head was fuzzy.

Lonny stood up. "You have something to say?" His words were slow, but his tone harsh.

"You've been hovering around your mentor all night, just like you did as a kid, lapping around his ankles, eating up every word he utters about his glorious achievements."

"That's not true." He hid himself behind a drink.

I looked at Martin who was quiet, and then to Oliver who was beaming.

"Something eating at you, Carpenter?" Oliver leaned back as he spoke. "Other than the fact that I made something of myself."

Dale didn't answer.

"Is that why you planned this reunion?" I asked. "To gloat in front of us about your wonderful life?"

He stood up, seeming taller than before, and strode to the bar casting glances at all of us.

"In the club, you all looked up to me as a leader. I came here to see how you all turned out. But what I see when I look around disappoints me."

"I guess the games are over," Martin tossed his cards on the table, as he stood up and moved into the den.

"No," Dale said. "I think the games are just beginning."

Oliver laughed.

I got up and went into the den also. Everyone soon followed.

"Everything is a game to you," Dale continued. "You play your hand, always have something up your sleeve and you do whatever you have to win."

"I strive to excel. It's what got me where I am today. You could all learn a lesson from it."

"Maybe we're happy where we are," Martin said.

"At least I give the others credit for getting away from this dump of a town. But you Peak, you're stuck here, you're going to die here. And what's worse, you're content with that. You live your life, raise your chickens and you're happy. You still live with your mother for Christ's sakes."

"Ducks," Martin mumbled under his breath, barely audible. "They're ducks, not chickens." He looked at us. "And my mother is ill. She needs someone to take care of her."

Oliver turned to Lonny. "Make yourself useful and bring the bar in here."

"There you go," Dale said as Lonny turned.

"I'm doing it because I want to," he responded, "not because I have to."

Oliver chuckled.

"This is a game to you," I said. "One you really enjoy playing."

"You're the one that really surprises me, Thorn. I thought that if anyone was going to make something of themselves it was you. Were all those years of talking about what a great writer you were going to be just talk?"

That hurt. "As a matter of fact, I'm working on a book now."

Lonny wheeled the bar into the den.

"It's about us."

"Us?" Oliver questioned.

"The Jokers Club."

"Fiction or non-fiction?" Oliver looked upset.

"A little of both." I smiled.

"Is Jason going to be in it?" Lonny's glass shook as he loaded his ice cubes.

"He would have to be a big part of the story."

Oliver's fingers clenched on his glass. "Nightingale was never a real member of the Jokers Club."

"Are you really writing about us?" Dale asked.

I nodded. Even though I had only started it today, I wanted them to think I was actively working on it. "It's one of the reasons I came here. To get the feel of what things were like."

"And how do things feel?" Oliver asked.

"Very bitter."

"Better be careful what you write about me. I might have to sue your ass off." He chuckled and gulped his drink.

"Oh, you're a very special character."

"I won't hold my breath waiting for an advance copy. Because when it comes right down to it, I don't think you could get published on a bathroom stall. You're no better off than the rest of the losers here."

"Don't be so hard on him," Lonny said.

"You," Oliver replied to Lonny, "you turned out to be a really pathetic case."

Lonny's face blushed. He slammed his glass down on the bar.

"How can you treat me like this? All those years, there wasn't anything I wouldn't do for you."

"I always despised you for that. You were like a puppet. I pulled your strings for you. You never had a spine of your own." He turned to us. "You know what he had the nerve to ask me for tonight."

"Don't!" Lonny demanded.

"He came crawling to me –"

"I said don't!"

" — to beg me for money."

Lonny rushed Oliver, reaching out to grab him. Oliver was quicker, spinning him around and pinning him up against the wall.

I stood up but didn't feel compelled to interfere.

"All I asked you for was some help." Lonny's words came out part angry, part sobbing.

Oliver gripped tightly to his collar and moved his face close to Lonny's, breathing on him through gritted teeth.

"The only reason you came here is you figured you could mooch something off me. You're nothing but a phony." He grabbed the hair on the top of Lonny's head and pulled up. "You're even afraid to admit you've lost your hair." The hairpiece peeled back, revealing bare scalp.

Dale stepped between them and backed Oliver off.

"Easy, Carpenter," Oliver said, brushing his hands away.

"You don't know what it's like," Lonny said. "The pressures I'm under. I've got kids, responsibility. The bills come in. I got to make money. I can't sell an insurance policy every day."

"I thought you sold cars," I said.

"That's right." He waved his arms. "I sell cars. It ain't easy. I come home from work, supper's done, the kids are in bed by seven. There I am stuck in the house, nothing to do but stare at my wife and talk to the walls. I'm so bored, I want to scream. But the pressures are there. I feel like I can't even breathe. It hurts my head so much sometimes. I thought, maybe if I got a little help from you, my friend."

"I earned what I got."

"Enough!" Martin screamed out and we all turned to face him where he stood on the other side of the room. I don't think I, nor anyone else for that matter, had ever heard him raise his voice like this. I was skeptical it was him who had even spoken.

"You're all making me sick. Why did you come here? You all moved away and I was the only one who stayed behind. But that was fine by me. But then you had to come back. I knew this was a mistake. I wish none of you had bothered." He turned and left the room. There was a brief gush of air as the front door opened, then closed.

I hesitated for a moment and then went after him.

I caught up in the parking lot as he was about to get into his car.

"Are you all right?" I asked.

He sighed, looking all around him at the surrounding night, looking everywhere but into my eyes. "I just think it would be better if you all went back to where you came from."

I am back, I thought.

"It was just a chance for us to get together, reminisce about the old days. We had some good times."

"We also had some bad times."

"Yeah, but we shouldn't dwell on those."

"But they've never really gone away."

I bunched my hands in my pants pockets to warm them from the slight chill in the fall air. "I just wish I knew why Woody didn't show up tonight."

"He was the only smart one."

I shrugged. "Are you going to get together with us again this weekend?"

"I don't know. Maybe. I'm not sure what the point is."

We were both silent for an awkward moment, neither, I guess, knowing what to say. I broke the silence.

"I just wish things could be the way they used to be. I miss that. I miss the town, us as friends. I miss Meg."

He looked at me like I was crazed and then shook his head. "Why don't you grow up?" he yelled. I was taken aback. Who was this guy? "Why don't you stop living in the past and get on with your life?" He hopped in his car, started it up and drove away, tires spitting gravel.

"I can't help it," I said to nobody. "The past is all I have left now."

Back in the inn, things had quieted down. Dale sat on the couch; Oliver was standing by the fireplace; Lonny stood by the bar making himself a fresh drink. I joined Dale on the couch.

"How about making me another one," I said to Lonny.

"Make it yourself," he said sourly.

Dale chuckled.

The front door opened and closed, and there were footsteps in the hall. Thinking it was Martin coming back, I turned to look and saw a young, attractive woman with long, wavy brown hair. It was Meg, I thought, come to find me and take me away from this mess. She smiled a pleasant smile, and then disappeared up the steps.

No, not Meg. This was the woman guest Wolfe had mentioned, the one I had seen in the window. That was why she looked familiar then. This wasn't the first time I had seen a brunette and thought it was Meg. It had happened many times in the city. Everywhere I looked, there she was.

"Well," Oliver said. "I wasn't aware we were sharing our accommodations with something that lovely."

"Why don't you make a play for her," Dale scoffed. "You can put another notch on your belt buckle."

"Quite possible, Carpenter, but actually I've made other arrangements tonight."

"We're not ending the night already?" Lonny asked.

"This night ended before it started," Dale replied.

The tail end of Dale's sentence faded in volume with each word so I had to look at him to make sure his mouth was still moving. His face blurred and I closed my eyes hoping to clear my head. Pain slowly, but steadily built in the lower back left corner of my head. *Not again,* I thought.

Luckily my drink was empty because the glass slipped from my fingers and plopped softly onto the braided rug in front of the couch, spilling only a harmless couple of ice cubes.

I felt Dale's hand on my shoulder and heard him ask if I was all right.

"Yeah," I said, opening my eyes to a clearer vision of my surroundings. "Sure." The headache was still intense, concentrated so heavily on the left side of my skull that I thought my skull would tip over. I wanted to stand, but was afraid I'd go sprawling onto the rug beside my glass and the two quickly melting ice cubes.

"Just a little auto lag, I think," I said.

"You're getting old, Thorn," Oliver grinned. "You can't handle the booze like you used to."

"Are you sure you're okay?" Dale asked.

Their voices, coupled with the throbbing of the headache, felt like someone was slugging the side of my head with a mallet.

"I think I'll just call it a night and go upstairs and lay down." I wanted to get away from everybody, not let them see me like this.

"That's probably a good idea," Dale said.

"I was hoping you were going to cap the night with a scary story," Oliver said. "Just like you used to in the clubhouse."

I wasn't sure if he was mocking me or not. It did bring to mind a story I had written about this house and the Peas sisters and all their cats that had devoured the last sister and how, even though the police thought they destroyed all the cats, some still roamed these halls and rooms looking for fresh flesh to feast on.

"No," I shook my head. "There'll be time for stories later."

I made my way hesitantly up the stairs, aware of the watchful eyes upon me. When I got out of their sight at the top of the first landing, I paused, bending over and gripping my head in my hands. After a few deep breaths, I straightened, looking up at the moose head on the wall.

"What are you staring at?"

I moved down the hall, aware of the moose's eyes following me.

Once in my room, I lay down on my bed. I wasn't sleepy, so I just stared up at the pattern of the tin ceiling and did not think of anything, keeping my mind clear until the pain flushed itself out of my throbbing temple as quickly as it came.

I thought about returning downstairs to the others, but the way the night had gone didn't encourage me. Even though I had been remembering how much fun we had in the Jokers Club, tonight reminded me of some of the friction that arose from time to time. It was almost as if I had chosen not to remember it, like selective reminiscence.

Oliver's mention of Jason not really being part of the club reminded me of the incident with the house of cards. That was the catalyst of all the events that followed.

I sat up in bed and looked at the typewriter, then to the clock on the nightstand. It wasn't working. I wasn't sure if it was past quiet time, but it wasn't my fault the clock didn't work. I couldn't be blamed.

I got off the bed and went to the desk, rolling in a fresh piece of paper and closing my eyes to picture a tall structure of playing cards. My fingers started pecking at the keys before I reopened my eyes.

I wasn't sure how much time had passed when I stopped. I leaned back in the chair and stared at the small pile of paper for about five minutes, trying to remember what I had just written. When the knock came at the door, I was sure it was Mr. Wolfe come to scold me for typing past the "lights out" hour.

"Come in," I said, and when the door slowly opened, it was Dale's head that peeked in.

"I heard the typing stop, so I thought it was safe to intrude."

"Sure."

"I guess you're feeling better."

"It was just a headache, they come and go. I shouldn't have left the party so abruptly."

"Well, it wasn't much of a party anymore. Lonny's still downstairs, but Oliver's gone off somewhere."

"Some reunion." I laughed.

"Well, the only reason I came was to see you." He pulled a half-empty bottle of whiskey out from under his coat. "Want to join me out on the porch for a bit?"

* * *

We sat on the porch swing. The night was cool, but comfortable.

"Let's just hope we don't do this every year," Dale said, taking a swig from the bottle. He handed it to me.

My head already felt waterlogged, like a soaking wet sponge that couldn't absorb any more fluid. But I took the bottle and forced down a snort. It burned inside.

Lonny came out onto the porch. He also had a bottle in tow. I couldn't tell what it was.

"What are you up to?" Dale asked.

"Thought I'd just go for a walk."

"At this time of night?" I said, still not really sure how late it was.

He shrugged his shoulders. "Insomnia. Had it a couple of years now. Just can't seem to sleep. I try and try to force myself, can't do it. It's not that I'm not sleepy. God, I get so damn tired." He took a long gulp from his bottle. "Now, I usually just drink until I pass out. Seems about the only way I can get any rest. Trouble is, I wake up so hung over and tired the next morning, doesn't feel like it's done me any good." He took another gulp.

He looked out toward the town.

"You know, I used to love the nighttime. When Pam and I first got married, before we had the kids, we would go out at night all the time, have drinks, play pool, listen to a band. Once the kids came along, that all changed. Kids had to be in early. Put in bed by the time night fell. Then we'd be stuck in the house. I felt trapped. Like my home had become my prison. Though I could look out the windows and see the night, I couldn't get to it. It was out of reach." He took a swig from his bottle and wiped his lips with the back of his left hand. "Now it taunts me. I lie awake all night long, trying to get to sleep, just staring up at the dark ceiling, looking out the bedroom window at the night beyond. I have come to hate the night, knowing what restlessness it will bring. I dread that moment when I climb into bed, hoping sleep will come, knowing it isn't going to. The night has become my demon."

"That sucks," I mumbled, not really knowing what else to say. "Where are you going to walk to?"

He shrugged. "Don't know. Maybe down to the boardwalk. Look at the lake. As long as Heifer don't catch me and throw me in the drunk tank."

"Heifer?" Dale questioned. "Is he still chief?"

"Some things never change."

Lonny hesitated. "You know, I'm just having some financial problems, and I thought, since Oliver was doing so well, that a loan, just a loan, that's all I was asking for."

"It's okay," Dale said. "Don't worry about it."

"That's all I seem to do lately. Worry. I worry about money, worry about sleeping. Maybe it's the worrying about money that keeps me from sleeping. I don't know. I feel so desperate sometimes."

"Things will work out," I said, feeling sorry for him. But I doubted my own words. He didn't look like he had too firm a grip on things.

"Is my hair on straight?"

"Yes," I lied.

He turned, walked down the porch steps bottle held close to his side and disappeared into the night.

Our own bottle passed back and forth between Dale and me a few more times. I was nervous each time I took it. The tip seemed to waver in the air. I was afraid I was going to drop it.

"It was worth coming here just to see you," Dale offered again.

"There were so many things I wanted to accomplish this weekend."

"Like your book."

I nodded and then took the bottle. "There's a story I need to tell, and it has to be told here." I handed him the liquor. "Speaking of telling. Why didn't you tell me about your marriage being in trouble?"

He shrugged. "I was going to. Just waiting for the right moment I guess."

"Oliver always seems to find the right moment."

"Yeah."

"So what happened."

"We just can't seem to get along. All we do is bicker at each other. We don't really fight, but every single day we pick back and forth, usually about nothing." He drank from the bottle. "It's like we don't even have normal conversations. As if we forgot how to talk to each other. I'd come home from work every day and we'd be sitting in our condo and I would try to think of something to say to her but nothing would come. We'd just sit there in silence."

He looked down and shook his head. "You know, I used to enjoy lying in bed at night with her. We'd chat, make love, spoon like couples are supposed to. But then, more and more we started laying back to back. More like forks and knives." He chuckled. "I mean, we still have good times, but there isn't a day that goes by that one of us doesn't get uptight about something with the other. It just isn't fun anymore. I think the real problem is that I love her, but I don't really like her. And I think she likes me, she just doesn't love me."

"I'm sorry to hear that." I wanted to say more.

"It's funny. I had even stopped drinking from the day we got back from the honeymoon. I was figuring I was really going to try hard to settle down and be a responsible adult and husband. But that didn't help at all. This is practically the first time I've drank since. I guess it's my coming out party." He hoisted the bottle to his lips.

"And you're really between jobs?"

"Yeah, well sort of. I was actually downsized."

"That sucks. That stress couldn't have helped the marriage any."

"That was kind of the final straw. I didn't tell her right away."

"You didn't?"

"No. I couldn't bring myself to. I was embarrassed, at my age to be losing my job. So I got up every morning, put on my shirt and tie, grabbed my briefcase and drove off like I did every morning. I just didn't have any place to go."

"And she didn't suspect?"

"Nope. It worked for a few weeks, till she called the office one day and was shocked to find out I hadn't worked there for a while."

"What are you going to do now?"

He smiled. "Oh, I don't know, maybe move back here and milk cows for a living."

"What?"

He broke out laughing. "Just kidding. Actually, that's really the reason I came to this reunion, to talk to you about it. I thought I could come to New York, stay with you and look for a job. We could be roommates."

I didn't know what to tell him. If only. ... If only.

"It'll be like old times, you and me together. An adventure in the city. Think of the times we could have."

... If only I had time.

I thought back to that day in Dr. Cutler's office, driven there after the headaches wouldn't cease. And after all the X-rays and tests he had sat me down in his office and told me about the tumor. He described in precise medical detail the exact location of it in the back lower left portion of my brain and all I could think of was the little attic room the Joker inhabited.

It was malignant and feasting on my brain, he had said. An operation was necessary and he wanted to do it as soon as possible. There were no guarantees though. It was only a fifty-fifty chance, but without it, he doubted I'd last another year.

I told him I needed time to think about it, sort it all out, and he seemed shocked. Time was not an ally, but I had an important decision to make and that's why I think I really came back to Malton. Not to see how Woody was doing, not to see Dale and the others, not to find Meg, but to see if I really wanted to stop this thing.

The bottle went back and forth and so did my head, swaying as if it would fall off. Dale's face got serious and he began talking, but I couldn't hear him. I concentrated hard to see his lips move and hear the words coming out of them, tried to read them as they let loose from his mouth, but they were getting lost in the air. I squeezed my eyes shut and shook my head, trying to clear it, but everything began to spin, and I gripped hard with both hands on the banister as I found myself making my way up the stairs to the second floor. There was a relentless pounding in my forehead (*Don't open it*), and the going was tough. Bile began to rise in my throat. I thought I was going to vomit, but it subsided. The pounding continued. Each step was slow as my feet felt weighted. I had to keep both hands on the rail for fear of swaying too far sideways or backwards and tumbling down the stairs. I could see cats all over the steps, the Peas sisters' cats, and I had to be careful not to step on them as I made my way up each step. They were all around my feet. I could only see them out of the fringes of my vision and whenever I tried to look directly at one, it was gone, replaced by another just barely in sight.

The pounding in my head would not stop. I literally pulled myself along the banister, up the steps that seemed to get steeper the higher I got. The beating seemed to fade slightly, and I realized it was not coming from my head, but from somewhere below, from off to the left. The den maybe. But no, beyond it, the dining room, or further back in the inn.

At the first floor landing, I could have sworn the moose head's eyes followed me again as I made my way up the next flight of steps. I reached the landing on the third floor and used the wall to guide me to my room. Once inside, I closed the door and leaned against it, a rest for my reward for my mountainous assault.

I heard footsteps in the hall. Cats? No, the steps were too heavy. I turned and opened the door, just a crack, an eyeball's width.

The sound came from the steps leading to the fourth floor tower room. A figure emerged down the stairs. It must be Sandy, Wolfe's niece, carefully tucking in the front of her blouse and buttoning the top button. This was what Oliver meant by something else planned to cap the night. I closed the door and made my way to the desk. I picked up the pile of paper I had typed a short while ago. Or was it a long time ago?

I started to read it, though it was hard keeping the words in focus. I thought it was good. Hoped it was. I remembered in college how some of my best papers were written when I was drunk.

I put the papers down and nearly tumbled into the bed.

Maybe I should check underneath for cats?

I closed my eyes and thought about how far I had gotten in the story.

The pounding echoed in my ears.

THE FALL OF THE JOKERS CLUB

Dale had walked his bike to the boardwalk where Martin, Geoff and Jason were waiting astride their bikes watching the early summer activity on the beach.

Jason let out a deep sigh. "This school year seems like it's never going to end."

"The older we get, the longer they seem," Martin replied.

"Every year feels like a prison term," Dale said, popping a wheelie on his bike, the front tire slamming down on the boardwalk causing it to rumble. He glanced over his shoulder toward one end of the wood planks and smiled. "Hey, look who's heading this way."

They all looked in his direction.

"Carrothead."

None of them knew Carrothead's real name. There were many stories about how he got to be like he was, but one was more common than the others.

He used to be normal, the story went, and in fact was a star athlete in high school. But one summer he was out with a group of teens at the rope swing on the east side of the lake. The story went that he was swinging on the rope out toward the water when, at the apex of his swing, he released the rope and attempted to do a mid-air summersault. As he body twisted around it became entangled in the rope which wrapped around his legs and neck. He hung there in the rope, swinging back and forth over the water like a pendulum while his friends frantically attempted to cut him down. They managed to free him in time to save his life, but the oxygen to his brain had been cut off long enough to cause permanent brain damage. The rope had also damaged the circulation in his left leg that left him walking with a jerky, shuffling movement.

That was how the story went, anyway.

No one was quite sure exactly how old he was – most likely mid-twenties – but to Dale and the others, he appeared child-like. He lived with his mother somewhere off Autumn Avenue, and people said she was just as nutty as he. He always dressed in a pair of blue overalls, and whether he owned several or just the one, no one could be sure. He usually wandered the streets, spending day and night on the boardwalk, but he never bothered anybody so nobody bothered him, except for the kids who sometimes teased him. He kept a walkie-talkie with him that he constantly talked into, and no one knew for sure whether there was anybody else on the other end. Maybe it was his mother, telling him when to come home for lunch or dinner or to take out the garbage.

Carrothead came shuffling down the boardwalk toward the four boys. He looked all around him, first over his left shoulder, then over his right. He clutched the walkie-talkie to his chest with both hands as if afraid someone would snatch it from him. He brought it to his mouth and spoke softly into it.

His eyes lifted over the device without bringing it down. They scanned from left to right, from one boy's face to the next. His lips moved as he spoke into the mouthpiece, too low to hear.

"Let's go," Geoff said, and the four boys pushed their bikes along the boardwalk past Carrothead. When Dale was a step or two past him, he stopped and turned around.

"Who's there?" he asked.

Carrothead looked at him. His face scrunched up as he spoke. "It's the other side. They want to know if it's safe to come out."

Dale stared in curiosity for a moment, then reached out and grabbed the walkie-talkie. "Let me talk to them."

Geoff and the others had stopped ten feet further down and watched. Before Dale got a chance to utter a sound into the walkie-talkie, two stone-like hands grabbed onto his wrists.

"Don't you touch it!" Carrothead screamed, his face red, his mouth twisted. His hands pried the coveted apparatus from Dale's.

"Leave him alone," Geoff yelled to Dale.

"They won't talk to you!" Carrothead spat out of his scrunched face. "They only talk to me!"

Dale took a step back. Drool had begun to run out of the corner of Carrothead's mouth.

"You'll see them in time! Don't worry!" A long string of spit hung down past his chest.

"Let's get out of here," Geoff called to Dale.

"Yeah," he answered, turning his bike and taking a step, but then he stopped and looked back.

"They know about you!" Carrothead yelled. "I've told them all about you! They know everything."

"Come on, Dale!" Geoff screamed. "Move it."

"I'm coming." He ran, pushing his bike, and caught up with them. "I've never seen him act like that before."

"He gives me the creeps," Jason said.

"We really shouldn't bother him," Geoff responded as they mounted their bikes and raced down Autumn Avenue. When they got to the clubhouse, Oliver and Lonny were already there.

"Don't anyone dare breathe," Oliver said.

Before them, on the cable spool, stood the biggest house of cards Dale had ever seen. It was seven stories high and must have taken three or four decks of cards to build.

"Wow," someone said, and he could see the walls of one side flutter from the breath. Oliver turned his head slowly toward them.

"Who did that?" he asked in a whisper, but turned back to the house without waiting for an answer.

Dale watched as Oliver slowly placed another card onto the top of the house, admiring the steadiness in his fingers. Then he sensed movement beside him and turned to tell Jason he better stand still but knew right away it was too late as Jason's left leg struck the open trap door in the floor of the clubhouse. It slammed shut with a loud, reverberating thump.

Jason froze.

Oliver looked toward him in horror, then back at the house of cards.

The whole structure began to vibrate like a giant mound of gelatin. Then Dale saw one card in the middle of the stack slip and tumble downward, almost in slow motion. Oliver reached both hands out, as if to try and steady the building, but in a sudden flash, the cards fluttered to the table top.

"Oh my god, oh my god," Jason said, "I'm –"

Oliver turned.

"You dillhole!" he screamed, his face red. His hands rose up in fists and he started to take a step toward Jason.

Dale saw what was about to happen and stepped between them. "It was an accident," he said. "It's over. Nothing you can do about it now."

Oliver looked at him, then over his shoulder at Jason. Dale could almost see the color in his face drain, as if some chemical reaction was taking place in his head.

"You owe me big time, Florence," he said and went to his seat and slumped down. Nobody said a word for a while. Nobody dared. They all just sat and kept quiet, looking from one to another.

"Anything going on, boys?" Oliver asked, calm now. It was as if the whole incident never happened.

"Carrothead's freaking out on the boardwalk," Dale answered.

"We should do something really good to that retard one of these days."

"He doesn't bother anyone," Geoff said.

"He bothers me by breathing." He scooped up a handful of cards from the table and dropped them back down with a sigh of boredom. "I almost gave up on you guys getting here."

"What's up?"

"I've got a treat." He reached over, grabbed a brown paper bag and pulled a handful of cigars from it.

"Cool! Where'd you get those?" Dale asked.

"I lifted them from the five and ten," Lonny said, smiling.

"I've already chewed the idiot out for not getting the kind that comes in their own tubes," Oliver began to hand them out. "At least he didn't get those wussy kinds that have the tips."

"Good thing Woody isn't here, he'd probably eat them," Dale said, taking his.

"I don't want one," Jason said when Oliver got to him.

"Come on Florence," Oliver waved the cigar under his nose. "It'll make a real man out of you."

Jason sighed. "Fine."

A book of matches was produced and they began lighting up. It took nearly half the book for them to successfully light the cigars. Soon, smoke and coughs filled the confines of the clubhouse.

"Is your father home?" Jason asked, looking out the window. "Cause he might be able to see the smoke coming out."

"Nobody's home. Don't be a pussy."

"I'm not sure I'm doing this right," Geoff said, a cough wrenching from his throat. "I think I'm gonna spit my lungs out."

"Don't worry, Thorn," Oliver said, puffing away. "You'll get the-"

"Jesus Christ!"

Martin screamed this, louder than he had ever sounded before. He was standing and pointing.

There was so much smoke from the cigars that Dale didn't notice anything at first. Then he looked at the pile of comic books in the corner, and the flame rising from the top.

"Holy shit!" Oliver jumped to his feet. He shoved Lonny. "Quick, put it out."

"Not me!"

They stood, stunned for a second, as the pile, in a flash, became engulfed. The flames crawled up the wall toward the clubhouse ceiling, as if the whole structure were made of paper.

Martin was the first one out the trapdoor, before Dale even knew he was gone. Lonny moved toward it but was shoved out of the way by Oliver, who scrambled out. As Dale waited for Geoff and Lonny to get out, his heart thumping wildly inside of him, he thought how lucky they were that Woody wasn't here, for it would have been now that the fatso would have gotten stuck in the door before the rest of them had a chance to get out first.

When Lonny's frightened face disappeared, Dale swung his feet out. He could see the flames stretching across the wall. He looked behind him.

Jason sat there, staring at the raging fire.

"Come on, Jason! Out!"

The boy was frozen.

Dale could feel the heat on the side of his face, giving him an instant sunburn. The flames were spreading across the clubhouse ceiling.

"JASON!"

The boy looked at him, mouth open a bit, but nothing came out. His eyes were unrecognizable.

"Please," Dale said.

A piece of wood cracked with a loud snap and it shook Jason out of his trance. He moved toward the trap door. Before Dale ducked out of the door, he looked up at the wall with the drawing his sister made of the Joker and saw it blacken and curl up in a grasp of red. The Joker seemed to be screaming in pain ... or madness.

When the boys were all on the ground below, they grabbed their bikes and moved away from the huge maple tree. They stood and watched as the searing heat completely engulfed the clubhouse and began dripping onto the branches of the tree. Martin was crying.

"My mother's going to kill me," he said.

"What are we going to do, Oliver?" Lonny cried, his voice high-pitched with fear.

"Shut up! Let me think." It only took him a second. "Let's just get the hell out of here. Now!"

They were on their bikes and racing down the street. Nobody knew where they were going, they just followed Oliver. In no time they were on the boardwalk by the lake, gasping for air from their frenzied flight. Oliver got off his bike and paced back and forth. Dale and the rest stood hunched over their bikes, some of them holding their guts and panting. A siren broke the air and they saw the fire truck screaming around the corner and up Autumn Avenue. Normally they would have chased after it, hoping for a chance to see something so cool. Not this time.

"We've really done it now," Martin said. He had stopped crying, but his eyes were red.

"We've been right here," Oliver said. He had stopped pacing.

"What?" Dale asked.

"We weren't in the clubhouse at all today. We stay right here. Pretend we've been here all the time. They won't be able to prove we did anything."

"They'll know," Martin said.

"They won't know nothing. Not if we stick together."

"I don't know," Dale said, shaking his head.

"It'll work if we stick together. We have to swear not to say anything about what happened."

They all agreed.

"I mean it," Oliver said to Jason, who was strangely quiet. He looked pale.

"Yeah," he answered.

"Oliver! Oliver!"

Dale looked up Autumn Avenue and saw Woody racing madly toward them on his bike. He skidded to a halt when he got to them and almost fell off. He tried to speak but was gasping for air and couldn't get any words out. No one said a word as they waited for his voice to catch up to his lungs.

"Christ, Oliver! The clubhouse is on fire! The whole damn thing is burning to bits! Tree and all!" This all came out in sputtered gasps. He was so excited, Dale thought he might pass out.

"We know," Oliver said.

The gasping stopped. "What?"

They filled him in on what happened, and then swore him to secrecy also.

"What are we going to do without a clubhouse?" Lonny asked.

"I don't know," was all Oliver could answer.

* * *

It was only a few days later that they all found themselves at the fire station in Chief Burns' office. All of them except Jason. Dale wondered why he wasn't here.

Chief Hooper stood behind the desk, right beside Chief Burns who was lecturing about the dangers of fire. One thought kept running through Dale's mind: *They can't know, they can't know, they can't know.* Hooper had a smug look on his fat face, as if he wanted to break into a smile, but knew that a stern look was best to intimidate and frighten the boys. When Burns was done, Hooper walked around the desk and stood in front, looking them up and down.

He's just trying to scare us, Dale thought. There's no way he can know anything.

"Would anyone care for a cigar?" he asked.

* * *

"Look at Oliver!" Lonny screamed. He was standing in the middle of Maple Street, pointing across the way at the Rench house. Dale was sitting with Geoff and Woody on the curb across the street. He looked up at Lonny's cry and saw Oliver crossing his front yard and heading down Maple to Shadow Drive, toward Jason's house.

They all ran to him and when they were close, Dale could see the black and blue all around his left eye and cheek. His lip was cut and trickled blood.

"I'm going to kill that bastard!" Oliver screamed, fighting back tears he refused to show.

Dale at first assumed he was talking about his father. They had all on numerous occasions heard the screams and yells coming from the Rench household and knew Oliver was getting beat upon, especially if Mr. Rench had been drinking. It was nothing new to them, but the severity had never been this extreme. Usually it didn't show.

"Wait up, Oliver," Lonny said, reaching out and grabbing his arm.

Oliver spun around and gave him a shove that sent him sprawling on his ass. "Don't touch me!"

The whole left side of his face was puffed out and swollen. Three-quarters of the white of his eye was bright red. The look in both eyes was mad.

Dale didn't dare speak.

"That son of a bitch is going to regret the day he was born."

"Your father?" Dale questioned.

"Jason!" Oliver screamed. "He ratted us out! He squealed the whole story to his dad!"

The others looked at each other with shock on their faces. No one in the group had ever squealed before. Lonny got up from the ground.

"The little prick," he said.

"I can't believe it," Woody said.

"Well, believe it," Oliver bellowed.

"What are you going to do?" Dale asked.

"I'm gonna tear his friggin' head off!" He started down the street. Dale thought about the praying mantis in the jar.

"He's not home," he said. Oliver stopped and turned around. "We looked for him before."

Disappointment spread over his face. "Lucky for him," Oliver said. "Damn lucky!"

"Now what?" Dale asked.

"It'll give me time to think." Oliver rubbed his fist in his hand. "We've got to fix him real good."

The black and blue image of Oliver's face stuck in Dale's mind that night as he lay in bed. Dark, brooding colors. He thought about his own father's reaction when he heard about how the clubhouse caught fire. Dale had remained secluded in his bedroom, dreading the moment when his father would arrive home from work. His sister enjoyed teasing him about how he was going to "get it when dad got home." Maybe she was mad her work of art had gone up in flames.

Dale heard the sound of the car pulling into the driveway and the opening and closing of car and house doors. His stomach trembled as he lay on his bed, listening to the muffled voices of his parents, not able to make out any of the words spoken. Then he heard footsteps on the stairs.

Dale nearly jumped off the bed when the door burst open. The look on his father's face was something he had never seen before. It was like a stranger had stormed into his room. A mad man.

He began yelling and screaming and all Dale could do was cringe and shrug his shoulders, giving soft answers of "I don't know" to the questions spewing from his father's enraged face.

Dale tried to crack a smile, because whenever his father was upset with him over something, Dale would try to lighten the situation and his father always ended up smiling along and everything would be all right again.

But this time, he saw his father raise his hand and an open palm swept across his face, wiping the half-smile away.

He hit me.

Dale watched in shock as his father turned and left the room. His left cheek stung and he lifted his hand to feel the warm, tender skin.

That had never happened before. His father had never hit him. Never. That was something Oliver's father did, not his own. His father couldn't be like Oliver's, could he?

A short time later, Dale crept quietly down the hallway and sat at the top of the staircase. From below, he could hear soft sobs. He wondered why his mother was crying, but then realized it was coming from his father.

His father was crying.

He could hear him tell his mother how ashamed he felt for hitting him. Dale's stomach ached with guilt. Two firsts in one day: He had made his father hit him and made him cry. He wished he could take it all back, but it was too late. It was all his fault.

No.

It was Jason's fault. He had caused this.

Now, lying in bed, the image of Oliver's face with him, he thought of what Oliver had said and agreed.

We've got to fix him real good.

CHAPTER THREE

Pounding. The pounding in my head won't stop.

I opened my eyes and the room swirled around me. I squeezed them shut, waited a few seconds, tried opening them again. The room oscillated back and forth like a pendulum, then slowed to a stop. The shade was open in my room and I could see the sun was just coming up, bringing what little light there was to the new day.

Why was I up so early?

The pounding in my head. That's what woke me up. But it wasn't the kind of beating headache I've been having lately or the kind a hangover brings. The pounding felt like it was coming from elsewhere, as if something, somewhere, wanted to be let in. Or out. (*Don't open it*).

I realized I'd slept in my clothes, but had only vague recollections of even going to bed. My mouth and throat were dry, and I felt an urgent need for fresh air.

Vertigo hit me momentarily when I stood up. I paused, closing my eyes until it went away, then gingerly made my way to the window and with strained effort, raised the sash. I sucked the air in deeply. It was cool and quenching, as if I were sucking the moisture off the surface of the lake, and I decided I needed more.

Not bothering to change my clothes, I went quietly down the hall to the bathroom on our floor. I could feel the frigid tiles through the thin fabric of my socks as I stood before a white pedestal sink. I turned the brass lever with the "C" on it and filled the sink with cold water, rubbing it into my face and eyes, taking handfuls into my eager mouth, feeling it cascade down my throat and scrape away the dryness. I looked at myself in the mirror, tried to make some semblance out of my disheveled hair, but gave up. I brushed my teeth and gums furiously to get the alcohol-laden taste and odor out of my mouth, gargling with the frothy lather before spitting it into the sink.

I made my way down the stairs after slipping my sneakers on. My body still felt unstable. I held onto the rail for support.

The inn was quiet.

I wondered if anyone else was up. As I reached the bottom of the steps, I noticed the basket of apples by the check-in counter and went over to it. I grabbed one, shining it on my shirt front and bit deeply, anticipating its moistness. Instead of a sharp snap, my teeth sunk into something soft and mushy. I pulled away the apple, staring into its brown interior. Rotten. I took the small piece out of my mouth, looked in vain for a garbage pail, and then stuck it in my front pants pocket. I heard footsteps and quickly returned the apple to the basket, bite-side down.

Bob Wolfe came out of the dining room door followed by the scent of fresh brewed coffee. The look on his face was surprise, either because I was up so early, or I looked worse than I thought.

"One of your friends is asleep on the porch swing," he said, his tone bitter. "Could you wake him?"

It wasn't really a question.

I grunted or nodded, maybe both, then headed for the door. When I stepped onto the porch, the air felt more invigorating than before. I looked at the porch swing and saw Dale sitting in it, head leaning back. At his feet lay the bottle we had been drinking, tipped on its side, a dark patch beside it where a puddle had formed and soaked into the floorboards.

I snuck up behind him carefully, trying not to make a sound. I gave the back of the swing a shove.

"Wake up you drunken loser!"

I moved around to the front.

The swing moved back and forth with a rusty creaking squeak.

Dale's eyes met mine.

I looked at the bottle by his feet, at the wet patch beside it. The patch was red.

I lifted my eyes and couldn't take them off the cut that ran from the top of Dale's chest, down to his belly. The soaked red clothing was ripped open. The jagged edge of the skin formed a long, deep crevasse. Pink muscle and innards showed through.

His eyes never left mine.

The porch swing continued to sway slowly back and forth, the chains it was suspended from crying out softly in rhythm: *creak ... creak ... creak.*

Something thick bubbled up from the base of my throat, maybe vomit, struggling as it rose 'till it reached the surface and erupted from my mouth as, not puke, but a scream.

*   *   *

I sat on the front lawn in one of the white metal patio chairs, my back to the front porch of the inn and the horror resting on it. I stared out at the calm of the lake beyond, two completely polar scenes. Mr. Wolfe had heard my scream, as did everyone else in the inn, and they took up various positions around the porch, keeping a reasonable distance from the body as we all awaited the arrival of the authorities. Nobody came near me at my front lawn outpost, as if they were afraid.

I didn't dare look behind me. I had seen the horror and now I just wanted to stare at the serenity of the lake. It reminded me of summer vacations during high school when I would hang out a lot at Meg's house on the west side of town. Her front lawn had a beautiful view of the water, and we would sometimes sit in wooden Adirondack chairs soaking up the sun. Usually I would give her one of my stories to read, and we would sit quietly, feeling the breeze float up while I waited with enthusiastic anticipation for her to finish and give me her critique. I was always a little nervous about what she would think. I wanted her to like my writing.

I remembered one time, when she read a tale I had crafted about an abandoned well at an old Wiccan's farmhouse and a trio of boys who summon a demon that crawls up from its depths. She smiled, she always smiled when she finished, and her milky brown eyes glowed.

"It's different," she said at last.

"What do you mean?" I asked.

"It's good, don't get me wrong. I like it."

"But ..." I hung on her words in anticipation.

"It's not like your usual stuff."

"Hmm," I said, pondering. "How so?"

She fanned herself with the pages, thinking, and I was sure she was trying to find a delicate way of putting it. That's Meg, never wanting to say something bad, always looking for the good angle.

"The ending is pretty creepy," she continued, "and gave me chills, even here in the bright daylight. I guess," she shrugged her shoulders and tossed her wavy brown hair, "it's just not as gruesome as you usually write."

I looked at her in silence, thinking it over.

I remembered the story I wrote about the fishermen in the lake, trying to catch what turns out to be a prehistoric fish. I got pretty graphic with that one, with dismembered limbs and blood-churned waters and the jaws of the lake creature chomping on the helpless fishermen. Yeah, that one was a bit gory.

At some point the gore seemed to lose its bite. Maybe it was because of that one summer when I came face-to-face with true horror. That had been real and diminished all the grotesque blood-drenched images my mind had conjured up. The Joker in that attic room in my mind had helped me conjure up those visions. He seemed to relish the most absurd demented tortures any soul could bear and laughed as I wrote them down.

When I entered through the door into that attic room, the Joker was the one really in charge. He knew. He guided me, helping me wade through the tide of blood.

"That's what they want," he'd say. "They want blood. Deep red blood." And he would grin, his teeth shining, and I would write.

But once I had seen real horror, I realized the Joker's tapestry of terror was not nearly as unsettling as what deeper, darker things could scare the human mind. For a while I couldn't even write at all, thought maybe I'd never be able to again. But the Joker was always there to help me and eventually I was able to get back to it. But things were different now. Maybe it disappointed my muse, maybe the Joker understood, but I tried to write my stories with a truer sense of what was really frightening.

"Maybe I've matured," I finally said, looking at Meg. "Don't need to always go for the guts."

She leaned over and pressed her soft lips against my cheek.

"Well, it's subtle, I like it. I think it's great progress." She leaned back in her chair smiling and I just marveled at how adorable she was and how lucky I was to have her.

But now I had seen real horror once again, right there behind me on that porch swing. Meg had it all wrong; the Joker was right. There was nothing subtle about horror. It was gruesome and grotesque and Dale's blood soaked the wood of the swing and the floorboards beneath and you could see the ragged tearing of his flesh and the innards through the opening in his abdomen.

No, nothing subtle about that. That was horror.

And no matter how much I stared out at the beauty of the lake, I couldn't ignore it. Not when the wail of the sirens approached to remind of what was going on behind me. I had to turn around and face it. There was no other choice.

* * *

Police Chief Hooper hadn't changed at all. He was just as fat and ugly as I remembered. We all stood at one end of the porch: Lonny, Oliver, Martin and myself. I looked at the faces around me. They were all pale, and I imagined my own to be the same. Nobody spoke.

A little further away from us stood Bob Wolfe, Sandy the chambermaid, Professor Bonz and the woman guest. They too were silent.

In the middle of the porch were Hooper and several other police officers, all standing around the swing. With them was a medical examiner looking over the body. One of the police officers was taking pictures from a variety of angles.

Dale remained seated, unaware of everything going on around him. Like the rest of us, he too was silent, would always be. It was crazy. He couldn't be dead. I was sitting there right beside him on that swing just hours ago. And now he was still there. But he wasn't ever going to get off of it. Not on his own. Dead. Murdered. It was all a dream. No more spooning peanut butter from jars snatched from our mothers' kitchens. No more racing through the ravine during a game of Relievo. If I could just shake his body hard enough to wake him.

The officer with the camera continued taking pictures. I wanted to grab the camera from him and smash it into his face. Didn't he realize Dale didn't want to be photographed?

His eyes were open. That freaked me out the most. He looked right at me. How could he not see me? How could he not know what was going on now?

The doctor took a step back from the body. He looked at Chief Hooper.

"Notice the ragged edges of the skin along the wound?"

The chief nodded.

"Most likely a knife with a serrated edge. Judging from the size and depth of the opening, a rather large blade I'd say."

"Maybe a hunting knife?" the chief questioned.

"Could be."

The cop with the camera kept shooting.

"It doesn't look like he put up any struggle," the doctor continued. "No defensive wounds on the hands."

He did look peaceful, I thought.

"Could it be," the chief said, "that the killer came up behind him?"

The examiner nodded. "Possible." He rubbed his chin. "Most likely they wouldn't have gotten much blood on themselves that way."

"No," I said.

All heads turned toward me.

"The killer wasn't behind him. He would have been in front. Dale saw the killer. You can see it in his eyes."

His eyes *were* looking at something. They weren't just vacant eyes. Even in death they held something.

The chief glared angrily at me. He conferred with the examiner some more in an inaudible conversation. Then he signaled for the ambulance attendants, who had been patiently standing nearby, to proceed with their end of the business.

I watched as they callously laid Dale's body out on the outspread plastic bag. I couldn't take my eyes away. I realized this would be the last time I would see Dale. I wanted to reach out to him, tell him I wouldn't forget him.

One of the attendants pressed his eyelids closed.

No, I thought. Don't shut out his world. Don't close off his last look.

But I realized he could look no more.

I turned my head when they began to zip up the plastic bag. I did not want to see that, but the metallic sound ripped through my body like an icy blade.

After the ambulance pulled out, I opened my eyes and looked at the others. Martin's head hung down, exposing more of his bare scalp;

Lonny's hands kept twitching as his fingers continuously moved to his head to adjust his hairpiece. It didn't help.

Even Oliver seemed shaky. He kept exhaling deep breaths.

I listened as Hooper questioned Professor Bonz and the two women. They had all gone to bed early they told him, the professor accentuating his need to rise early to get onto the lake for his studies and expressing frustration at this current interruption.

I remembered seeing the female guest going upstairs to her room while we were still in the den. I also remembered the chambermaid, Sandy, coming down from Oliver's room. What did she consider early? How long had I sat out on the porch with Dale? How late was it when I went up to my room? Nothing was clear to me.

Hooper thanked them and let them go about their business. Then he turned his attention to us.

As he crossed the porch approaching us, the floorboards emitting a strained creak with each step, he removed from his front pocket a plastic bag and pulled out of it a hunk of pepperoni. He bit off a huge chunk, gnawing it as he replaced the remainder in his pocket. He tugged on his belt when he stopped in front of our group.

The way he glared reminded me of the many times he would approach us as kids and accuse us of some mischievous activity. Like the time Oliver caught a duck with a fishing net and we put it in Hooper's car. The next morning, the bird flew out as soon as Hooper opened his door. But it had left behind a gooey mess all over the car's seats.

He had stared at us then in hopes one of our members would finally crack and admit our guilt. But no one ever did. Except that one time Jason Nightingale squealed.

"I knew you were all back in town." He glanced from one to another.

Nobody said anything.

"You probably didn't have any idea I knew what was going on. I know more than you think. I didn't like the idea of you guys coming back here one bit. I haven't forgotten all the trouble you and that stupid club of yours caused. Don't think for one second that I have." He chewed as he talked and a bit of drool poked out of one corner of his mouth. He wiped it away with the back of his hairy hand. "You've left some black scars on this town. You've never been nothing but trouble to me. And here it is years later, and you're still at it."

"You got a point?" Oliver asked.

Hooper looked at him. "I don't like any of you, never have. And if I pin this on one of you, it'd make me very happy."

"You don't think –" Lonny began, but a look from the chief stopped him from finishing and caused him to play with his hair some more.

Hooper turned to me.

"You were the last one to see him?" His breath stunk of pepperoni.

"Yes."

"What time?"

I shrugged. "I really don't remember."

"About?"

I thought real hard, but the whole night was blurry; I just couldn't remember. I really didn't remember even leaving him to go upstairs. I just had vague recollections of climbing the stairs to my room. Time was a total blank.

"I really don't know. We had quite a bit to drink."

He bowed his head and shook it slowly, then with hands on hips, looked up at the porch roof and wheezed a slow sigh. "And you were the last one up?"

Wait a minute, I thought. Lonny had still been out. He couldn't sleep and had been out walking the streets. He would have come up later. He would have had to walk right by Dale.

"Yes," I lied. "I was the last one up, except for Dale."

"Why didn't he go up?"

Why? If only he had this wouldn't have happened. Everything would be all right. Why had I gone inside and not he? What had we been talking about? He had been telling me something. What was it? Why couldn't I remember?

I looked over at the porch swing and the red streaks on its white paint, the splotch of red on the floorboards beneath it.

"I don't know," was all I could answer.

He huffed and another wave of pepperoni smacked me.

"I know Mr. Wolfe would prefer you all got out of his inn, but I'll have a talk with him. I want you all around for a few days while we investigate this."

"We have these rooms booked through Sunday night, chief," Oliver said. "Unless you want to charge us with something, we are free to go as we please."

"You're still a wise-ass." He scratched his fat belly. "Just remember. You're not kids anymore."

No, I thought. If only we were.

The chief started to walk away, and then turned back.

"I notice Mr. Woodman isn't here."

"He didn't show," I said.

"I guess I'll have to look into that."

* * *

After Hooper and the other cops left, we gathered in the inn's den. We were all seated except for Lonny, who paced in front of the fireplace. Everyone was silent at first. I just shook my head, trying not to believe all this was happening. Dale was gone. His body was wrapped in plastic and on its way to some morgue where they'll throw him on a cold steel slab to perform the autopsy. At least his body was already split open down the middle; that should make their work easier. They'll rip out all his internal organs to get a sample and slice them up like vegetables for a salad.

This shouldn't be happening.

I couldn't stop thinking about his eyes, the way they were looking at me. I started thinking about when I first saw those eyes, when I turned around in class in second grade and saw the little blond-haired, gap-toothed kid looking back at me, smiling. The teacher introduced him as a new student in town.

At recess, while I played with some of my friends, I noticed him off by himself, watching us. He was still smiling, and I wanted to invite him to join in but was a little too shy to ask.

When school ended that day, I noticed him in line for the same bus as mine. He sat a few seats behind me and I kept wondering where he lived. Whenever I looked back, his eyes met mine and we both smiled. When I got to my stop and got off, so did he. As I headed down Maple Street, I watched as he went up Autumn Avenue and then turned down Elm. I raced all the way home to tell my mother there was a new boy in the neighborhood.

It was hard to believe that smiling seven-year-old boy carrying a lunch box and a pencil case would eventually end up having his abdomen sliced open with the serrated edge of a knife.

A strange thought occurred to me. This incident could give the story I wanted to write a new direction. This was like a natural progression of events. It was as if the story was starting to write itself. Maybe it's why I came here. Maybe it's whey we were all brought here.

Lonny broke the silence. "Why would anyone want to kill Dale?"

"I don't know," I said.

"Could be some maniac drifter," Martin offered. "Just doing it for the thrill."

"They'd have to be nuts," Lonny said. "The way they butchered him."

Oliver cleared his throat. "I think we should all realize that this may not be a random act."

"What are you getting at?" I asked.

He stood up from his chair.

"Just, maybe he was killed for a reason. Maybe someone wanted him dead."

"No," Lonny exclaimed, as if it never occurred to him. "You think so?"

"But who?" Martin asked.

"And why?" I added.

"Why? I don't know. But maybe the chief's right, maybe it's one of us."

He almost smiled as he said this. We all looked at each other.

Yes, I thought. This would fit in with the story.

"You mean one of us wanted to get rid of him?" Lonny said. "Are you crazy?"

"Someone is."

Something I had forgotten came to me. "Lonny, didn't you see Dale on the porch when you came in last night?"

"That's been really bugging me. I remember being down by the marina, drinking that bottle I had. I'm pretty sure I finished it, cause I remember chucking it into the lake." He began to pace. "I was really drunk. I know I headed back to the inn." He stared at the floor. "I came in the front door. I had trouble opening it for some reason. And I went up to my room." He looked up at us. "But I don't remember if I saw him or not. He could have been awake, maybe I even talked to him. I don't recall. Maybe he was passed out." His body trembled. "Or maybe he was already dead and I walked right by him without noticing."

"Do you have any idea what time it was?" I asked.

"What are you getting at?" His voice rose. "Are you trying to say I did it?"

"I'm just asking –"

"Why would I want to kill him?"

"You're the one desperate for money," Oliver offered.

"He wasn't robbed!" Lonny's face turned red.

"No, but you begged me for money yesterday. Maybe this is some way of threatening me, scare me into paying you off?"

"You're nuts! I always thought you were smart. You're just an idiot!"

"If Dale was brought here to be killed," Martin said to Oliver. "Remember, it was you who invited us to this reunion."

He laughed. "Why would I need to kill anybody? I've got everything I want."

"Maybe that's it," I said, leaning forward. "You're the most successful one of us here. Maybe you're afraid of exactly what you said about Lonny, that one of us will take advantage of your success and try to blackmail you. Maybe you brought us all here to get rid of us."

"That's ludicrous. Blackmail me with what?"

"A horrible wrong committed long ago."

He approached me and leaned over. "I did nothing wrong."

"You still believe that? Is that what you keep telling yourself?"

"I don't even think about it anymore."

"Don't you?"

He turned and walked across the room.

"Besides, I may have sent the invitations, but this reunion wasn't my idea."

"Oh, whose then?"

He turned around. "It was Woody's."

"Woody's?" I said, surprised.

"He wrote me awhile back, suggested that we all get together. I took it from there."

"Why should I believe you?"

"I don't care if you do."

"Do you think Woody's here?" Lonny suggested.

I thought about it, about what Woody said to me when I last visited him.

"I suggest we all keep our eyes open," Oliver said.

"It won't matter," I responded. "We can't control our destiny in this thing. This whole thing is like a story. And we're all just characters. We'll just have to let the tale play out."

"And just who might be writing this story, Thorn?" Oliver asked. "You, perhaps."

"If only I was this creative."

Lonny let out a deep breath and shook his head. "This certainly isn't going to help my insomnia."

"There's one thing we haven't considered," I said.

"What?" Martin asked.

"Maybe this reunion is more complete than we thought."

Oliver looked irritated. "What are you driving at?"

"Maybe Jason is here."

"You're not serious?" Lonny looked up, his voice half laughing, half quivering. "I mean, you really don't think so? Do you?"

"Why not?"

"You're a bigger fool than I thought you were," Oliver grunted. "Jason Nightingale is dead."

"You don't have to remind me," I said. "We're the ones who killed him."

HOUSE OF THE TIN MAN

Woody shone his flashlight out his dark bedroom window onto Geoff's window at the house next door.

Come on, Geoff, he thought. *Hurry.*

Finally, the shade lifted and Geoff stuck his head out.

"What are we going to do, Geoff?" His voice was loud enough to travel across the lawn separating their houses but quiet enough so his parents downstairs wouldn't hear.

"I don't know," Geoff shrugged.

"We've got to do something. We can't leave him out there all night."

Geoff lowered his head, as if he were concentrating real hard.

"Meet me outside," he finally said. "And bring your flashlight."

Woody knew where they were going: back to the Tin Man's house.

The house was mired at the end of Shadow Drive. Not to either side of the dead-end street, but directly at the end, so that if the road were to continue, it would go straight through the front door. It was a lonely old house, badly in need of repairs. A rusty gutter hung unevenly from the front edge of the roof, the left side dangling as if it would give way with the slightest accumulation of rain. Behind the dust-covered windowpanes on both floors were dark green shades pulled down, obstructing any view, in or out. The house hadn't seen a paint job in years and not a flake remained of whatever color it had been. There were only dingy gray clapboards cracked and calloused like the owner's dried skin.

His name was Emeric Rust. He seemed a century old. He'd lived in the house forever, Woody had been told. His face was a mass of wrinkles, resembling a mountainous region on a topographical map. Round eyes appeared to bulge out of his head. His crown was topped with, surprising for his ancient years, thick white hair.

He rarely made an appearance outside the house, except for the occasions when he would chase members of the Jokers Club with a long-handled spade shovel, yelling, "Keep out of my yard!" The only other times Woody saw him was when one of the green shades would suddenly shoot up and his bulging eyeballs would peer out of the dusty windows, ping-ponging back and forth until, just as suddenly, the shade would jerk down.

His name was Emeric Rust, but to all the kids, he was the Tin Man.

His name originated from the condition of his back yard. Amidst the tangles of the overgrown lawn was an ever-expanding pile of junk. It had grown continuously over the years. It was now a mountainous mound coated with rust. Amid the heap were old tire rims, bicycle frames, an aged mailbox, electric fans (box and oscillating), toasters and other small kitchen appliances, rakes, hoes, the guts of a washing machine, tin cans, a television set with an exploded picture tube, a baby carriage, a lawn mower and the blades of a snow blower. Near the top was a box spring with the padding long worn away, leaving only the skeletal remains of springs and frame.

There were things that seemed to be growing out of the pile as if through some form of metallic gestation. Some stuff appeared to melt together to form one object, and other things were so dripping in rust as to be indecipherable. It seemed as if everything and anything had found its way onto the pile. At the very top there was even a kitchen sink.

Beside the junk pile there was also an old black junked car, resting on rusted rims, the trunk open, the hood missing (probably buried in the junk pile), a spider-web crack splattered across the windshield, the back window blown out completely, and the vinyl seats shredded and spilling out stuffing.

It was between the car and the junk pile that the seven boys had stood earlier that day. They were playing Relievo, a game of capture the enemy played between two teams. A cross between hide and seek and tag. One team pursued another. The goal was to elude the pursuers for an allotted time period. If members were captured, they were held in a designated "cell" and could not escape unless a member who hadn't been caught was able to sneak up to the cell and tag a teammate yelling, "Relievo!" The prisoners would run free and the pursuit would continue. Only when all the members were captured could the pursuing team claim victory.

The Jokers Club members considered themselves experts at the game, and they accepted challenges from anyone who wanted to dethrone them. This time the challenge came from a group of kids from a neighborhood on the west side of the lake. As usual, Oliver had chosen the Jokers Club to be the ones pursued.

Jason Nightingale was with them. He had avoided them for the first couple of weeks after the clubhouse fire, but, living right down the street from them, it became difficult. Shortly after school let out for the summer, he came to them and apologized. He said his father had pressured him into telling the truth about the clubhouse fire.

They had all agreed not to have anything more to do with Jason Nightingale. All of them had gotten in deep trouble because of him and suffered a variety of punishments, though none as severe as Oliver's.

Woody was stunned at first when Oliver decided to accept the apology. Eventually he realized something was up Oliver's sleeve. He was biding his time till the right moment arose. He had no idea when or what, but he knew something would happen.

Five minutes before the Relievo game was to begin, the Jokers Club all looked to Oliver.

"What's the plan?" they asked.

Oliver looked them over, and then glanced around.

"We need a shadow," he finally said.

Woody saw the confusion on Jason's face. They explained it to him. The shadow was a tactic they sometimes used in the game. One of the players would remain completely concealed in a hiding spot so even if the rest of the team was captured, he could remain hidden until the game was over. At one time or another they had all been the shadow, with the exception of Oliver.

"This time," Oliver said, "it can be you, Nightingale."

Jason started to utter a protest, but wisely halted.

"Where do I go?"

Woody looked at the trunk of the junk car. They had used it a few times, and he himself had lain in its darkness, being the shadow, being obscured by the dark. Oliver even took a step toward the car, but then spun on his heels and pointed.

"There!"

Woody turned and followed his outreached arm and extended index finger to a spot halfway up the south face of the junk pile.

There stood, embedded in the surround metal and tilted backwards, an old refrigerator. Its whiteness had dulled and there were blood-like splotches of orange as if it had been fired upon with rust bullets.

Jason looked at it, then at the others and finally at Oliver. "In there?"

"They'll never find you."

Jason hesitated momentarily, looking at the others as if for some clue as to how he could back out. No one said anything. He looked back at Oliver.

"We don't have much time."

The footing was tenuous to say the least. Some bits of metal scrap held more firmly than others, but Jason reluctantly picked his way up the hill of junk.

Woody looked at Geoff's face, then the others. They just looked back. Nobody knew what Oliver was up to; nobody knew what to do.

Jason's sneaker gave way on the side of an empty paint can and he lost his balance, his arms wind-milling like a cartoon character, but he reached out and grabbed a protruding piece of lead pipe and steadied himself. He looked down at the others.

"I don't know about this, Oliver," he said.

"Florence," was the sneering response and that was enough to spur him on till he reached the refrigerator. With a tug he opened it.

From where Woody stood, he thought he saw something in the shadow of the inside of the refrigerator, something shifting. He wanted to call out, but knew it was only his imagination and he kept quiet.

"Not much time," Oliver said.

Jason stepped into it and swung the door closed behind him with a thud that echoed in Woody's ears.

Nobody moved for a moment, as if that thud had frozen them all. A muffled voice came from beyond the door.

"It don't open from this side!"

"We'll let you out when the time is up!" Oliver yelled.

He turned his back to the pile and stepped away from it.

"Is he gonna be okay in there?" Dale asked.

"Sure," Oliver said, turning and facing them.

Woody could see the glint in his eyes.

"What are you up to?" Geoff asked.

"He's gonna stay in there. All night."

Lonny smiled. "Yeah."

"How long?" Woody asked.

"We'll let him out in the morning."

Woody looked at the others, not knowing what to do.

"You gotta be with me on this," Oliver yelled. "He ratted on us." He looked from face to face. "We all got punished, now it's his turn." The tone of his voice elevated. "It's his turn to be punished. Right guys?"

Woody thought about it. It was true. They had resented him when he squealed. No one in the club had ever done anything like that before. Jason deserved what he was going to get.

"But he is gonna be all right?" Woody asked.

"Sure. He spends the night, cries a lot, then we let him out in the morning and kick his ass out of the club."

Woody thought about it for a moment, as he was sure the others did. Jason hadn't been a part of the club for very long. It wasn't like the two of them had made any special connection. Jason had always seemed more interested in Geoff and Dale. It could be easy not to be friends anymore. And he did deserve it.

Oliver took the silence as agreement and gave them one last order. "Scatter."

*   *   *

They had won the game of course, like always. Afterwards, Woody and the others stood silently in Oliver's back yard, as if not sure what to do next.

"Are you really going to leave him there all night?" Geoff asked.

"You're damn right," Oliver replied.

"Hasn't he had enough?"

"No!" Oliver's face flushed. "He could never have enough."

"We let him out first thing in the morning," Dale assured.

"What if he tells his old man on us?" Woody asked.

Oliver went up to him and looked him in the face. "He wouldn't dare!" He turned to look at the others. "We go home. Nobody says a word. Nobody lets him out till morning."

Quietly, they all went to their own houses as night came on.

Woody thought about Jason in the refrigerator. He imagined time would be crawling slowly for him, wondering when they would come for him. *If* they would come. Panic would set in and it would dawn on him that he wouldn't be getting out. He imagined Jason, trapped inside that white coffin, pounding on the door, screaming for help. But there would be no one to hear him. Or would there? Maybe the Tin Man would hear his calls and come for him. But once he let Jason out, what would he do to him then?

He felt sorry for Jason, but it was his own fault. No one in the club had ever squealed before. It just didn't happen.

Unable to sleep, he had looked at the clock and saw it was just before midnight. Sleep was not going to come. That was when he grabbed his flashlight and signaled to Geoff's window.

Now the two of them found themselves walking down the sidewalk on Shadow Drive. The night was hot and clear and eerily silent. No cars turned down Shadow Drive. No one was about in the neighborhood at this late hour. Stars spattered the black sky above, helping the moon to light darkened air. The shambling house at the end of the road moved closer toward them, as if it rested on wheels that were slowly rolling down the quiet street. The boys could almost imagine the sound of the tires squeaking, for indeed they would be old, worn and rusted rims like the rest of the house and like the junk pile in the back yard that was their destination.

As the house moved closer to them, the pace of their steps slowed. When they first left they had been running, as if urgency were their utmost concern. But now that their arrival at the Tin Man's home was imminent, the need to hurry did not seem as important.

Before they knew it, the structure was upon them, seemingly leaning out over them like some lumbering beast, stretching its creaking timbers and beams. Geoff motioned for Woody to be quiet as they crept around the side of one wall with caution, as if the sound of sneakers on grass would be noise enough to wake the rotting hulk. Once out back they saw the junk pile, looking twice its size in the moonlight, one complete entity instead of being made of multitudes of organisms, like a giant beast rising up from the dark earth.

They stood beside each other in front of the pile, not speaking. Woody flicked the flashlight on and guided its beam up the sloping surface. Weird twisted shapes jumped out as the spotlight shone on them, like macabre performers on a ghastly stage. The junk seemed even more unrecognizable in the dimness of the interrupted dark.

It's gone, Woody thought as he frantically played the beam over the pile searching for the refrigerator. Maybe the junk beast had swallowed it whole, Jason and all. But then he saw it, higher up than he remembered, and pinned his beam on the reflective surface.

At the end of the flashlight's tunneled vision the refrigerator looked as if it were bobbing on an ocean wave. Its surface appeared gray and looked cold to the touch even in the hot summer night. There was an unnatural silence that surrounded the box that had become Jason's prison.

Woody heard a gasp and it took him a moment to realize it came from himself. He forgot Geoff was even with him till he felt a hand grip his arm. He turned and looked into his friend's face. He was met with nervous eyes and rapid breaths. They both looked back up, at the refrigerator.

"Jason," Geoff whispered. There was no answer.

"Jason!" Woody yelled out loud. Geoff clamped a hand over his mouth. The name echoed around them in the darkness.

"Quiet. The Tin Man might hear you." They turned and looked back at the house. The dark green shades were all drawn as usual.

They returned their gaze to the junk pile.

"Maybe the Tin Man already got him," Woody said.

"Maybe. But he probably just fell asleep. He's been in there a long time."

"Well, we better hurry."

"Yeah."

Woody aimed the flashlight beam to guide Geoffrey who began climbing the metal mound. He proceeded cautiously as if he was uncertain about the foothold for each step he took. Woody had visions of him planting his foot on a sharp metal shard and having it come right up through the top of his sneaker, or of losing his balance and falling backwards and impaling himself on a jutting pointed spike that rips through his back and out his chest.

The higher Geoff got, the easier the going seemed, and he moved quicker. He was almost within reach of the refrigerator. With his next step there was a sudden screech of metal as his right foot sank into the pile.

"Geoff?" Woody called from below, this time in a lower voice than earlier.

"I'm okay." He pulled on his leg. "I'm stuck, though." He looked back, but Woody only looked up at him helplessly. Geoff was close to the refrigerator. He leaned forward and stretched his arm out. The handle was just five or six inches from his fingertips.

"I can't reach."

There was a sound in the night air that froze Woody. It was a flapping sound. Could it have been a bird, he thought, or a bat, flying overhead? But it sounded more like the raising of a window shade.

Slowly he turned and, lifting a shaky arm, scanned the flashlight beam across the windows at the back of the house, petrified he'd see the image of that cragged face staring out at him. But the window shades were all drawn. He turned back around quickly.

Stupid, he thought. Shining the light in the windows might stir the old man.

"Did you hear that?" Woody asked.

"I think so."

"Hurry up," he called to Geoff.

He pulled on his leg, again to no avail. "You're gonna have to come up here. I can't budge it."

"Are you kidding?"

"Hurry up so we can get the hell out of here."

To his surprise Woody had little trouble making his way up the side of the pile lighting the way with the flashlight. When he reached Geoff, he grabbed onto his leg and pulled hard on it. It gave a little, but did not come free.

"You're stuck good," Woody said, letting go of the constrained limb.

"Get Jason out and he can help."

Woody handed the flashlight to Geoff and moved up to the refrigerator. He put his ear to the door and rapped his knuckles on it.

"Rise and shine, Jason."

"Come on, Woody," Geoff said, keeping the light trained on the refrigerator, "just open the door."

He grabbed the cold metal handle tightly and pulled. There was a sound of rushing air as the door swung open.

The light shone directly on the figure in the refrigerator. Jason was slumped down inside it, his eyes wide open, the skin on his face a purplish hue. His mouth was also open, a blackened, swollen tongue protruding from it. Long jagged gouges, caked with dried blood, ran down his neck all around it. His hands lay frozen in front of him, twisted into claws, the fingernails tipped with blood and bits and pieces of flesh. These were the hands that had ripped and torn at his own throat as he tried to get air to breathe. *He couldn't breathe. My God,* Woody thought, he couldn't breathe. The whole time in there, and he couldn't breathe.

Then Woody screamed.

It was a scream that pierced the air with a crack. Geoff dropped the flashlight and the light flicked out on impact, but the glow of the moonlight still framed that horrid face. Woody started to back down the pile, but before he got any further, he stopped to do something – for what reason he had no idea. He reached up with his hand and threw the door shut. Maybe so those eyes wouldn't see him.

He turned and saw the horror on Geoff's face and felt he was looking into a mirror and seeing his own reaction. He moved down the pile quickly, as if his feet touched nothing but air. Geoff must have gotten his leg free because he soon heard running feet behind him. At least he hoped it was Geoff behind him as he raced down Shadow Drive, but he did not dare look over his shoulder. He was afraid one of Jason's bloodied, clawed hands was reaching out to grab him.

CHAPTER FOUR

After writing, I left the inn and took a walk down to the beach. It was sunny and warm enough that I was glad I left my jacket in my room. I even pushed my sleeves up to my elbows. Indian summer. It reminded me of youthful hot days, school vacation and playing outdoors. But that made me think of Jason and the chapter I had just completed. There were very few days for him, Indian or otherwise.

As I stepped onto the beach, I looked at my watch. It had stopped. I shook my wrist and held it up to my ear, but no ticking.

The soft sand yielded to my every step and my balance felt beyond my complete control. It dawned on me that I had been walking on concrete so much the past few years that the beach felt like an alien surface. Just like I had forgotten what it was like to be a kid until this weekend, I had forgotten what it was like to walk on sand. As I approached the edge of the water, I was able to get on firmer ground and steady myself.

Someone was at the opposite end of the beach walking in my direction. Otherwise the immediate area was deserted. Out in the middle of the lake sat Professor Bonz in his boat. A slight breeze brushed across the lake, causing the water to reach the edge with a soft lapping sound at my feet. It was all so peaceful here, not the type of scene that would include such a vicious act of violence. Maybe in my stories, but not here. Not in real life.

I reached into my pocket and felt something soft and wet. I pulled it out and saw it was the rotten piece of apple I had hastily put in there and forgotten. I hurled it into the lake.

There were footsteps on the boardwalk and I turned to see Carrothead. He shuffled slowly along the wooden planks. I could hear the faint sound of his voice, mingled with static from the walkie-talkie in his hand, but none of the words he was saying were clear. He didn't look any older. Maybe his mind was so damaged that he didn't know he was supposed to age.

Didn't anybody grow old in this town? Everyone looked exactly as I remembered them when I was a kid. As if they had frozen, waiting for me to return. Like the town only existed when I was here, and when I left, everything stopped, so nothing grew older.

Dale wouldn't get old, I thought. He was trapped in the town now, forever frozen in his youthful look.

The figure on the beach was getting closer, its gender indeterminable. It appeared to be wearing a baggy jumpsuit and a strange hat.

Again I thought of Jason Nightingale.

The morning after Woody and my grisly discovery, we all went to Oliver, asking him what to do. We gathered behind his house near the fire-scorched tree that was the sole remainder of our clubhouse. Martin was crying. Woody had a distant look in his eyes, as if he were somewhere else. That's where I wanted to be and I implored him with my eyes, *take me too, wherever it is you are. I don't want to be here.*

We all waited for Oliver to tell us what to do, but even he seemed unsure. He finally decided we would do nothing. We would pretend nothing happened. We couldn't find Jason after the game and assumed he had gone home. Let someone else find him. Oliver even started to smile, as if this was the most ingenious plan he had ever devised. Or maybe he was smiling from relief, now that he had found a way out of our situation. Even I felt some sort of release of the tension gripping me that had brought on a tremendous headache and queasy stomach.

Oliver made us all take an oath and swear that none of us would ever tell a soul about what we did. Cross our heart, hope to die, stick a needle in our eye.

We all swore. It would be the hardest thing to do, but fear of what would happen to us sealed the oath.

When Jason was reported missing, Hooper questioned us. We all stuck to our story. A search party canvassed the neighborhood. I remembered looking out my bedroom window and seeing them going through the area. I wanted to scream at the top of my lungs, *Look behind the*

Tin Man's house. But they went about their mission, going door to door, combing the ravine and the woods and fields out beyond the ballpark and cemetery. I looked across at Woody's house and saw him also at his bedroom window. Our eyes met. Our eyes that had seen what no one else on Earth had seen. Without a gesture of any kind, he pulled his window shade down.

A couple of days went by without a trace of Jason Nightingale. Fliers went up around town. Fliers with the smiling face of a young boy. But I knew what that face looked like right now in that dark tomb of the refrigerator. I knew the expression etched into skin that was as far from smiling as humanly possible. It was a face of terror, madness and horrible death.

The waiting and anticipation was driving me crazy. I would lie in bed at night and think about Jason being out there, think about his parents staring out their window and wondering when or if he was coming home.

Woody wouldn't come outside his house. Whenever I looked up at his window, his shade was down.

I thought maybe they would never find Jason. They would give up and stop the search. The case would go unsolved. The years would go by and they would never realize how close he was, his body sitting in that refrigerator rotting away like a piece of leftover meat forgotten on a back shelf. I didn't want that to happen. It seemed too lonely. I didn't want his family to never know what happened to him. That would be too cruel.

But they did find him.

They finally searched through the Tin Man's junk pile. Finally climbed that mound and opened that refrigerator door and saw what Woody and I had seen that night.

The funeral was the worst.

I remember standing in the cemetery looking at that little coffin. It was hot and my body sweated and itched beneath the suit I wore. The tie was noosed tight around my neck and my fingers tore at it, trying to get some air. There was sobbing. I looked across the coffin at Jason's parents and his younger sister who clutched tightly to her mother's hand, a vacant look on her face. I wanted to go up to his sister and take her other hand and tell her how sorry I was that I caused her brother's death. But she probably wouldn't understand. Probably never would.

Back in the present I heard a faint jingling sound, almost like sleigh bells, coming from the distance. Pain started to inch its way into my head, and I felt dizzy, my vision blurring. I didn't want to have one of my spells. I squeezed my eyes shut. I wished I could put my hand through my skull and rip the tumor from my brain, throw it on the ground and stomp on it.

When the headaches came, I imagined them originating in the same spot in my brain where I had built that attic room. That was where the tumor was. I could feel it. It was as if all the horrifying and evil thoughts that I had developed within that space for my stories had created the tumor. I was really starting to believe it. The horrors in my thoughts had created a real sickness in my brain: a sickness that was killing me, my own imagination poisoning me.

Yes, I could believe that.

The jingling sound grew louder, and I wondered if it was coming from my head. Real or imagined? But it originated from my left and I turned and opened my eyes. The figure on the beach was getting closer to me. It looked like someone dressed in a clown costume. I stared in wonder as the figure approached.

When I realized what it was, numbness spread through my body, right down my legs to my feet and the sand seemed to shift beneath my soles as I thought my balance was finally giving way.

"Expecting me?" the stranger said.

The figure was dressed in a black-and-white striped court jester's costume. The jingling had come from the bells attached to his head piece. His face was painted white with the exception of his black lips and black eyebrows. His long, narrow face ended in a pointed, jutting chin. His nose was also long and pointed with flaring nostrils. His ears stuck out, with thick dangling lobes.

I knew this person.

It was the Joker. The spitting image of the joker from the deck of cards we used, from the drawing that used to hang on the clubhouse wall.

"Aren't you happy to see me, Geoffrey?"

"This isn't funny." I managed to keep my balance. "Who the hell are you and how do you know my name?"

He was grinning madly. "Come on, Geoffrey. It took me so long to get here. Don't act like this. You know who I am."

I looked at him long and hard. I thought about Dr. Cutler and what he said about the spells: headaches, dizziness, blackouts and hallucinations. But this was ridiculous.

"You're not real," I said.

His grin reversed itself. "But I'm here. I'm talking to you."

"Why are you here?"

"Because I want to be."

"I don't want you here." I turned around, hoping the image would go away.

"You need me."

I was wrong. I turned back and saw him grinning again.

"What do you want?"

"Want? Do I have to want anything? I sense how you're feeling. I thought I could help."

I started walking at a slow pace along the shoreline. The Joker followed alongside.

"How do I feel?" I asked him.

"You're pretty torn up inside. Heck, you just lost your best friend."

"I still can't believe it happened. I can't believe he's dead. Not just dead, but murdered. Killed like that. I never knew anyone who was murdered."

"Oh, no?" He looked at me with a puzzling stare. I knew what he was thinking.

"That wasn't murder. That was an accident."

"Is that what you believe?"

I stopped and looked at him. Of course I believed it. "We didn't want to kill him. We just wanted to punish him, make him suffer. We had no idea there wouldn't be any air in there. At least, I didn't. What we did was wrong. We made a mistake, but we were just kids."

"Do you think that was how Jason felt?"

I lowered my eyes. "I try not to think about that."

"But you have to now. Seems like the past is catching up to you."

"I can't escape the past. It's all around me." I looked from the lake to the woods to the boardwalk and the town beyond it. "It's everywhere here."

I continued walking, the Joker still beside me.

"I keep thinking about the possibility we were brought here on purpose," I said. "But I'm not sure I can accept the fact that one of us might be the killer."

"Why not?"

I shrugged. "It just seems too contrived."

"Like one of your stories?"

I looked at him with surprise. "My stories weren't contrived."

"Then how come you never sold any?"

I laughed. "I used to think I was going to be a great writer. When I was young, thoughts seemed to flow out of my head. When I left here, I think I left them behind."

"That was your mistake."

"But now that I'm back, I feel like I'm immersed in a story."

We stopped at the end of the beach at the marina. The sound of the water slapping the wooden pylons competed with our voices.

"So, what happens next?" the Joker asked.

"Figure out a suspect. If Oliver was telling the truth, and Woody was the one who suggested the reunion, that would make him the obvious choice." I shook my head. "Even with all he's been through, I can't see him doing something like this."

"Jeepers, why not? He's a frickin' lunatic! He was in the funny farm."

"Oliver, but he's a successful businessman."

"And a vicious bastard who cares for nobody but himself."

"Lonny –"

"An insomniac drunk, who's desperate and on the edge."

"Martin. It couldn't be Martin."

"How can you be so sure about Martin? He resents that you all returned."

"He wouldn't hurt a fly."

"The quiet, meek ones are always the crazy ones."

I stared down at the sand around my feet.

"Are you forgetting someone?" The Joker asked.

I looked up at him. "Huh?"

"What about you?"

I stared in disbelief at his mad grinning face. I stepped backwards away from him.

"No," I said, backpedaling some more, slowly. "NO!" I turned and ran, my feet digging into the soft sand, trying to propel myself as fast as possible, but hampered by the supple surface of the terrain. I did not look back as I ran. I did not want to.

When I climbed the steps to the boardwalk, I felt I was going to pass out. I got down on my knees and clutched at my stomach as I gasped deeply for breaths. I looked over my shoulder at the beach.

It was empty. Only my footprints marked the sand.

Footsteps approached, echoing off the wood and I looked up. Carrothead stood over me.

"I was watching you," he said.

A strand of drool descended from the corner of his mouth, and I got out of its way and stood up. I wanted to ask him if he saw me talking to someone, but I was a bit afraid of what the answer would be. "That's nice." I started to walk away.

"I remember you." He laughed.

I stopped and turned around. "You do?"

"And he remembers you." He indicated his walkie-talkie.

"Who?"

"The one on the other side. In the shadows. He's watching you. He's coming soon."

"Then I'd better be going." I turned to leave.

"You shouldn't be laughing at me!" he screamed, startling me.

"I wouldn't laugh at you."

"He tells me it's not nice to tease," he said, his head cocked sideways.

I remembered one late summer night when we followed Oliver up Autumn Avenue on our bikes. Lonny was carrying two cartons of eggs in a grocery bag, trying to be careful not to crush them. We didn't know where Oliver was leading us; he was being very secretive. But his face could hardly contain his grin.

We took a left when the road forked. I thought I had been to just about every part of town in my young life, but hadn't remembered ever coming this way. We came to a narrow dirt road that was barely noticeable and turned left onto it.

Just before a sharp bend, Oliver told us to stash our bikes behind some bushes. He signaled to be quiet and led us on foot down the dirt road. It didn't seem possible there'd be a living soul out here; the place seemed desolate, but as soon as we rounded the corner, I could see a house.

Calling it a house was being kind. I had seen sheds in better shape. It was tiny, barely the size of a two-car garage. Weeds grew up around the base of the walls, as if nature were trying to hide the blue paint that was chipped and peeling in spots, like the house had been dipped in corrosive acid. What few windows it had were tiny and could not have let in much sunlight. A rusted furnace pipe stuck up out of the middle of a sagging black-shingled roof.

It was depressing to look at, to think someone actually lived like this. Whatever excitement I had was dampened. I didn't know about the others, but I wanted to turn back and go home.

"Do you know who lives here?" Oliver asked, looking from one of us to the other. No one knew the answer.

"Carrothead."

The others were excited and started laughing. I had enjoyed teasing him as much as the rest, but now that I saw what he called his home, my heart wasn't in it. I wanted to say something but didn't dare.

We climbed a big pine tree nearby, one whose needles provided ample camouflage. Oliver let the first egg fly. It seemed to sail forever in the air, and then dropped like a rock with an audible splat as it hit the roof. Soon, another followed, then another. We each took aim, but several, including my own, fell short of the intended destination. I didn't really give it much effort.

When we were just about out of eggs, the front door opened and Carrothead stepped out.

"Hey!" he yelled, looking around but not knowing where we were. He turned back toward the house and noticed a glob of egg running down the clapboards. He stuck his finger in it and brought it close to his face to examine it, then stuck his finger in his mouth to taste it. When he turned back around, an egg slapped him in the side of his head. From our vantage point in the tree, we could see his face flush as his shoulders hunched and his right fist raised in the air.

He spotted us.

As we scrambled down, the last of the eggs were tossed, harmlessly landing at Carrothead's feet as he shuffled toward us.

I had been higher up in the trees that the others, and as I neared the lower branches, I could see them hit the ground and scatter. When I dropped, I landed hard on my left side. I immediately jumped to my feet, but before I could take a step, two arms wrapped around my body. I could feel warm stinky breath on the back of my neck and cold drops of saliva. The arms tightened, squeezing my chest. My mouth opened, not to scream, but to try and gather air. Nothing could get through the tight clamp on my chest. My eyes searched for the others, for some hope of help, but they were nowhere in sight. I was getting dizzy and thought I was about to pass out.

A voice suddenly yelled out behind us. It was Carrothead's mother.

The grip on me immediately loosened and air rushed into my lungs. I gathered strength in my legs and sprinted away to join the others waiting by our stashed bikes.

Once I was safe with my friends, my fear was gone, and I joined them in their laughter.

* * *

I stood on the boardwalk now and stared at Carrothead's bewildered face.

"I'm sorry," I said, remembering all those times. "We never meant any harm."

He lifted the walkie-talkie to his mouth and whispered something inaudible into it. Who was he talking to? The other side? Was Jason on the other side, telling him things? (*Don't let him out.*) I heard only static return a reply. I slowly walked away, keeping my eyes on him, but he just stood there, still talking into the walkie-talkie.

As I crossed the boulevard, I looked up at the town hall steeple to check the time. There was a large clock on all four sides of the steeple, but the two that were visible from my angle appeared to be broken. They both had different times, and neither of them could be remotely correct.

I crossed Main Street when I spied the phone booth outside the barber shop. There was a call I wanted – no, needed to make and my cell phone wasn't getting a signal. I did not want to make it but felt I should.

Nick the barber stood outside his shop, wearing his white smock and holding a pair of scissors. He smiled at me.

"I have a seat available," he said, gesturing inside.

I looked down and saw two small red dots on his smock.

"No thanks," I said and stepped into the booth. Across the street, I heard the pinging sound of a chisel on stone coming from Mr. Under's headstone shop. Could he be carving out Dale's name already? No, it was too soon. I closed the door, shutting out the noise.

I took out my address book and looked up Dale's number, thinking about how many times in New York I did the same, but never made the calls. I always put it off, hoping he'd call me first. Now it was too late. Now I dialed the number for the last time, dropping the correct change in as instructed. I counted the rings, really hoping no one would answer. I was about to hang up, even though it only rung a few times.

The ringing stopped.

"Hello?" The familiar voice of his wife came from across the miles. It gave me chills. I couldn't find my voice. I just stood there holding the receiver in one sweaty hand.

"Hello?" she said again, irritation in her voice. "Is someone there?"

"Hi," I finally uttered. "It's Geoff, Thorn."

"Oh, hi." She was definitely thrown off guard by this. "Where are you calling from?"

"I'm in Malton. I needed to tell you something."

"Well, listen. If Dale put you up to this, forget it."

"No, you don't understand." My palms sweated.

"I hope you're all having fun, getting drunk and whatever the hell else it is you're doing there." Her voice was angry.

"Listen, please –"

"I'm kind of busy if you don't mind –" her voice was cut off and I could hear someone talking to her in the background. It was a man's voice. She had a man over. Dale was lying dead in a morgue and she had a man with her. I stared at the phone, fuming. I slammed the receiver down. For the first time that day I began to cry, inside that phone booth all alone.

I don't know why I chose that moment to break down. Things were happening in my life with such turbulence and disorder, it was making me dizzy. Something was wrong in this town. I came back here for some kind of stability, in the dazed state my mind had been in from learning about my tumor, to the town that had always remained a constant. But everything I looked at seemed cockeyed.

I drifted along the streets, wherever my legs took me and they carried me back to the old neighborhood that had been the starting point of everything. I could feel the echoes. I wanted to reach out at the curtain of time and grab hold and pull it back, to run through the streets and woods again in a moment when there was no awareness of evil and dark things that crawl out of the cracks, except for the ones my own imagination generated in that attic room where the Joker lived.

It wasn't fair that something that happened so long ago should affect the lives of others now.

I walked down Shadow Drive, toward the ancient and decrepit house that was rooted at the end. There was no one else on the street. Why was this neighborhood so quiet? It was as if, now that the Jokers Club was all gone, there was nothing else left.

The green shades were still drawn in all the windows. I wondered if it was possible the Tin Man was still alive. But he couldn't be; he had been so old then. But nobody seemed to age here. It was as if the whole town was stuck in time, stuck waiting for us to come back. Waiting for the long-delayed justice to be dispensed.

I thought back.

* * *

When they found Jason's body in the old man's refrigerator, all the parents pointed their fingers at the Tin Man. He was strange, they said. He spooked everybody. He was always chasing the kids out of his yard with that spade shovel of his. He had to be the one. He must have caught Jason in his yard and decided to teach him a lesson.

The whole neighborhood stood on their front steps or porches and watched when Hooper came to arrest Emeric Rust. What evidence they had, who knew. But it was an answer that would satisfy the restless residents.

At the inquiry, I was the first one called to testify before the grand jury. It was hot in the county courthouse that day. They had the wide multi-paneled windows open all the way, but all it let in was hot air from outside. The ceiling fans were going, but they just pushed the searing heat that rose back down upon us. One of the fans had a rhythmic squeak, not loud enough to drown out anyone's voice, but noticeable enough to stick in my ear like a buzzing fly I couldn't swat away.

I was so nervous I was nauseous. I just wanted this all to be over. All eyes in the room were on me as I sat on the stand wearing the same suit I wore at the funeral. The only suit I owned. The one I wore to church on Sundays. And here I was about to lie after swearing an oath to tell the truth. But I had sworn another oath: *cross my heart ... hope to die.* I don't know which urge was stronger, the one to cry or the one to vomit.

When they asked me when was the last time I had seen Jason Nightingale, I glanced over at the table where Emeric Rust sat. The whole time in the courtroom I had avoided looking at him. I thought the only way I could go through with it was if I didn't see his eyes. But now I couldn't help but look at the pathetic old man as he sat there with his head bowed and staring down at his wrinkled and knobby fingers.

He glanced up and his eyes met mine, freezing me like two animals suddenly crossing paths. I thought about the noise that night that sounded like a shade being rolled up. Had those eyes looked out the window and seen Woody and me in the darkness?

If they did, they showed no sign of it.

I told the county prosecutor that the last time I saw Jason Nightingale, he was running down Shadow Drive.

Oliver and Lonny were the only others of the club they called forth. Luckily they didn't call Martin or Woody, because I think they would have fallen apart on the stand. But the three of us stuck to the story that we were playing the game and then went home afterward without seeing Jason. They didn't grill us too hard, didn't think there was a reason to I guess. We were just kids.

Emeric Rust remained silent throughout the entire inquiry. He would not utter one word in his own defense. Everyone said it proved he was crazy.

But the evidence, or rather, lack of evidence, convinced the grand jury there was no reason to indict him. They let him go free, deciding it was most likely Jason accidentally crawled into the refrigerator to hide during the game and couldn't get out. His parents were upset and less than a year later moved out of town.

I remembered when Emeric Rust left the courthouse that day. I was standing on the sidewalk. My parents and some of the others were standing in a group off to one side, conversing quietly. Outside there was no relief from the smothering heat. With the proceedings over, I had undone my tie and it hung loosely around my neck. I saw Jason's family driving away, but averted watching them, looking down at the worn leather on the tip of my shoes as I tapped the edge of the stone wall with my right foot. I didn't want to face them, but they were going back to the same neighborhood I was. How could I help but meet them sometime? Our paths were bound to intersect.

Hooper led Emeric Rust down those stone steps to his car to give him a ride back to his house. Oliver's father began yelling and swearing at him until a police officer quieted him down. When Rust got near me, he stopped and stared down at my cringing frame. He bent over and, in a whisper that still managed to roar in my ears said,

"Keep out of my yard!"

I stood there quivering as he turned away, led by Hooper who gave me a puzzling look. I was afraid everyone had heard him. But no one could have heard. No one, except …

* * *

My mind returning to the present day, I turned and saw Hooper in his patrol car, looking at me. I had been so engrossed in my remembrances, I hadn't heard him pull up. He got out and approached me.

"Whatcha doing?" he asked.

"How did you know I was here?"

"I'm keeping my eyes on you boys, you can be sure of that."

I looked back at the old man's house. "I was just checking out the old neighborhood. Surprised to see this place still standing."

"I'm surprised to see him still standing."

"You mean he's still alive?" I was shocked, but shouldn't have been.

"As far as I know. No one sees him around much, but the undertakers haven't collected him yet. I guess he just doesn't get out often." He grinned at me, but it wasn't a happy grin.

"Got any leads?" I asked.

"That's what brings me here." He walked to the Tin Man's front door and knocked. "Checking things out." There was a rusted metal doorknocker, but Hooper ignored it and just pounded on the door with his fist.

"You don't think he has anything to do with it?"

"Exploring every avenue. You boys put him through quite an ordeal." He pounded again, this time louder, then shrugged. "Don't think he'd answer even if he did hear me." He walked back to where I stood.

"You think it's one of us, don't you?"

"That seems most likely." He looked off to the woods at the Pines. "But heck, maybe it's just some psycho wandering around town. I've got my men checking the vacant cabins on the other side of the lake. Sometimes drifters passing through shack up in them for a while, before moving on."

"But that's just another one of those avenues you're exploring?"

He looked at me, squinting, licking his lips.

"They say murder with a knife is a rather intimate kind of killing. Your friend wasn't robbed. That makes the motive rather a mystery, don't you think?"

"It is interesting."

He walked back to his car but stopped.

"I'll tell you another thing that's interesting," he said. "I checked up on your friend, Paul Woodman."

If he was waiting for my attention, he had it.

"Seems he's been missing for about a month or so."

"Really?"

"Seems he had settled in a town up north near a girlfriend. But he hasn't shown up for work, hasn't been at his apartment. Just vanished. No one filed a missing persons report though, so no one's really looking for him. I've asked the local police to check on the girlfriend, but they haven't been able to track her down yet."

"Do you think he's here?"

"What do you think?"

He didn't let me answer, just got in his car and drove off. But I wasn't sure how I'd have answered him. I wasn't sure what I thought. I wasn't sure where the story was going.

*   *   *

A wind began to blow, kicking up leaves all over the ground. They danced around my feet, sounding like screeching animals as the crisp ones scraped the pavement. It was getting cold and I thought of heading back to the inn, but there were other places my legs wanted to take me, other things to see. There just wasn't enough time.

I found myself heading out to the cemetery beyond the Pines and the Little League field. I noticed the headstones were creeping closer and closer to the outfield fence of the ball field, as if the two of them were fighting for territory, as if death were overtaking the ground where youth once held reign. I could almost picture a future scene where outfielders would have to dodge concrete slabs while shagging a fly ball.

I visited my parents' graves, wishing I had brought some flowers because I think, in the back of my mind I knew I was coming here. They had both died of cancer just a few years apart. It must run in the family. My father succumbed while I was in college; my mother died a few years after I graduated, before I left for New York City. I had no reason to stay. No family, no Meg, no work. It was as good a time as any to get (run) away.

The headstones looked cold, the plot lonely. This was where I could be soon, beside them, a family again. If they knew what I was facing they could comfort me. They could tell me it was all right, that it wouldn't be so bad. But here I was, their little boy, and he was very frightened. *I don't want to do it alone.*

The breeze kicked up, chilling me and I wrapped my arms around myself. Was it death that made this place so icy?

I heard a car door and saw, over to the east side of the cemetery, a man emerging from a vehicle. I also saw a figure moving along the birch tree covered slope on the northern end of the cemetery. I felt this was an invasion of my privacy. I wanted this whole place to myself. These people had no right to intrude.

The man from the car stood in front of a grave and as I stared, I noticed it was Oliver. I started walking in that direction, but then slowed.

Maybe I shouldn't disturb him. Let him have his private moment. But I had the sudden urge to talk to him, so picked up my pace. When he turned and noticed me, he smiled.

In that instant, when his expression was framed in my mind, I was reminded of my first memory of Oliver. I was about five years old and wandered out into my new neighborhood and saw the scruffy looking kid with the black hair dangling in his eyes look up at me from behind a sand castle in the middle of his sandbox, smile at me and ask me if I wanted to help him build it. We had spent the better part of the afternoon piling the sand higher and higher until we had a castle King Arthur would have been proud to call home.

I remember that smile and wondered what could make an innocent young boy grow up to be such a hard man. Then I looked down at the grave he stood in front of: his father's.

He had died a few years back when he was drunk. His car went off the road at a high rate of speed on a rainy evening, slamming into a tree and splitting in two.

There was no empty plot on either side of Mr. Rench's reserved for Oliver's mother. She had deserted the family long ago, leaving Mr. Rench alone with the three boys. That had happened not long after the bicycle incident. It had been the summer Oliver was nine. His father had lost his license for drunken driving. Chief Hooper was the one who pulled him over early one evening right as Mr. Rench was turning onto Maple Street on his way home. Hooper wasn't even on duty. He was on his way to his house on Elm Street and was driving behind Mr. Rench. Oliver's father had pleaded with Hooper to let him off, since he was less than a hundred yards from his house and offered to walk from there. But Hooper arrested him and his license was revoked. I think that was the start of Oliver deciding to play pranks on Hooper. It was a way to get back at him — torture him for revenge.

Shortly after Mr. Rench lost his license, his wife came home with a brand new bicycle. She parked it in the driveway on its kickstand and called out to Oliver's father. I guess she figured during the nice weather he could ride it to work until he got his license back.

I remember staring out my living room window and watching Mr. Rench glare silently at the bike. From across the street I could see his face redden. Then he exploded. He turned to his wife and began screaming and swearing. My father came into the room and we both watched silently as Mr. Rench picked up the bicycle and raised it over his head and with a clatter of steel, slammed it down on the asphalt. He jumped up and down on top of the bicycle with his big heavy work boots, spokes snapping and popping, and stomping it as if trying to sink it out of sight beneath the surface of the tar.

His cowering wife turned and fled into the house and Mr. Rench soon followed. The screaming was louder when they were inside. My father went to the phone and picked up the receiver, fingers hesitating before the numbers pad. I saw the deep furrows on his forehead as he thought about what to do. Then he hung the phone up and told me to come away from the window.

Oliver and I stared at his father's grave, and then I decided I should be the one to break the silence.

"I'm surprised to see you here," I said.

He laughed. "I come here once a year. I don't bring flowers though. I may have hated the bastard, but I respected him. He made me what I am today."

"Is that what you want to be?"

"He made me tough, and that's how you have to be to survive, because it's a tough world."

"And you're happy?"

"I've got everything I want, and I'm only going to get more. There's no stopping me."

"Oh?" I knew something that could stop him dead in his tracks. He read my mind.

"That?" he laughed. "That doesn't worry me. I'm not afraid."

I'm not either, I thought. It didn't matter to me, I realized. *I'm already dead.*

"I keep tossing it back and forth in my head," I said, "that maybe the killer isn't one of us. Maybe the whole thing is just some random, senseless murder."

"Is that what you really believe?"

"The more I think of it, I doubt it." I looked around the cemetery, still seeing the man standing amongst the birches. "The killer is close to us. I can feel it."

"You think it's me, don't you?" His face studied mine looking for some kind of reaction. If anything, my expression showed puzzlement.

"I'm just not sure about you anymore."

"Don't trust anybody, that's my motto."

Then I asked a question that had festered in the back of my mind for a very long time. "You knew he wouldn't be able to breathe in that refrigerator, didn't you? You knew it would kill him."

"Is that what you believe?"

Don't play games with me, I thought. Just tell me. I want to hear it.

"What about you?" he asked. "Ask yourself if you didn't know what would happen."

No. I had no idea what was going to happen. I'm sure of it. I never would have let it get that far if I had known. I'm sure.

"I know I'm no killer," Oliver said. "But I will kill if I have to, to protect myself."

I decided to tell him what Hooper told me about Woody.

"Well that's an interesting twist," he replied.

"I can't help but think about something he said to me when I visited him, about having to pay for what we did. Maybe he's right. Maybe we should be punished."

Oliver burst out laughing. "Do our penance? That's the way it is?" He shook his head. "You don't think we can't go through life unpunished for our dirty deeds? God, you're so naïve."

"I really believe it's why we're here."

"What about the killer then?" he asked. "If it's one of us, and he kills us off, then he'll be left. He'll go unpunished."

"What makes you think he hasn't been punished already?"

He looked at me queerly.

"What's going on in that head of yours?"

I don't know, I thought. Something very strange.

He walked away, as if unsure of who I was, and headed to his car, not taking his eyes off me. When he opened the door, he stopped.

"Do you want a ride back to the inn?"

It was still cool and the thought of a ride back to the warm inn was tempting, but I didn't want to get in the car with him, and I think he was just as glad I declined.

As he drove away, I began to meander through the cemetery, working my way along the pathways toward the northern end. I took in the names on each tombstone as I passed. These could be my new neighbors soon. I should get familiar with them. Some names I recognized, could even picture the faces that went along with them. Here was a guy from high school who had drowned trying to swim all the way across the lake on a dare one hot summer night. Here was a young man who was accidentally shot by his father in a hunting accident. There was the headstone of a girl who had lived only five years before riding her tricycle into the road and getting run over by a garbage truck. I remembered the whole town mourning that day.

Would the whole town be mourning my death when it came? Or would I be placed here in my designated spot, to be forgotten with all the others. This cemetery was growing, stretching itself out, like the tumor that clung barnacle-like to my brain. Soon, would it outgrow the whole town? Death was something that would not stop.

I moved down a path parallel to the slope rising gently to my right. As I glanced up, I saw a man who moved slowly behind the birch trees. I stopped. The man, who was thin like the trees that nearly concealed him, emerged from the cover of a birch and looked at me.

I froze, not from the chilled air that engulfed my body, but from a sudden shock that numbed my soul.

"Woody!" I screamed.

He turned and ran.

It was him. His face was smudged with dirt, his loose clothes covered with pine needles and dead leaves, as if he had been crawling along the ground, but there was no mistaking it. It was Woody.

I ran after him, zigzagging around the trunks and headstones. The incline made my footing slow. My legs were numb and aching from walking all day long. I wasn't gaining on him. He moved swiftly, but I could see him in the distance ahead.

"Wait, Woody!" I cried, using up almost all the breath my lungs held. "Stop!"

I came to the top of the rise, where the trees ended in a clearing of graves, and stopped. As my breath sputtered in rapid bursts that stung the bottom of my lungs, my eyes searched. There was no sign of him. Beyond the clearing began the thick brush and woods that led to the Colonel's hidden tomb. I closed my eyes and listened, hoping to hear the sound of Woody's movement through the undergrowth. When the echo of my breathing dimmed in my ears there was only silence.

Then they picked up the sound of jingling bells.

It came from somewhere off to my left. I moved toward the sound. I saw its origin as I neared. My body trembled. What was going on in my head?

The Joker stood in an open grave, spade shovel in hand, digging out shovelfuls of dirt and throwing them on a pile beside the grave. He went about his work, not looking at me as I approached the side of the grave and peered down.

"What are you doing?" I asked.

"Digging," he replied, still not looking up. He was almost completely below ground level. I looked at the name on the headstone.

JASON NIGHTINGALE

I cringed.

"Why are you digging?"

He stopped and looked up. His black lips were spread in a wide grin. "Why, to get to the bottom of course." He dug the tip of the shovel into the dirt and tossed it over his shoulder.

"But why are you digging here?"

"Can you think of a better place to dig?"

How about the plot that's reserved for me? I thought.

I heard the thump as his shovel struck something hard. I closed my eyes tight. Make this vision go away please.

"Ha, ha," he laughed. I heard the scraping sound of dirt being brushed off the lid of the coffin. I opened my eyes to see the Joker climb out of the hole. He stood beside the pile of dirt he had removed, one hand leaning on the shovel, the other extended out toward the hole, palm open.

"There you are," he said.

"I don't want to look."

His smile faded. "What are you afraid of?"

I was afraid of everything. But my body did move, it did take small steps to the edge of that hole. I looked down.

I wanted to scream.

There was no coffin. Instead, lying in its place was a refrigerator.

"Don't do this to me," I cried.

"But I didn't do anything," the Joker said. "I had nothing to do with this."

I fell to my knees beside the hole. Every muscle in my body trembled in spasmodic fits. I put my face in my hands, trying to hold the tears in.

"I don't want to remember."

"Geoffrey," came a voice. It sounded like it came from a great distance. It wasn't the Joker's voice. It was higher pitched. It was a youthful voice; it sounded like it came from ...

I took my hands away from my face, staring from behind watery eyes into the hole.

"Geoffrey!" came the muffled voice from inside the refrigerator.

It was Jason's voice.

"Help me," it said.

I stared, afraid to move.

"Don't just sit there," the Joker said. "He needs your help."

"Please, help me." The voice was louder.

Frantically, I jumped into the hole, onto the refrigerator, grabbing the door handle and pulling it. It wouldn't open.

"Geoffrey!" the voice screamed. "Let me out!"

I yanked on the handle, but it still would not open.

"I can hardly breathe, Geoff." The voice was growing weaker.

"Hang on, Jason!" I screamed. "I'll get you out!" I kept jerking the handle back with all my might, but it wouldn't budge.

"I ... can't ... breathe." The voice was fading.

I began pounding my fists on the door, smashing them one after the other.

"Open dammit! Open!" No sound came from the other side. "No!" I screamed. "I can't be too late! Not again! Please no!" I collapsed on the door, shaking, heaving tears from my eyes, one fist still pounding in ever slowing thumps, like the beats of the heart fading on the other side of the door. I pushed myself up onto my knees.

"This can't be happening!" I screamed to the sky above.

The Joker looked down at me, smiling.

"Leave me alone!" I jumped up and scrambled frantically up the side of the grave, momentarily panicking that I wouldn't be able to get out. Once on the ground, I ran as fast as I could, away from that grave, away from that refrigerator. Just like I had run those many years ago.

SEARCHING FOR JASON NIGHTINGALE

Martin Peak was nervous. He lay on his bed in his room, sweating, his whole body shaking; he could feel his heart drumming in his chest. What had they done? This was a nightmare. This couldn't be happening. Could it?

He closed his eyes and kept repeating to himself: *It's only a dream; it didn't happen.*

"Martin!" his mother called from downstairs. His eyes opened. No, he wasn't dreaming. Oh, how he wished he was.

"Martin!"

He slid off his bed and shuffled to his bedroom door, opening it and leaning out into the hall. From the master bedroom to the right he could hear the deep breathing of his father and the puffs of air from his oxygen tank.

His father wasn't long for this world. Years of smoking had scarred his lungs for good, and he relied heavily on the oxygen tank that pumped air into those damaged organs. But he wouldn't be able to suck on that tank for long. Soon the air would run out for him.

Just like the air had run out for Jason Nightingale in that refrigerator. But Martin's father was pushing seventy, and Jason had been a young kid just starting out in life.

It wasn't fair.

Martin always felt odd having such an old father, and one who seemed to have been sick for as long as he could remember. In fact, it seemed like his father (always father, never dad) had been sick for Martin's entire life.

When he was gone, it would just be his mother and him. His older brother, Richard, lived in the Midwest and had his own family to take care of. He was fifteen years older than Martin, so he hardly felt like a brother at all, more like a young uncle. He was off to college before Martin could even remember him living at home. Then a job, marriage, kids. Yeah, it wasn't like really having a brother. Not someone you could turn to when you were in trouble.

And boy was he in trouble now, very big trouble. And he couldn't stop shaking. He needed to talk to somebody. The authorities were looking for Jason Nightingale, and eventually they would find him. And then what?

His mother called again. "Why don't you answer me?"

When his father was gone, he would be left caring for his mother, who wasn't in the best of health either. Even as his father's lungs deteriorated, his mother kept puffing away at her own cigarettes, sometimes right in the same room with his father and the oxygen tank. It was a wonder the house didn't just blow up.

Martin often thought his birth was an accident. Why else would they wait fifteen years to have another child? But then he began to wonder if his birth wasn't planned after all. That maybe his parents realized his brother Richard would be going off to school in a few years and moving on, and who would there be to take care of them? It would be just like his father to plan his birth so when he was gone, Martin could take care of his mother.

But what he really needed right now was for someone to take care of him, because something really bad had happened, and he hadn't done anything to stop it.

And you could have, he told himself. That's what tormented him the most. You could have spoken up. Someone should have spoken up. Geoff or Dale should have spoken up, but it could have just as easily been you, he told himself. You didn't always have to be the quiet one. Sometimes you deserved to be heard. Sometimes you did have something to say. And maybe just this once you could have made somebody listen to you.

"Come down here right now. There's someone here that needs to talk to you."

Martin crept to the top of the stairs. Who? Who was here? Had Jason got out of the refrigerator and come for him? Was his angry rotting corpse waiting for him on the couch downstairs, waiting to make him pay for not speaking up to the others? Make him pay for always being the quiet one.

The stairs looked incredibly steep as he stared down them, wondering who was waiting for him down there. He plopped one foot on the first tread, then, like a Slinky, plodded one step at a time down the stairs to the bottom.

Chief Hooper stood in his living room.

God, he knows, Martin thought. Now his heart wasn't pounding anymore. It had stopped completely in his ribcage. Sweat beaded up along his temple.

His mother stared at him. "The chief needs to ask you something," she said.

Hooper glared at him, eyes burning into his and Martin wanted to look away, but he felt frozen in place.

"Jason Nightingale is missing," his mother said, before the chief could even open his mouth. "Did you know that?"

"Missing?" Martin said in a fractured voice.

"Yes," Chief Hooper said. "He was supposed to be spending last night at Lonny Mudge's house but apparently didn't. His parents were expecting him to come home in the morning. But he didn't do that either. Did you see him yesterday afternoon?"

The chief glared again.

Remember, Martin thought. Remember the story Oliver told them to say. Stick to the story and we'll be okay.

"Yeah," he managed. "We, uh, were playing. Then, um. I don't remember seeing him after that." Gosh, you idiot, that sounded stupid. You're a stupid liar, Can't you even lie right? "I guess, I thought he must have just gone home."

The chief was silent for a moment.

"Are you sure," his mother asked.

Martin nodded, not trusting his voice to try to speak anymore.

"Well, that's the same story the other kids in the neighborhood have said." He looked at Martin. "If you – remember – anything else, you be sure to let me know."

Martin nodded again.

The chief turned to his mother. "Thank you, Mrs. Peak."

After he left, Martin's heart started beating again.

Once his heart got moving, Martin did too. He had to find someone to talk to. He couldn't keep this to himself. He needed to share the panic.

Running down Maple Street, he could see Geoff up ahead in his front yard. He yelled and waved his arms and Geoff spotted him. Martin was nearly out of breath when he got to him.

"Hooper was at my house," he finally managed to spout, hands on his knees, bent over, catching his breath.

"Yeah, he was here too," Geoff said. He seemed calmer. God, how could anyone be calm in this situation?

"I thought he could tell I was lying," Martin said.

"Why? What'd he say?"

"Nothing." Now Martin began to cry. "It's just … I don't know." Tears rolled down his cheeks. "I don't think I was too convincing. I was really scared, Geoff."

"Come on. I'm meeting Dale at the Pines."

They raced through the ravine and out the other end onto Elm Street and then up the hill to the Pines. There Dale was already waiting for them. The three of them sat against the big boulder.

All below them they could see groups of people canvassing the area out in the fields beyond the cemetery and along the shores of the lake. A marine patrol boat even cruised along the surface of the water.

"They certainly don't think he's a runaway," Dale said.

"No." Geoff responded.

"They definitely think something happened to him."

"Maybe we should make a call," Martin suggested.

"What?" Dale asked. "Are you kidding?"

"Well, it can be, you know, anonymous," Martin explained. "One of us could go down to the pay phone in town and just call, tell them where to look, and hang up."

"That's crazy, Martin," Geoff said. "Then they'll know somebody did something to him."

"But we did."

"Martin," Dale said, frustrated. "They have to find him themselves. They have to think it was an accident."

"But it WAS an accident!" Martin screamed.

"Shut up!" Dale yelled. "We have to keep cool."

"Easy, Dale," Geoff said. "Nobody's going to hear us up here."

Dale looked around, as if expecting someone to come around the corner of the boulder. Martin began crying again. It made him feel like a baby, but he couldn't help it. He was scared. He wished he could be as cool as Dale or as calm as Geoff, but he just couldn't do it. It wasn't in him.

"What a mess," Dale said, shaking his head.

Martin stood up and took a few steps over to the side of the hill. He couldn't sit still. From here he could see the Tin Man's house and behind it, the pile of junk. There was the refrigerator nestled among it, holding its gruesome contents. Martin felt like screaming at the top of his lungs, *Look over there!*

But of course he didn't. No. He had to do what Oliver said. They always did what Oliver said. Wasn't that how they got into this mess in the first place? Doing what Oliver said?

Martin never felt the courage to stand up to Oliver. That he could blame himself for. But Geoff and Dale were smarter, stronger and cooler.

Shouldn't they have stood up to Oliver? Shouldn't they have said something to stop what happened? Damn them. They could have and they should have.

A few days later, Martin and Geoff went out fishing on the lake. Martin's father had a canoe. In Martin's whole life, he had never known his father to use it; it just hung abandoned on the wall in the garage. He often wondered why his father had it, and then found out one day that he used to take Richard out on the lake to go fishing in it. Of course, Martin thought. His father was probably healthier then and could do things like that with Richard. But he could no longer do those things with Martin. Of course not.

So he and Geoff took the canoe down and carried it, with their fishing poles and some night crawlers, over to the lake. They paddled out into the middle to where they figured it was the deepest. They hoped that's where they'd have the best chance to catch Behemoth, the lake trout that was a legend around here for its size. Several people had supposedly hooked it before, or so they would say, but it always outfought the fisherman and got away. And now it roamed the lake with two or three hooks still imbedded in its mouth.

It had inspired Geoff to write a story about a prehistoric fish that attacks some fishermen in a boat. Geoff had read it to the gang in the clubhouse one night. Martin thought it was a pretty cool story. It was more gory though than scary, with the fish chomping the hell out of a couple of the fishermen.

Martin didn't care about catching a fish, prehistoric or otherwise. He just didn't want to be alone. And being at home with his parents didn't count. Bringing food and drinks up to his father's bedroom and getting his mother a fresh pack of cigarettes wasn't the kind of companionship he needed. He might as well be alone for all that would do for him.

But being with Geoff was good. Sitting out here on the lake, his problems seemed so far away. But it was never too far. At some point they would have to reel in their lines and paddle back to shore and it would still be there, hanging over them.

Geoff baited the lines for him, because Martin hated putting the night crawlers on. He hated even touching the things. That's what Geoff should write a story about, a giant night crawler, because they had nasty teeth. That thing could eat up the town, just like one of the movies they would watch on television on Saturday afternoons.

They cast their lines and watched them sink into the depths of the lake. Then they just sat there silently. What could they say? What do you talk about when you caused someone's death?

"This isn't going to end good," Martin said.

"Huh?" Geoff looked up from his line, in a daze.

"They will find him and something bad will happen to us."

"I know they'll find him."

Martin looked up at him. He seemed so calm.

"What will happen?" he asked.

Geoff sighed. "I don't know. Oliver says ..."

"Who cares what Oliver says," Martin yelled. "He doesn't know everything."

Geoff stared back, silent.

"I can't tell you what's going to happen," he finally said. "I just don't know."

Martin thought for a moment. "Well, pretend it's one of your stories you're writing. What would you write that would happen."

Martin could see Geoff thinking deeply, mulling it over. Then he shrugged his shoulders.

"I guess, I dunno, maybe I'd have the police finally search the Tin Man's junk pile and open that door and then ..."

"And?"

He looked at him. Geoff's face was pale, and he looked deep in thought, then the color flushed back in. Geoff finally spoke. "They'd figure Jason was finding a place to hide and didn't realize he couldn't get out. And they wouldn't think any more about it."

Martin thought about this. Sure, that was Oliver's ending, not the ending writer Geoffrey Thorn would really come up with.

"No," he finally said to Geoff. "That's not how you'd write the story. In your story, Jason would come back from the grave. And he'd come after us, one by one, and get his revenge. His dead hands would strangle us in our sleep, choking the breath out of us with his bloody fingers, just like his breath was choked out of him by that refrigerator."

Martin shuddered.

"This isn't one of my stories," Geoff said.

They sat in silence for most of the rest of the morning. Martin didn't know what else to say. It was hard to talk about the summer or Little League. None of that seemed to matter anymore. This was going to be a crappy summer. Maybe every summer was always going to be crappy from now on. Maybe every year. Would life ever be the same for him? For any of them?

It was around noontime (because a band was playing in the gazebo for the lunch crowd) when they heard someone yelling from the shore.

Martin looked over toward Autumn Avenue and there was Woody, jumping up and down and waving his arms. He couldn't make out what Woody was saying, the words getting lost in the air by the time they reached the middle of the lake, so he and Geoff reeled in their lines and began paddling back to the shore.

By the time they got close enough, they could hear what Woody was yelling.

"They found him!"

They pulled the canoe out of the water as Woody continued to blabber between sobs and gasping breaths.

"Oh god, they found him," he cried. "They finally found him!"

"Calm down!" Geoff said.

Woody instantly shut up, though he still sobbed and hacked.

Martin looked at Geoff, waiting for him to say something. Anything. Geoff just stood silent, thinking.

"Oliver wants us to meet him in the ravine."

Geoff nodded. "Okay, let's go."

Of course, Martin thought, Oliver's in control as usual.

They left the canoe by the shore and followed Woody on his bike to the neighborhood.

The ravine between Maple and Elm streets was crisscrossed with paths and clearings, where kids had traversed the crossing between the two streets and hid out during games of Relievo or hide and seek.

In one of the clearings on a felled log sat Oliver, Lonny and Dale. They all looked pretty sullen. Even Lonny looked pale. Oliver got up and paced.

"Okay," he said, looking from one to another. "We knew this day would come. Now is the real important part."

"And what's that?" Lonny asked.

"Don't be stupid! We have to really stick to our story. Cause they'll probably be asking us again about what happened. And we can't sound stupid."

"This ain't good," Martin said, feeling sick to his stomach.

"It will work if nobody screws up!" His face was fuming. "Do you understand?"

Oliver looked right at him, and all Martin could do was nod.

"Okay. Now there's cop cars, ambulances and everything over on Shadow Drive. Normally we'd go check stuff like that out, so that's what we've got to do."

"Oh no," Woody said, "I can't go there."

"We have to!" Oliver said, frustrated.

"He's right," Dale said. "It's what we'd usually do."

"Then let's go and get it over with," Geoff said.

The six of them climbed out of the ravine and crossed between a couple of houses onto Elm Street. Then, under Oliver's command, they ran down Elm and onto Shadow Drive, Woody trailing far behind Martin. Martin didn't blame him. He himself was in no hurry to get there.

There was a crowd of people gathered before the Tin Man's house. They stopped and stood among the spectators gawking to see what was going on. Whispers ran among the crowd. People wondered if the Tin Man had done this.

Martin craned his neck, not sure what he was trying to catch a glimpse of. But then he could see Emeric Rust, standing near a couple of cops. He looked skittish and confused. Of course he should be, Martin thought. He had no idea how this young boy ended up in his junk pile. No, only we know, Martin thought. But how long would that last? That was the real question.

Then the paramedics wheeled a stretcher out from the back yard toward the ambulance parked in the driveway. A black plastic bag lay on the stretcher.

Oh my god, Martin thought. Jason Nightingale is in there. He was glad the body was covered, but it still gave him the creeps. *Jason is in there.* He felt sick, like he might pass out. He suddenly felt hot, and the crowd around him made him nervous. I've got to get out of here. He needed air; much like his father with his oxygen tank, he needed to get some air.

He pushed his way out of the crowd, nudging aside Woody (who also looked like he might pass out), and stepped away.

Martin bent over, hands on his knees, gasping. He looked up in time to see them load the stretcher into the back of the ambulance. Then he saw Hooper standing beside the Tin Man, talking to him. Hooper turned his head and looked out at the crowd on the street.

Martin could have sworn he was looking right at him.

CHAPTER FIVE

I sat at the bar in the Loon Tavern, a beer in front of me, my hand clenched tightly to the handle of the mug. I stared into that golden-amber liquid, watching the bubbles rise to the surface and burst.

The beer tasted good, ice cold and sparkling as it went down my throat. My head was already feeling light, but that was good. At least it wasn't aching anymore. My mouth craved more so I drained my mug and then signaled the bartender for another. My fourth I think. The first three I had to wash down the burger and onion rings I just finished. I wanted to have another and another. It didn't matter. I wanted to drink and try and forget what was happening to me. I wanted to try Lonny's method and get drunk, go back to my room at the inn and pass out, even if it would make me an easy target for the killer. It didn't matter anymore. I just wanted to go to sleep.

My head was all mixed up. When I got back to the inn from the cemetery I tried to lie down and rest. My body had been exhausted, but my brain was all jittery; sleep had been sporadic. I woke with fits and starts, images bouncing around my head. I woke more tired than when I lay down. I came to the tavern to get something to eat, but drink was what I really needed.

My mind was playing tricks on me, and I felt I was losing touch with reality. Maybe the tumor was getting worse. Maybe my time was running out. It was scary, not being in control of my mind. I was confused. I'm pretty sure I know what *isn't* real. But I'm not quite sure what *is* real.

What was it Oliver has said to me earlier? *I lived in a dreamland.* I always daydreamed, but was there a fine line when daydreams end and fantasizing begins? Maybe the tumor was causing my fantasies to become uncontrollable. What if no one from the Jokers Club were even here in town?

What if Dale wasn't killed? Maybe the tumor had created all this as just another of my fantasies without my even being aware of it. Was any of this really happening, or was I just creating it for my book? Was I writing this story, or was it being written for me? I often daydreamed of the way I wanted things to be. But what was happening now wasn't how I wanted things to be. Is it? Or was it the way things should be? Poetic justice? A morality play? Had everything in my life been leading to this point since the day Jason Nightingale stepped into that refrigerator? Did I want this to be the way the story ends?

My skull hurt. I thanked the bartender when he brought over a fresh mug, then glanced at the clock on the wall behind the bar. Its hands were set at twenty past three and I knew that wasn't right. It was still early I judged, maybe around seven. I still had my watch on even though it wasn't working. Habit I guess.

A figure moved onto the bar stool two down from mine. I turned to my left and saw it was the woman staying at the inn. She wore jeans and a rust-colored sweater that settled smoothly over the curves of her breasts and hips. The sweater had a cowl neck and her auburn hair spilled over it. She had a familiar attractiveness about her, sort of reminding me of someone. Was it Meg? Of course. Who did most women remind me of?

She caught me looking at her and smiled. "Hi," she said. Her cheeks looked soft and smooth and I had a sudden urge to reach out and stroke them lightly with my finger.

I smiled back and returned the greeting. I tried to think of some clever line to start a conversation with, but I felt like an awestruck high school kid. This was my problem in New York, never quite confident enough to just talk to a strange woman, never quite sure what to say. I thought some companionship would be nice, someone different to talk to. I racked my brain trying to come up with something, anything, but she spoke first to break the silence.

"I'm sorry about your friend."

My smile dropped. Not because I thought of Dale, but because I felt guilty about being attracted to a woman after losing my best friend earlier in the day.

"Thanks," I said, then tried smiling again "I still find it hard to believe."

"I'm sorry," she said, almost blushing. "I shouldn't have bothered you."

"No, that's all right." I tried not to look too pathetic. "Can I buy you a drink?"

"I have one," she said. I looked on the bar in front of her and she did. "But how about if you let me buy you one? You look ready."

I looked at my mug and saw it was empty again.

"Sure," I said, and slid over onto the bar stool separating us. "My name is Geoff Thorn." I extended my hand and she took it. Hers was warm and soft, like I knew it would be. I was sure mine was damp and cold from clinging to a beer mug all evening.

"Mary Torr," she said. "Pleased to meet you."

She ordered a beer and I thanked her when it came.

"So what brings you to the Tower House Inn?" I asked.

"Oh, just visiting really."

"Why here?"

"I used to live in Malton."

"Oh, really? Did you go to school here? You seem familiar."

"Oh, no," she said. "I moved away when I was young. I just thought," she shrugged her shoulders. "I don't know. Maybe it would be fun to come back and visit. Especially in the fall when it's so beautiful." She had a little girl nature about her.

"Do you remember much about the town?"

"Not a lot. But some of it's coming back now that I'm here. Some memories really stick out."

Yes, I thought. That I could certainly agree with.

This time she was ready for a drink, and I ordered her one along with another for myself.

"Do the police have any idea who killed your friend?"

I shook my head. "No, but Hooper isn't the smartest cop you'll ever meet. He may not be the stupidest, but he'll come pretty darn close."

"Do you have any idea why someone would do this?"

Sure, I thought to myself, a few ideas. I had a sudden urge to tell her about what happened. It would feel so good to open up to someone, not to keep it bottled inside for as long as I had. But we had taken an oath, had sworn to it. Cross my heart ... and hope to die.

"I wish I knew," was all I said.

A hand fell on my shoulder and I turned to my right.

"Geoff," Lonny said, "I've been looking for you everywhere." He sat down on the bar stool on my right. He looked over at Mary. "Excuse me," he said to her, then to me: "We need to talk."

"That's okay," Mary said, getting up from her seat. "I really should be going anyway."

I was disappointed.

"Thank you for the drink."

I watched her walk out the door.

"Gee," Lonny said. "Hope I didn't spoil anything for you?"

"No," I was still looking at the door she had just exited. *Just another missed opportunity*, I thought. My life was full of them.

Lonny ordered a drink. I thought he would notice mine was empty and ask if I needed one, but he didn't, so I ordered my own.

"What's up?" I asked, sipping my beer.

He gulped his beer, and then looked around the bar. "Have you seen Oliver?"

"Not since this afternoon."

"Yeah, me neither." He smelled of cigarettes.

"So where have you been all day?"

"Around. Here and there. You know. Doing things." His hands were shaky.

"So, why were you looking for me?" He stunk of booze and I figured he'd been drinking most of the day. But I myself had quite a bit to drink tonight already and was sure it showed.

"I've been doing some thinking," he said, tapping his finger on the bar. "About tonight."

"What about tonight?"

"I don't think it's safe."

"No?"

He glanced around the bar again and then leaned closer.

"We all know what's happening, don't we?"

"Do we?"

He nodded. His eyes narrowed. "It's one of us, and it's going to happen again. And I'll tell you, I'm kind of scared."

I believed him. "Yes."

"I know who it is."

I ordered another drink, purposely not ordering one for him, though I saw his mug was empty. "Who?" I asked when the bartender placed the mug in front of me.

"Oliver."

"Why him?"

"I just know it. I feel it." He ordered another drink. "I know it's not me. I'm sure it's not Martin or you. I don't think it could be Woody. It's just got to be Oliver. That guy is a crazy bastard. I wouldn't put anything past him."

I thought about telling Lonny what Hooper said about Woody being missing and my seeing Woody at the cemetery. But, did I really see him? I wasn't sure. I wasn't sure about anything anymore.

"He may be sick and twisted," I said, "but capable of murder? I don't know."

"Do you remember the lamb?"

I stopped with my mug just a breath away from my lips. That was something I hadn't thought about in a long time. I set the mug down, not wanting to taste anything at that moment.

"I remember," I said, then shook my head. "That doesn't mean anything."

"It means the guy's got something warped in his head."

I thought maybe Lonny was just upset about what Oliver did to him last night.

"You know," he continued. "I'm starting to doubt what happened to Jason was an accident."

That seemed to be the question of the day. "You think it was intentional?"

"I think Oliver's had a sick mind for a long time. There's something that happened back then. Something I've never told anyone." He sipped from his drink, and then looked around the bar again. "It was a few days after Jason's funeral. I was over Oliver's house one afternoon. There was nobody there but the two of us. He said to me, 'watch this,' and he grabbed the telephone and started dialing. He called the Nightingales' house. I didn't know what he was up to. I think he expected the parents to answer, but it was Jason's little sister who picked up the phone." He paused and shook his head, looking down at the floor. "When I think back, I can't believe what he did." He looked at me. His eyes appeared watery. "He disguised his voice and said: 'It's Jason, help me, I can't breathe! Please help me, I can't breathe, help!'" Lonny looked as if he were going to start crying. "Can you imagine how that little girl must have felt? He hung up the phone and started laughing. I didn't know what to do. I just couldn't believe it. He made me promise never to tell anyone, threatened to beat the crap out of me. And I didn't tell a soul ... until now."

I was shocked, as if it had just happened in front of me now. I could picture Oliver's face, see him laughing. He was sick. There was almost no doubt in my mind now that he knew what would happen to Jason when he sent him into that refrigerator.

"But would he jeopardize everything he's got just to get rid of us? It doesn't make sense."

"Of course it doesn't, that's the point. He's not right. There's something wrong with him, and you could see it through the years as he was growing up." He took one last gulp of his drink and started drumming his thumbs on the bar. I wanted to reach out and grab them, stop them. It was so annoying. "I guess if you take a beating all those years like he did from his old man, it'd have to mess you up."

I had enough. I wanted to go back to the inn, back to my room and, even though it was early, crawl into bed and sleep. I told Lonny I had to leave and started to get up from my stool. He grabbed my arm.

"Don't worry," he said. "I've got a plan."

"A plan for what?" I wanted to go, wasn't sure I wanted to listen to him anymore.

"I'm going to be the shadow."

"What are you talking about?"

"The shadow. Remember? In Relievo. I'm going to stay up tonight and hide out somewhere. Move around in secret. Watch over things."

"Don't be crazy."

"I can't sleep anyway. I might as well stay up all night. I'll keep my eye on the inn. On everybody. See what happens. You don't have to worry."

"I've got to go," I said.

"I know it's not you," he said. I think he waited for an answer from me, but I didn't know what to say. "Well, thanks for the vote of confidence," he said in reply to my silence, disgust in his voice.

I turned to go, then stopped and looked back.

"Be careful out there," I said.

He smiled. "Thanks."

When I got back to the inn, I looked inside the den to see if Oliver was there. Professor Bonz sat in a chair reading a newspaper.

"Hello," he said, eyeing me with suspicion, although his tone was pleasant.

"Good evening," I replied. "Just looking for a friend."

"Those can be hard to find."

I smiled. "That's for sure." He went back to his newspaper, and I proceeded upstairs. When I reached the second floor landing I stopped. I thought about Mary and wondered which room was hers. Maybe I could knock on her door and see if she'd like some company. I stood in the middle of the hall and looked at all the doors. Did she come back here after leaving the tavern? There were three rooms on this floor and the professor and her's were the only ones occupied. I saw no sign of light through the crack on the bottom of any of the doors, but I did hear the sound of movement beyond one of them. That had to be her room. I moved closer and stood in silence. I listened to her mulling around in darkness and wondered what she was doing. Was she getting ready for bed this early? It seemed strange, but I was planning the same thing myself, though I doubted she had the kind of day I had. I thought again about knocking, even raised my hand, knuckles poised, but decided it was stupid.

I turned and climbed the stairs to my floor.

Once inside my room, I went to the window. A slight breeze blew in, billowing the curtains. The street was quiet, as was the lake beyond. The only sound was the raspy twitching noise of the few leaves still remaining on the trees as the wind rattled their branches. A sudden cry of a loon joined that sound. I wondered if Lonny was still at the tavern or if he had begun his night watch. I really didn't know if it made me feel safer knowing Lonny was somewhere out there, lurking in the shadows.

I closed the window, locking it, not caring if it made the room stuffy. I drew the shade and undressed.

I hoped the alcohol in me would allow me fall asleep right away. I tried to empty my head of all thoughts, but something Lonny had mentioned earlier stuck in my mind and refused to go away: the image of a lamb.

Pounding. Pounding.

I broke from my sleep and bolted up in bed. My breathing was heavy, sweat covered my body. The beating reverberated in my ears. It felt like my skull was being struck as pain cracked across its base.

I threw the covers from me and walked across the cold wooden floorboards to the window. The room was definitely now stuffy. I fumbled with the window, which I forgot I had locked, and pushed it open as a cool breeze swept in, lifting the sweat from my bare chest. I sucked in the fresh air, leaning out the window to get more. A lone sound drifted up from below. A slow metallic creaking that I knew could only be the porch swing blowing in the wind. I felt a chill around me – no, within me – that I knew wasn't from the crisp biting air.

I closed the window, turned around and leaned against it. The sound was shut out but another sound lurked nearby, assaulting my senses: The pounding that I thought had been part of a dream, I now realized was coming from somewhere in the inn.

Was someone trying to get in? But, wait, why would they knock? The door should be unlocked.

I quickly dressed and went into the hallway. Pausing outside my door, I listened carefully. This floor was quiet, and I realized I was the only one on it. Dale wouldn't be needing his room anymore, and Lonny was somewhere out there in the night. No sound came from the stairs that led to Oliver's room. I wondered where he was.

The pounding emanated from below.

I descended to the second floor. This floor, too, was quiet. I wondered how late it was. Were the professor and Mary out, or were they asleep in their rooms?

I could still hear the pounding clearly in my head. It still came from below. As I passed the moose head at the top of the landing, I sensed movement. I looked at the creature. Did its eyes move? Were they following me?

No. But I kept its gaze for a moment, backing away from it slowly, then turned and proceeded down the steps till I reached the lobby. The inn was dark except for what moonlight filtered in through the windows. The pounding wasn't coming from the front door. I stood there letting the sound come to me, then I followed it into the den, to the doors that lead to the dining room, past the tables where we had so recently – or was it long ago? – gathered to play cards, to the door that led to the kitchen. The sound seemed to pull me along as if I were sleepwalking. I let it take me, lead me to … the refrigerator.

The pounding was coming from inside.

I stood in the dark, not knowing what to do.

When someone knocks, you let them in. Or in this case, out.

I grasped the cold handle and pulled the door open.

Hands shot out at me, wrapping cold fingers around my throat that squeezed, locking onto my neck like metal prongs, cutting off my breath, digging into my flesh. I couldn't have screamed if I'd wanted too. The face behind the hands loomed out of the dark pit of the refrigerator. White, bulbous, bloodshot eyes stared out from a purplish face, black tongue lolling out.

I dropped to my knees, tearing at Jason's arms as his hands continued crushing my throat. The arms were like stone. The hands pulled me closer to its dead face, as if trying to drag me into the box with him. I could feel the constriction inside me as my blood tried to move up my head but met with the obstruction at my throat. My body felt like it was going to burst. My head grew dizzy, black spots bursting around my eyes. My lungs pounded, struggling for air that was not there. Jason's face began to fade to black as I felt myself slipping from consciousness, my body continuing to struggle but my mind giving up. Blackness was everywhere.

Hands grabbed my shoulders and my body was shaken.

The blackness thinned. I could see bottles and jars on the refrigerator shelves in front of me. My breathing relaxed as I released my own hands from my neck. My arms shook. There were hands still on my shoulders. I turned to look behind me.

"What the hell are you doing?" Bob Wolfe yelled. His voice was angry, his face showing fear. Fear of me.

I didn't blame him. I looked down at my hands. I'm not in control, I thought.

"I must have been sleepwalking," I said, looking back at him and rising to my feet.

He took a step back from me.

"I don't like people creeping around my inn in the middle of the night. Awake or asleep."

"How late is it?"

"Just after midnight."

I closed the refrigerator door and mumbled an apology. I didn't want to go back to my room. I was too disturbed. I needed to sort things out. I needed a drink.

When I stepped out onto the porch, I thought about going back to grab a jacket but decided not to. It was cool but not cold enough to raise goose-bumps; there were other things in the night capable of that. As I walked to the edge of the porch, there came a sudden sound behind me that froze me where I stood. A creaking sound. I turned around slowly.

The porch swing swayed back and forth, pushed by a gentle breeze, each backward swing producing a painful groan from the chains suspended from the wooden beam in the porch roof.

I thought of Dale, sitting there on the swing. I could see him, his chest and gut split open, his eyes staring (at what?) straight ahead as the swing oscillated to its cryptic rhythm.

"I'm sorry," I said to him. "I wish I could have done something for you."

"Don't go out there," he said, raising an arm and pointing out toward the night beyond the porch. "It isn't safe."

I turned and looked to where he pointed, at the lake and town that was laid out before me. This is my hometown, I thought. This is the one place I really should feel safe. I stepped off the porch, not turning to look behind me, and walked toward somewhere, anywhere. The sound of the creaking porch swing becoming fainter with each stride I took.

I crossed Autumn Avenue and got on the boardwalk. The moonlight struck the lake on my right giving it the image of a dark sheet of glass. Most of the town was shadowy, but I could see the lights from the Loon Tavern on the other side of Main Street. I felt alone in the town, as if I had woken up and everyone was gone. But then my footsteps on the boardwalk were joined by another's, a shadowy figure at the other end walking toward me. I could also see someone standing in the middle of the gazebo, the dark outline of what I presumed to be a man. I couldn't even tell if it was his back or front I was seeing.

I kept my eyes on the figure on the boardwalk. He appeared to be holding something in his hand. As I studied his movement, an awkward stride, I realized who it was: Carrothead. I wanted to avoid a confrontation, so I stepped off the wooden surface and veered across Main Street. As I got closer to the gazebo on my left, I could tell that the figure – indeed it was a man – was facing me. I wondered what he was doing, only momentarily, and quickened my pace.

"Pssst," he called from the gazebo.

I stopped, looked around, but knew it was directed at me. There was no one else here but Carrothead. But why was the man whispering? There was no one to hear him. And what did he want with me?

He motioned with his arm for me to approach.

I did not move.

"Geoff, come here."

It was Lonny. I approached the gazebo, cautiously, and ascended the steps. We were both drenched in the shadows of the structure. He appeared nervous, looking over both shoulders, not making eye contact with me.

"What is it?" I asked.

He rubbed his mustache, and then finally looked at me.

"I know."

"What?"

"I know who the killer is."

I looked at him curiously, and then took half a step back, suddenly feeling very uneasy around him.

"How? Who?" I asked.

"It's –"

A blade came out of the darkness.

I jumped back and watched as it was drawn across Lonny's throat. His eyes nearly jumped out of his head. Blood spurted from the slit in his throat, pulsing out in repeated waves. He stood there, still trying to utter the words he'd been about to tell me, but they were caught in the gurgling liquid in his throat. I could see the two edges of the cut open and close, as if they were a pair of lips trying to say the name his own lips could not, but the only thing that came from them was another wave of blood that washed down the front of his shirt. He fell to his knees, then face down onto the wooden floor.

The Joker stood there holding a bloody knife and a wild grin.

"Who is it?" he laughed madly.

I stumbled backwards, shaking my head.

"Is it me?" he asked, raising his eyebrows, a grin stretched across his white face. He held the dripping knife out toward me. "Or is it you?"

"NO!" I screamed. I staggered back down the gazebo steps and ran to the tavern, not looking back.

I burst through the front door, nearly barreling over a man who was leaving. There was a scattering of patrons in the bar and most of them stared at my rude entrance. I ignored them and tried to calmly make my way through the tables to the bar. In one chair I passed sat Mr. Under and in another Nick the barber. Mr. Under smiled and nodded at me, but I ignored his gesture and clumsily collapsed on a bar stool. Beer wouldn't do right now, so I ordered a shot of whisky, stuttering out the request with a shaky voice. When the drink came, the shot glass was filled to its tip and unsteady hands spilled a few drops as I brought it to my mouth and downed it. My eyes winced closed as the liquid burned my throat. I swore I could feel it seep into my blood vessels and race to my brain where it tingled my nerve cells.

I opened my eyes and my mouth, letting air cool my fiery throat. I ordered another shot, my fingers trembling playfully on the bar as I awaited it. When it came, I downed it as quickly as the first, once again closing my eyes, bracing for its impact.

I sat still on the bar stool, barely breathing as I tried to let my body ease into relaxation. When I finally stopped shaking, I ordered a beer.

I can't tell anymore, I thought to myself. I can't tell what's real and what isn't. Maybe I'm not even sitting here right now?

I heard the jingling and a white gloved hand set a bloody knife down on the bar beside my drink.

I brought the mug up to my lips as the Joker climbed onto the stool next to mine.

"Is it over?" I said, setting my mug back down.

"Over?" he queried. "It's just beginning."

I looked at him. He had a drink in his hand.

"When will it end?" I asked.

"Why don't you tell me?" He grinned.

"How should I know? I haven't done anything."

"Can you be sure about that?"

"I can't be sure about anything anymore." I looked at him while he sipped his drink. "I'm not even sure what you are. I don't know if what I saw really happened. Is Lonny dead?"

"Why don't you tell me?"

"I don't know!" I said, slamming my mug on the bar. Heads turned in my direction, and I looked at the faces staring at me. I knew they were only seeing me. I saw Nick sitting at his table. He was still wearing his barber's smock. Had he been cutting hair this late? There were large dark splotches on the front of his smock, and I was sure they were blood stains. Didn't anyone else notice this? He caught my glance and smiled a toothless grin. I turned away. Maybe he had just spilled a drink on his smock.

I ordered another beer and gulped half of it down when it came. The bartender had given me a strange look when he brought it, probably wondering whether to shut me off. I hadn't had too much. I hadn't had enough.

I turned to the Joker. "You have lots of questions, but I notice you don't have many answers."

"It wouldn't be fun if we knew all the answers."

"This isn't fun."

"No?" he puzzled. "It's feeding your imagination. Isn't that why you came here?"

"I'm not sure why I came here. I don't feel like I had any choice."

"We can't always choose what we want."

I looked at him and his silly grin.

"If you're my muse, then why don't you help me with this story?"

He frowned. "You mean I haven't been any help?"

"I think I've had enough of your company tonight," I said. I paid for my drinks and turned to leave. I was weaving as I walked, almost bumping into the table where Mr. Under and Nick, with his spotted smock, sat.

When I reached the door, the Joker called out to me.

"Geoffrey," came his voice from the bar. "Didn't you forget something?"

I turned and looked where he sat. He held the knife in his hand, blood dripping from its blade onto the bar.

I staggered onto the sidewalk. The gazebo loomed ahead of me, and I stumbled to it. I climbed the steps, needing a hand to steady myself. The gazebo was empty but darkness was splashed across the floor in its center. I looked down at my hands and saw that same darkness on them. I tried to wipe it off but realized it was only a shadow.

Where was Lonny? I thought. Was he alive or dead? Was he out there being stalked by someone? Or was he stalking someone, maybe me? I thought about looking for him, but felt blackness creeping over me. It was so dark and I only wanted to get back to the safety of the inn. If it indeed was safe at all.

I left the gazebo, darkness swirling all around me, not sure if I could make it back to my room. My head was pounding, there in that special place. My legs felt like they were going to collapse. I could hear footsteps on wood. I tried to fight the emptiness. Why did everything have to be so dark?

THE TIN MAN'S INQUEST

Lonny twitched as he sat on the stand in the county courthouse. It was his turn to be questioned. The county attorney had already talked to Oliver, who had managed to keep to the story as far as Lonny knew. Now he had to continue the lie. They had gone over the wording so many times with each other, it should be down pat, but Lonny was still worried. They weren't going to question Woody or Martin, and that was good because Oliver was really afraid they wouldn't be able to cut it. They probably would have cracked on the stand and broken down in tears.

So now Lonny was worried about himself. He didn't want to let Oliver down. He didn't want to be wimpy like Martin and Woody. Oliver was like a brother to him, no, even more than that.

Lonny only had sisters as siblings, two older and two younger. And his mother pretty much ran the household. His father was not a strong man. Lonny always wished he had a brother to help him in times like this. Oliver had older brothers, and though they picked on him a lot, he learned quite a bit from them. Who did Lonny have to learn things from? That was a void Oliver had filled. Oliver always showed him the ropes.

He remembered when they first built the clubhouse. Lonny had never cut a two-by-four or even hammered a nail. Though Oliver was sometimes impatient with him and got frustrated and called him names, he still showed him how to do those things. That was just Oliver's way.

By the time they were nailing the roof boards on the clubhouse, Lonny pounded those nails without bending one crooked or missing the beams beneath. He was proud when they finished. It was quite an accomplishment, something Lonny never would have been able to do with his family.

But now the clubhouse was gone. That proud symbol of accomplishment, something Lonny had helped build with his own two hands was destroyed. It made him sad. And when Jason Nightingale squealed on them, it made him mad.

Jason had got them into this mess, and now Lonny had to sit on that stand and try not to screw this up, because he didn't want to disappoint Oliver. He didn't want Oliver to get mad at him. But he was very nervous. He knew the story but wasn't sure he could make it convincing. He wasn't good at convincing people. Oliver was. Oliver made it sound easy.

Just the other day, he and Oliver had been on the beach at the lake, lying out in the sun with Geoff and Dale. They talked about the upcoming inquest, though Lonny didn't want to think about it at all. He wanted to just lie in the sun and forget all this was happening, because he didn't like the way it made his insides feel.

"We've gone over the story a hundred times," Oliver said. "It will be a piece of cake."

"I know," Lonny said. "It's just, what if they try to trip us up?"

"It's not like they suspect we did anything," Dale explained. "They just want to know what Jason was doing that day and how he ended up in the Tin Man's yard."

"Right," Oliver agreed. "They won't be grilling us. They'll just be asking simple questions."

It should be just natural, Lonny thought. Kids were always playing around in the Tin Man's back yard. Heck, Oliver and he got the screens for the clubhouse windows from the old man's junk pile.

Even though the old guy was kind of creepy, it didn't stop them from rummaging through his junk.

Lonny remembered one time playing Relievo and it was his turn to be the Shadow. He hid inside the trunk of the junk car that sat on its rims near the base of the pile. He had lain in the dark, stuffy, moldy trunk, biding his time so they could win. It was a pretty big trunk, as most of those old cars had, but it seemed to get more cramped the longer he stayed in there. Lonny squirmed, trying to find a comfortable position, but it was impossible. He couldn't lay still and it seemed to be getting hotter. Sweat seeped through his t-shirt and he wanted to rip it off, but he could barely move his arms. It seemed like the trunk was shrinking, closing in on him. He wanted to sit up, but there was just no room.

Finally, he heard movement outside. It must be Oliver and the gang, coming to tell him the game was over, and once again they had won.

Lonny pushed on the trunk lid and it sprung open.

Emeric Rust stared down at him with his bulging bug eyes, holding his spade shovel.

"What the hell you doing in there!" the old man yelled.

Lonny clambered out of the trunk, dropping to the ground and began running for his life. The old man ran after him, waving the shovel.

"Keep out of my yard!" he screamed.

Lonny could barely contain his laughter, but he was also a bit frightened. The old man was crazy, and though he looked weak, one wild swing from that shovel could knock his head off.

The guy was crazy.

"What do you think will happen to him?" Lonny asked.

"Who?" Oliver said.

"The Tin Man. What do you think they'll do to him?"

"Who cares, he's an old fart."

"They won't be able to prove anything," Geoff offered. "I mean, come on, he didn't even do anything, so they can't really even put him on trial."

"But you hear all the time about innocent people being put in jail," Lonny said. "What if they think he did something?"

"That only happens in the movies," Dale said. "Or maybe in one of Geoff's stories."

Geoff laughed. "I would never write about something corny like that."

"No?" Dale asked. "The Tin Man's a pretty freaky character. Look at all that crap they found in his house."

Lonny remembered hearing about the search through the Tin Man's house after they took him away. The house was filled with all kinds of electric appliances and junk. They found dozens of toasters, blenders, stereos, tape recorders, microwaves, televisions, hair dryers, vacuum cleaners and radios. They were crammed all over the house, stacked on countertops, piled on the floor, stuffed into closets. The whole house was filled with electrical gadgets, some dismantled, their components scattered throughout the rooms.

"Why was he collecting all that junk?" Lonny wondered.

Geoff smiled at that. "I think I know."

"You do?" Dale asked.

"Yeah," Geoff laughed. "Maybe he was trying to build killer robots."

Lonny started laughing along with him. "Killer robots?"

"Yeah," Geoff said, sitting up on his beach towel. "I started thinking about a story idea. That Emeric Rust used to be some kind of scientist, and he collected all these electric gadgets and stuff so he could continue his experiments and build robots that he can program and seek revenge on all the people that bother him."

"Like people who trespass on his property?" Oliver asked. "Like Jason Nightingale?"

Geoff lay back down. "Well it was just an idea."

Lonny wished they hadn't gotten back on this subject. He was happier thinking about Geoff's killer robots. That's the kind of stuff kids their age should be thinking about. Not about a twelve-year-old boy dying a horrible gruesome death, but some mechanical monstrosity with circular saw hands tearing apart some burglar who breaks into the Tin Man's house in the middle of the night to steal televisions.

Yeah, that'd be cool.

"Maybe you should build a robot," Lonny said to Geoff.

"Why?"

"So you can build one that looks just like you and you can program it to go over there and talk to Meg Rand, since you don't have the guts."

They all laughed and Geoff blushed.

Meg Rand was on the beach with a few other girls on a blanket about fifty feet away. Lonny noticed she seemed to look this way a couple of times. Geoff talked nonstop about Meg Rand, and everyone knew he had a big crush on her, but he just didn't do anything about it.

"What about it?" Dale said. "Just go over there now. Because if you keep chickening out, I'm going to ask her out."

"Now's not the time," Geoff said, glancing over at the girls.

"It's never time for you, Thorn," Oliver said. "You can't wait for the right time. You've got to take charge, make things happen."

"Everything's too weird right now, with this whole inquest and stuff." He looked away from them. "Maybe when everything dies down. Maybe when school starts up. Right now I just want to get this thing over with."

Lonny could agree with that. It seemed never ending. He wanted to put Jason Nightingale behind him and forget the bratty kid ever existed.

And sitting on the stand in the courthouse, Lonny thought that if he could get through this day, everything would be all right. He tried to keep his fingers interlocked, his hands resting on his lap. But his fingers refused to stay clasped, instead pulling apart, thumbs drumming on his thighs.

The county attorney approached and Lonny looked right into his eyes. He didn't want to look beyond him to where Emeric Rust sat. Lonny didn't want to meet the old man's sad confused face. The old man appeared to have no idea why he was here. Hell, he probably didn't. *It's because of us,* Lonny thought, you stupid old fart.

Yeah, that made him feel better.

"So tell me, Lonny," the county attorney began. "Can I call you Lonny?"

"Yes sir, that's me." There were muffled chuckles in the courtroom. Lonny smiled, but his right hand began grabbing at his tie, twisting it, and then he had to force himself to pull his hand away.

"You said in your police statement that Jason Nightingale was supposed to spend the night at your house the day he disappeared."

"That's right," Lonny said, trying to remember what Oliver had told him to say. "I had talked to him earlier in the day and asked him to see if he could sleep over at my house. He checked with his parents and it was okay." Lonny started touching the tips of his fingers in succession to his left thumb, index, middle, ring, pinky, then back again. It helped calm his nerves, gave his hands something to do while he sat there. "Later, he said they said it was okay."

"And did he sleep over your house?" the attorney asked.

Lonny shook his head, reaching up and scratching at the side of it with his right hand. "After we got done playing Relievo, I couldn't find him, so I just figured he changed his mind and went home."

"And you didn't see him again."

Lonny looked down at his hands as he tried to keep them together. "No sir."

"And you didn't go looking for him? Or call his parents to see where he was?"

The attorney waited in silence for an answer.

Once again Lonny shook his head. "No. I guess I should have, but I just thought he didn't want to sleep over."

The attorney stood before him without saying anything, then excused Lonny from the stand. His legs were numb and at first he though he wasn't going to be able to get up, but he forced himself to move. He wanted to get out of the hot seat and away from this place. He didn't like everyone looking at him. He was afraid they could tell he was lying.

Lonny walked slowly back to his seat, trying not to look at the old man, trying to keep his hands at his sides. But he did look, and was glad the old man wasn't looking up. *Keep your head down old man*, he thought. Don't you dare look at me, because if you do, then everyone might know I was lying and that would be bad. Oliver wouldn't like that.

But when he came closest to where Emeric Rust sat, the old man's head tilted upwards and slowly turned, eyes set deep within that wrinkled mass of flesh catching his and burning into them. Lonny tried to look away but couldn't, as if the old man possessed some hypnotic power and those eyes bore through his retina, burning a hole into his socket and along his optic nerve like a fuse, leading into his brain where he could read Lonny's thoughts and realize what really happened in the junk pile.

Lonny's right hand reached up to his scalp, grabbing a strand of hair in his bangs, twisting and pulling on it.

When all the testimony was done from whoever had anything to say, which really wasn't much at all, the grand jury decided there was no evidence to warrant a trial and the case was dismissed and Emeric Rust was free to go.

Lonny and the others were outside the courthouse when Chief Hooper walked the old man out. It didn't seem possible that the Tin Man could look any older, but Lonny thought he aged another ten years by the whole process.

Emeric Rust shuffled slowly down the walkway outside the courthouse. Hooper seemed to move his fat frame gracefully by contrast.

Oliver was disappointed they let the Tin Man go. He thought it'd be cool if he got sent to the electric chair.

"They don't use the electric chair in New Hampshire," Geoff said.

"Damn," Oliver said. "What do they use?"

"They still have hanging in the state, though it hasn't been used for over fifty years."

Geoff always seemed to know shit like that, Lonny thought. He was always reading about that kind of stuff for his stories: Poisons, executions, vivisections, autopsies, amputations. That kid had one weird mind.

"Hanging," Oliver muttered. "That'd be cool too."

Geoff shook his head, disgusted, and walked off.

Hooper led the old man past them on the sidewalk and once again Lonny averted his eyes. In fact he kept his gaze on Oliver, who looked right at the old man and smiled as he shuffled by.

Cool as a cucumber, Lonny thought. That's Oliver.

When the old man passed, Lonny turned and watched him walking away. Hooper was now several steps ahead of him, too impatient to maintain the old man's turgid pace.

Lonny saw the Tin Man stop when he got to where Geoff stood. Emeric Rust leaned over and whispered something to Geoff.

Oh shit, Lonny thought. He knows. He saw something. Lonny tried to swallow, but it felt like his Adams' apple grew double in size and blockaded his throat. The Tin Man saw something and didn't say anything. That didn't make sense. Unless, perhaps, the Tin Man was planning some sort of retribution of his own.

Lonny began tugging on his bangs.

CHAPTER SIX

Incoherent thoughts ran rampant through my aching mind when I awoke Sunday morning. It took a while for me to even realize what day it was; they all seemed to blur together, none having any more significance than the others. Time had no special meaning for me anymore, not here. It just kept on running. Mine was running out. I could sense it.

I didn't even remember coming back to the inn last night. The whole end of the evening was one big black cloud. I had vague recollections of working on the book. I looked down and noticed I had slept in my clothes. One of my first thoughts was to call Dr. Cutler, tell him about what had been happening. Not necessarily about Dale's murder but about what had been happening to my mind. The hallucinations and tricks it had been playing on me, my trouble distinguishing reality.

But if I did call him, I know he'd want me to come back to New York, back to the hospital and have the operation, remove the tumor. I couldn't do that. I still needed the tumor, I think. Things weren't finished here.

I thought about Lonny. I had to find him, find out if he was all right.

I stepped out into the hallway and went to Lonny's door, putting my ear against it. The room was silent. I knocked, lightly at first, then louder. There was no response, so I reached down to the knob and turned it. *(Don't open the door.)* I pushed the door open slightly and cautiously squeezed my head through. I was hoping so much to see him lying on his bed, asleep or more likely passed out.

His bed was empty, not even slept in.

I stepped into the room. It smelled of stale cigarette smoke and alcohol. An empty whiskey bottle sat on his nightstand.

Had he come back to the inn at all last night? Or was he still roaming the streets out there?

I looked around the room. Maybe I should go through his drawers, see if I find anything? Like what? A knife?

If you're going to do it, do it quickly, I told myself. I went to the bureau and opened the first drawer. Empty. I checked the second, then the third. All empty. I stood there for a moment, not even bothering to check the fourth. I didn't need to. It just occurred to me, Lonny had been wearing the same set of clothes all weekend. He had only come with one set. But why?

I heard a door slam somewhere in the inn and decided to get out of the room. I closed the door behind me and went back to my room to grab a fresh set of clothes. I went to the bathroom and showered quickly and changed. Heading downstairs I ran into Professor Bonz on the second-floor landing. He was heading out with an armload of equipment.

"Morning, Professor," I said. "How goes the fish hunting?"

He grunted, giving me a sour look. "Not too good," he said. "If I don't come up with something soon, I'm afraid I'll lose my funding."

I wondered how much funds that could be and who was paying it. "What are you using for bait?"

"Anything vegetable and animal I can get my hands on. Aside from human limbs."

I laughed.

"He must be feeding too low in the lake," he continued, "beyond the reach of my lines."

"Maybe he feeds at night?" I offered.

The professor stopped on the steps and looked at me. "That hadn't occurred to me."

I began to wonder if he really was a professor of anything. Maybe he was more like an outpatient from Acorn Estates. "Do you need a hand with that stuff?" I asked.

"No thanks," he said, continuing down the steps. "Mr. Wolfe said we should keep away from you and your gang." He gave me a queer look.

"You don't think I'm a killer do you?" I said this half in jest, but wondered how I appeared to a total stranger.

"You don't look much like one," he said as we reached the bottom of the stairs. "Not that looks ever counted for anything. But I'd much rather spend time with a carnivorous fish than a carnivorous man."

I held the front door for him, and he thanked me as he left.

The den was empty, so I checked the dining room to see if Lonny might be in there. Oliver sat at one of the tables, a plate of brown sugar covered pancakes before him. How could he possibly eat? My stomach was so twisted in knots, I couldn't imagine trying to force food down. Death had destroyed my appetite.

"Have you seen Lonny?" I asked.

He shook his head. "The idiot's probably passed out somewhere."

The two of us just stared at each other. *What have you done with him?*

"I haven't seen you around," I said.

"That makes two of us."

I smirked and then turned away.

I stepped out onto the porch to a warm, sunny autumn morning. There wasn't even a breeze to stir the leaves discarded across the front lawn. Without thinking, I sat down on the porch swing, in the exact spot I had two nights prior. When it dawned on me, I looked at the seat beside me. There were still a couple of small red stains on the wood. I turned away. I didn't want to think about it. I gently started to rock the swing but stopped as soon as I heard the creak of the chains that brought back an image of last night's apparition.

I looked out at the lake and immersed myself in the peaceful quiet that surrounded the place: warm sun, white friendly clouds dotting the bright blue sky, orange and yellow leaves dropping from the trees to flutter to the green grass beneath. It was all so relaxing.

My life shouldn't have turned out like this. It was all supposed to be different. Meg and I were going to be married, and we were going to live in a big house. A house like this one.

* * *

Yes. This *was* our house. And here I was sitting on the porch on a warm sunny day, resting before I went back inside to work on my latest novel. It was so nice to be successful enough to work at my own leisure.

I could hear the clattering of plates and glasses from inside. Meg must've been doing the breakfast dishes.

But that was the only sound I heard; otherwise it was strangely quiet. The children? Where were the children? I sat up, worried. But then I realized it was October. They must have been in school. That's why I didn't hear the familiar screeches and yelps of our kids as they played around the yard. I sat back and smiled. Life had been good to me. Meg, the kids, my writing: everything I'd dreamed about. It made me so happy.

The screen door opened and closed. Footsteps approached the swing and then there was a hand on my shoulder. A gentle, but trembling hand. Without looking I reached up to touch it. It was soft. I turned my head and looked up into her face, her beautiful smile, her lovely eyes.

"I love you, Meg."

Her hand slowly withdrew. The smile faded as her eyes averted.

"What's wrong?" I asked, rising from the swing.

She stepped away, not looking at me.

"I'm sorry," she said, "but I'm leaving."

"But why, I don't understand," my voice pleaded. "Don't you love me?"

She faced me. "Not like I used to."

There was sadness in her eyes. But was it sadness for herself? Or sadness for me?

"You can't do this to us," I implored.

"I have to go," she said, turning and walking down the porch steps.

I wanted to do something, but my mind and body were frozen. I couldn't think. I couldn't act. Halfway down the walk, she stopped and turned.

"Don't worry," she said. "In time, you'll find love again. Someday you'll be happy."

"Not for me," I cried out. "I'm dying."

But she didn't hear me. She was too far away.

"She's gone," a voice beside me said. I turned and saw the Joker. I looked back but could barely see Meg in the distance.

"This wasn't supposed to be your life," the Joker said.

"But I wanted it so much."

"It wasn't meant to be. You both have your own separate lives."

"We used to be a part of each other's. Now, I have no idea what her life is like, and she has no idea about mine." I let out a sigh. "I just wish –"

"What do you wish?" the Joker asked.

I looked at him. He was grinning, but this time it was a compassionate grin. I looked back to where Meg last was.

"If I had one last wish, it would be to see Meg again, hold her, tell her how much I've missed her."

I felt the Joker's hand on my shoulder.

"It's so distant now," I said. "I can barely remember what it was like with her. It's as if time is slowly white-washing it away. I can't even remember the color of her eyes." I thought hard for a moment. "I think they were –"

I turned around. "—brown," I said, staring into beautiful brown eyes as her hand withdrew from my shoulder.

"Are you okay, Geoff?" she asked.

I smiled, but then realized the eyes I was looking into belonged to Mary Torr.

"Oh," I said, stumbling a step back, shaking my head to clear it. "I'm terribly sorry."

"Do you feel all right?"

"Yes," I blurted. "I'm just, well, I guess I just got lost in my thoughts." I sat back down on the swing. "I guess I haven't been sleeping well." I was more embarrassed than anything. I also realized I hadn't cared too much about my appearance when I washed up this morning, so I imagined the way I looked, coupled with my actions, must have appeared very odd.

"I understand," she said. "I have difficulty sleeping too sometimes."

I figured she was just trying to appease me. I felt like an idiot.

"Are you going to be okay?" she asked.

"Yes," I said, looking up at her. Was she real, I thought? Or was she someone I created? Did my mind conjure her up in Meg's image to take her place? Is that why she seemed familiar to me?

"Try and get some rest," she said before excusing herself. I watched her walk away.

I knew now that I would not find Meg here. She was gone, like so many other things in my life. I couldn't dwell on thoughts of her. I had other tasks to concentrate on.

When Mary left my view, I leaned back on the swing, careful not to make it rock. I wanted to relax in the quiet of the moment, but that was broken by the car that pulled up in front of the inn. It was Chief Hooper.

The front door to the inn opened and I turned to see Oliver step onto the porch. He must have heard the car pull up.

"Hmmm," he almost smiled. "I wonder what Heifer wants with us now?"

I said nothing, only watched as Hooper climbed out of his car with a struggle and approached the inn, pulling up on a belt that his stomach kept pushing down. It was as if the two were in a confrontation. The stomach won.

He stopped a few feet from the porch. He was chewing on something and looked all around the inn, his eyes resting the longest on the parking lot. It was as if he were pretending not to notice us. I couldn't tell if he were chomping at the bit over something or waiting to finish chewing before talking. He swallowed and rubbed his chin. His eyes fixated on me with a look of distaste, and I thought maybe he didn't like where I was sitting. His gaze shifted to Oliver.

"Mr. Mudge around?"

"Haven't seen him," Oliver said. "Why?"

Hooper ignored this. He looked at me.

"I saw him last night," I answered, "but haven't seen him yet today."

"Where last night?"

"At Loon Tavern."

The chief looked over at the parking lot again. He stared as if deep in thought.

"What's going on?" I asked, thinking about last night.

The chief looked back at us and cleared his throat with a disgusting gurgling sound.

"I have a warrant for his arrest."

I stood up. "What?"

"A murder warrant?" Oliver asked.

"No such luck," the chief said, shaking his head.

"Then what?" I was confused.

"There's a warrant from Maine out on him," Hooper said. "Auto theft." He looked to the parking lot. "That car right over there." He indicated Lonny's car, the one with the dealer plates.

"But I thought that was his car? He's a car salesman."

"Was," the chief said, trying one more tug on his belt. "He got fired a few days ago. He was giving some customer a test ride when he got stopped for driving while intoxicated." The chief shook his head and laughed, but it was more of a pitiful laugh than humorous. "The company canned him, and he was supposed to return his dealer car." He scratched his head. "But it seems like he never did. Just took off with the car. His wife doesn't even know where he is. They issued a warrant for his arrest."

My god, I thought. What has Lonny gotten himself into? That explained the lack of clothes in his room. What could he have been thinking? What did he plan to do? I thought about something he had said the other night: *I'm desperate.* How desperate?

"What a pinhead," was all Oliver said.

"Well, I'm going to have my men come up and impound that car," Hooper said. "If Mr. Mudge shows up, you'd be advised to have him come see me." He nodded. "Before I find him." He turned and walked away, trying to saunter, but his body shape didn't allow for it.

"Chief," I called out after him. He stopped and turned. "Any word on Paul Woodman?"

"We still haven't been able to get a hold of him. I'm keeping on top of that."

I decided not to tell him about who, or what, I saw at the cemetery. I wasn't even sure myself if I really saw it. When Hooper was gone I turned to Oliver.

"What do we do?" It was as if he were still the leader.

"Nothing."

"Nothing?"

"Mudge is an idiot." He turned to go back inside. "Let him dig his own grave."

I couldn't just sit by. I had to do something, had to find Lonny. I got in my car and decided to drive around town, see if I could locate him. It was probably futile, but it was something. Besides, I had nothing else to do.

I figured I'd check Loon Tavern first; it was as good a place as any to start, but when I pulled onto the boulevard downtown, I noticed Hooper had beaten me to it. His car was parked outside the tavern. I pulled over into a parking spot next to the boardwalk and cut the engine. I waited to see if Hooper would come out with Lonny. It was only a minute or two then the chief stepped out, alone. He got in his car and drove off. I breathed a sigh of relief.

Hands shot into the passenger side window, grabbing my arm.

I twisted around sharply, my heart jumping in my throat. I looked in horror at the maniacal face before me.

"HEY!" Carrothead screamed, drool running down a face scrunched up like a clenched fist. "Tell your friend he's too old to play games!" His hands withdrew to the edge of the window. I remained pressed up against my door, afraid he'd reach out for me again.

"Do you hear me?" he screamed. His face was brighter than his hair. "He can't play games no more! Tell him he doesn't belong in the park!" He stepped back from the car, his mouth still frothing. "Tell him to stay away from the park!" he shrieked one last time, then turned and shuffled down the boardwalk.

I had been holding my breath the whole time and now released it. My body was shaking and I gripped the steering wheel to settle it. When the shakes were gone, I tried to figure out what Carrothead was ranting about.

The park? Games?

Did he mean the ball park? The Little League field out past our old neighborhood near the cemetery?

Had he been talking about Lonny or someone else? It could have meant nothing. But it was worth a look. I started the car.

As I headed up Autumn Avenue, I decided to take a cruise through our neighborhood, just on the off chance Lonny was wandering around there. I turned onto Maple and drove slowly down the quiet street. I looked at my old house once again and the one next to it that Woody lived in, thinking about the night Woody and I talked to each other from our bedroom windows and decided to go out to the Tin Man's house. I looked over at the blackened skeleton of a tree that stood in the Rench's old back yard and thought of the fire that inadvertently started this whole nightmare. A nightmare that still hadn't ended, apparently.

When I got to the end of the street, I turned left onto Shadow Drive, looking up at the house on the corner where the Nightingales lived. I imagined Jason's family was still haunted by the same memories we were.

I didn't drive all the way down Shadow Drive. I stopped at the spot where Elm Street intersected it. But I could see the end of the road. I could see the Tin Man's house. I sat in the car and stared at the windows of the house with the drawn green shades. I watched for movement behind those shades. After all these years. He was still alive. How could Emeric Rust have lived so long? What kept him alive? He was behind those windows somewhere, I could feel it. Was he watching me? What was he living for? What driving force kept him going?

I shook my head, as if to rid myself of the somnambulant trance I seemed to be yielding to and turned the car down Elm Street. I scanned the ravine behind the houses, not really expecting to find Lonny lurking there. I glanced at the house Hooper lived in and wondered if he still did. Probably.

I looked to my right, up the hill to the Pines and saw somebody.

I pulled over to the side of the street and stopped. I looked through the windshield and could see a figure standing amidst the trees on top of the hill. I got out of the car to get a better view.

The figure moved. A man.

He moved quickly along behind a row of trees creating a strobe effect on my vision. The man looked dirty and disheveled. He glanced down at me.

It looked like Woody.

"Hey!" I yelled. "Woody! Wait!"

He disappeared over the crest of the hill.

I thought of running up the hill after him but didn't. Maybe it wasn't him. Maybe my mind was playing tricks on me again.

I stood there for a minute, pondering, and then got back in the car. As I pulled out onto Autumn Avenue once again and got around to where I could see the other side of the hill, I looked over. There was no one there.

I dismissed it and pulled my car up by the Little League field. I surveyed the field as I stepped out of the vehicle. It looked much smaller than I remembered as a kid. Back then the outfield fence seemed impossibly far away, but now it looked like I could throw a ball over it from home plate.

There was no one around. The ballpark was in a state of rest for the upcoming winter ahead. The grass had grown thick and was turning brown. The concession stand was boarded up. The green paint on the wooden dugouts on either side of the field was cracked and peeling.

I walked toward the middle of the field, out to the pitcher's mound. The pitcher's rubber had been removed, but I stood where it had been. The mound seemed low. I looked at the infield and outfield around me.

At the players around me. My teammates.

It was the city Little League championship. I stood on the mound rubbing the ball into my glove. It was the bottom of the last inning and I was tired. My arm ached. I had pitched the whole game, but I didn't want to stop now. We were up by only a run with one out and no one on. I couldn't let the coach see I was tired. I wanted to get these two outs, wanted to finish the game, wanted to be the hero. If the coach saw I was tired, if he knew how sore my arm was, he would give me the hook.

A quick peek into the bleachers and I could see my dad's smiling face. I wanted to impress him, needed to make him proud of me. That's why I had to finish this game.

I stepped onto the rubber and looked at the batter. Glancing into the on-deck circle, Oliver Rench waited, swinging a weighted bat. I had to get these next two outs because I knew what awaited me after Oliver's turn: Chuckwagon.

I stared in at Woody behind the plate. He was setting his catcher's mitt up low and inside. I didn't want that. I didn't want to work too much to this guy. My arm couldn't take it. Nothing fancy. Just put it down the middle and let him hit it. Then hope for an out.

I wound up and threw as hard as I could right down the pipe.

The bat cracked and the ball lined way over my head. I spun around and watched as the center fielder ran in and caught the ball.

One more, I thought, removing my hat to wipe my forehead. I replaced my cap and caught the ball after it went around the horn.

Oliver stepped into the batter's box, and Chuckwagon stepped into the on-deck circle. He was built like a block of granite. Even his head looked square. He held three bats together and swung them back and forth.

"Keep it alive for me, Oliver," he hollered.

Oliver grinned at me, then at the plate.

I released a sigh and looked in at Woody. I had to get Oliver out. I didn't want to face Chuckwagon. He had hit more home runs than anybody in the league. If I could just get Oliver out, we'd be the champs. The pressure was sickening.

I wound up and threw the ball right down the middle of the plate. He took the ball for a strike.

I shook my head. I wanted him to swing. I was putting every bit of energy I could into my pitches. I didn't want to waste time throwing. I wanted him to just hit the ball and get it over with. My arm felt like lead.

I wound up and threw again. This pitch was high for a ball.

Come on, I said to myself. Just swing at the damn thing.

My arm gave out in the middle of the next pitch. It was accurate, right down the heart of the plate, but there was no power to it. It just floated to the bat.

Oliver swung and lined the ball into left field. A roar went up from the crowd and the opponent's dugout. I felt my heart slip a notch inside me.

Chuckwagon tossed two bats aside and strode up to the batter's box. The coach called time out and walked to the mound. Woody joined us.

"I'm all right," I said to the coach, before he even had a chance to speak.

"How's the arm?"

I was staring into the stands at my dad. "It feels great," I lied. "Really, I can get this guy."

The coach shook his head, as if not convinced by my plea, but then surprised me. "Okay," he said. "Do it."

Woody spoke up. "Maybe we should put this guy on, Coach?"

"No way," I said, emphatically. "That's the coward's way out."

"If we want this championship," coach said, "we're going to earn it."

Coach walked back to the dugout.

"Don't give him a treat like you've been feeding these other guys," Woody said.

"Don't worry," I nodded. Woody went back to the plate. He was right. I couldn't fool around with Chuckwagon. Anything down the middle of the plate would be out of here for sure. He already put one out on me earlier in the game that wound up in the cemetery. I would have to be a bit craftier.

"Take him out coach!" one of the parents yelled from the bleachers. It didn't sound like my dad.

I glanced over at the opposing dugout. The whole team was standing up at the chain link fence that covered the face of the dugout, hands gripping the metal fibers, eyes bugging out at the field. No one had even bothered to step into the on-deck circle. It was as if they were all certain Chuckwagon was going to end the game.

There was no doubt in my mind he was thinking home run all the way. He wouldn't settle for anything less.

I went into my windup and threw to the plate. I threw the ball low, hoping he'd be over anxious and bounce a grounder to the infield, but he just watched it and Woody bobbled the pitch and dropped it.

Out of my peripheral vision I saw Oliver take off for second. Woody was barely able to pick the ball up and his throw down to second was nowhere near in time. Oliver stood up from his slide laughing, brushing the dirt off his pants.

"Oliver!" Chuckwagon hollered. The whole park was jolted into silence. "Don't you dare take a chance like that again! This game is mine."

I looked at Oliver and his smile was gone. I had never seen a look of fright on Oliver like that before.

My next pitch was high and outside, but Chuckwagon's long arms and huge bat reached for it and connected.

I held my breath at the sound of that crack. He had gotten solid wood on it. I spun around and watched the ball sail out toward right field. I leaned way to the right, mentally trying to force the ball foul. I don't know if it helped, but the ball started to hook. My pitch must have been just outside enough. The ball went foul, well beyond the homerun fence.

There were oohs and ahhs from the crowd and I released my breath. My teammates cheered behind me.

Hmmmm babe. Hmmmm babe.

My arm was throbbing, so I thought I'd try a curve. I just didn't have the strength to have much faith in my fastball. As I released the ball, my arm spasmed. The ball was heading for his head and I didn't think it was going to break. At the last possible second before it met his helmet, he threw himself to the ground. The crowd gasped. I don't think anyone had ever seen Chuckwagon go down from a pitch. I think maybe the only reason he did was because he didn't want to get on base by being hit. He wanted that home run, could taste it.

He got up, shook off the dirt, and then glared at me, brandishing his lumber menacingly. The fire in his eyes dried up my throat.

I knew I had to forget about the curve. My control was shot.

I wound up and reared back, gripping the ball tightly, and heaved it with all my might. I think I garnered energy I thought was long gone. It was inside and he swung. He was over anxious I think and it jammed him. He fouled the ball back over the backstop.

The ump threw in a fresh ball and it turned out to be brand new. I pretended to accidentally drop it on the mound and, when I bent to pick it up, I dragged it in the dirt. I then rubbed the ball in my palms. I didn't need to give him a nice bright white target.

I think the last pitch totally exhausted every muscle I had. I didn't think I could throw another fastball. I figured maybe I could fool him with a breaking ball. Maybe he wouldn't expect it.

I tucked the ball deep into my palm. Chuckwagon was gripping the bat so tightly his knuckles were white. I wound up and threw, releasing that ball ever so lightly. It drifted down toward the plate, right down the middle, letter high. It must have looked as big as a beach ball to him. The ball seemed to take forever to get to the plate.

Chuckwagon gritted his teeth and swung with all his might.

There was a loud popping sound.

I shook my head.

The ball was in Woody's mitt.

I was dazed. I couldn't even lift my arms above my head to cheer. Everybody was on top of me. I was buried, but soon found myself hoisted up in the air and carried off the field. I turned and looked toward the stands, looking for my dad.

I wanted to see how proud he was of me.

But he wasn't proud of me. Because that wasn't the way it happened. That was the way I wished it had happened.

Someone else pitched that game. I watched the whole game from the bench in the dugout. I didn't get to pitch that game. I never got to pitch in Little League. I sat on the bench most games, and when I did play it was for a couple of innings in right field. That was where they stuck the players who were no good. Right field was where the fewest balls got hit, there were fewer chances to screw up.

We didn't even win the game that day. Chuckwagon hit the homerun. I remember Oliver rounding third base and making faces at me as I sat in the dugout. Chuckwagon ran the bases with his arm in the air, finger pointing skyward, waving it back and forth. My teammates slowly walked off the field, heads down. But I didn't care. I wasn't a part of it. Why should I have cared?

I stood on the mound remembering days best left forgotten when I realized I was being watched.

I didn't make any sudden movement. I was afraid to.

Someone was sitting in the dugout on the third base side watching me. I could see the figure of what looked like an old baldheaded man behind the chain link fence, sitting in the shadows of the dugout. Just sitting, staring out at me.

I suddenly felt an uncontrollable panic creep over me. My heart raced, but I tried to remain calm. It was broad daylight, nothing could happen to me. I inconspicuously glanced around. There was no one else here. Across the road from the ball park were a few houses, but there was no one visible in or by them. Why was this town so damn quiet?

I thought about sprinting for my car. He'd never catch me.

This is ridiculous, I thought. I was getting paranoid. It's probably just some old guy out for a leisurely Sunday walk who decided to stop and rest in the shade of the dugout.

But his stillness spooked me.

Maybe I should just go over there and talk to him, see who he was?

I stepped off the mound and gingerly approached the dugout. I tried to form some opening line in my head, something about the weather usually worked. As I got closer, I noticed that something didn't feel right.

I got to the dugout and peered through the fence. My heart was no longer beating furiously. It almost stopped in mid-beat. I ran around to the side and entered the dugout, though there was no need to hurry.

It was Lonny, sitting on the bench.

He was slumped there, one eye open, staring out onto the field. But he hadn't seen me on the mound. He wasn't seeing anything anymore. His throat was slit.

I approached slowly, not taking my eyes off the gaping gash in his throat and the dried blood that glazed the front of his shirt. My knees felt like they were going to buckle, so I sat down beside him.

I had thought he was an old man because his toupee was gone. Without it he looked much older, like a completely different person. He appeared utterly peaceful, except for the wide gash and the blood. Maybe he was at peace. His problems were behind him. At least now he could finally sleep.

This really was a nightmare, I thought. His glassy eye showed no horror. The one closed eye gave the impression of winking, as if he were trying to let me in on a secret, a secret only he now knew. What had that one eye seen? Whose eyes had he looked into when it happened?

"I'm so sorry, Lonny," I said. I wanted to believe he could hear me. I looked around the dugout for his toupee, figuring it must have fallen off in the struggle. But I couldn't find it. Besides, it didn't really look like there was any kind of a struggle.

Lonny had played the shadow to find the killer. At least he succeeded in the last endeavor of his life.

* * *

The three of us sat on the bleachers on the third base side of the field, near the dugout. Oliver was on my left, on the row halfway up the bleachers. Martin sat two rows behind us. His face was pale, his eyes stricken with shock and fear. Oliver showed little emotion. His face held a relaxed expression, almost serene. Was this man stone?

I looked down at my own hands and noticed they were shaking. There was no doubt now. Dale's murder was not random. Someone was stalking the Jokers Club.

I had called the police from one of the nearby houses, as my cell still couldn't get a signal. Hooper had rounded up Martin and Oliver (the usual suspects) and brought them out here. I could hear the chief and the medical examiner now, talking in the dugout as they looked over the body.

"It's not the same kind of wound as the other," the medical examiner said.

"Different weapon?" the chief asked.

"Not necessarily. It's a nice fine cut. They could have used the same knife, but this time used the smooth edge of the blade as opposed to the serrated edge used on the first body."

Their voices dropped and I could no longer hear them.

I thought about the hallucination I had of Lonny in the gazebo last night, about how similar it was to the way he was killed. It was too frightening a coincidence.

I turned sideways on the bench so I could see Martin and Oliver at the same time.

"I've been thinking," I said. "Maybe it's time we tell Heifer about what happened with Jason?"

Oliver's eyes widened. "NO! Don't even think of telling him that!"

"I just think it's about time we come clean with Heifer on everything. What about you Martin?"

He nodded. "I think you're right. It's gone on long enough."

"There's no need for Heifer to know," Oliver said.

"It could help him figure out what's happening here," I said.

"I'm not having my reputation ruined by something that happened nearly twenty years ago."

"How will your reputation be if you're dead?" His childish stubbornness angered me.

"No killer's going to get me." He sounded arrogant. "There's no need to dredge up that old stuff. Besides, we took an oath. Remember?"

Yes, I remembered. Cross our hearts and hope to die.

Chief Hooper came out of the dugout and stood in front of the bleachers. He looked us over, as if studying us. Maybe he actually thought he could stare one of us into a confession.

He finally spoke. "When did you see Mr. Mudge last?" The question wasn't posed to anyone in particular. Both Oliver and Martin responded that they hadn't seen him at all yesterday.

"I saw him last night, at Loon Tavern," I said. "Just like I told you earlier."

"That's right. What time was that?"

I shook my head. "I don't remember. Early evening."

"He was still there when you left?"

"Yes."

"And what'd you do?"

I thought for a moment. "Went back to the inn. Did some writing, and then went to sleep."

"That's it? You didn't go anywhere else?"

I told him how I had woken up in the middle of the night, couldn't sleep and went back to the tavern. But I said I didn't see Lonny that time. (That wasn't Lonny in the gazebo. Was he already dead then? Was that his ghost trying to warn me?)

The chief stared at me for a while.

"Funny," he said, his forehead furrowing. "Funny how you're the one who's discovered both bodies."

I explained to him how I happened to come to the ballpark.

"I think Carrothead's the one you should be talking to," I said.

His face flushed. "You're not trying to blame this on a helpless idiot?" he yelled.

"I didn't say that," I yelled back. "I'm just saying that obviously he saw Lonny here, saw something. Maybe he saw the killer with Lonny. I think you should just question him."

"Don't tell me how to do my job, mister! I've been chief in this town a helluva long time. I damn well know how to do my job!"

No, I thought. This wasn't your job. Your job was breaking up underage parties, handing out speeding tickets and maybe once in a while investigating a case of vandalism at one of the summer cabins. Murder was out of your league. There hadn't been a murder in Malton in nearly half a century. Not unless you considered Jason Nightingale's death a murder. I looked over at Oliver. They say the best planned murder is one no one considers a murder at all.

"What about Woody?" Oliver asked. "Any word on him?"

The chief's color returned to normal and he shook his head, almost in disgust.

"He's still listed as a missing person. There's been no trace of him at all."

"Any sign of Lonny's toupee?" I asked, Oliver snickering beside me.

"That's missing too. Damn weird."

"Chief," I started to say. Oliver shot me a threatening look, as if afraid of what I was going to say. I hesitated, unsure myself of what I was about to ask.

"Did you check Emeric Rust's house again?" I finally asked.

The chief looked disgusted. "Old men, retards. You're trying to look in every direction but the obvious one. I have no doubt the killer is sitting right here in these bleachers."

The three of us looked at each other.

The scary thing was, he was probably right.

I dropped Oliver off at the Tower House Inn and offered to give Martin a ride home. A tow truck was hooking up Lonny's dealer car when we got there, and we watched them haul it away. It made me think of Lonny's body being put into the plastic bag and hauled away. I wondered if that same fate was awaiting me soon.

I was disgusted with myself for not telling Hooper about the real story of what happened to Jason Nightingale. I don't know why we listened to Oliver. It was like, after all these years, he was still our leader. He was still telling us what to do. And we still listened.

I couldn't wait to get away from Oliver. I couldn't stand being around him. Martin didn't say a word the whole time during the drive to his house.

As we pulled into his driveway, I looked at his home. It was an old colonial farmhouse, probably a couple hundred years old, but it looked as if it could have been built yesterday. The clapboards looked freshly painted, a dark hunter green, and all the shutters hung perfectly straight. A couple of polished brass lanterns kept guard on either side of the old-fashioned wooden door.

I asked if I could come in for a moment.

He hesitated and I thought the answer would be no, but he nodded.

"Sure. But I've got to feed the ducks."

We stood in his back yard by a small duck pond. He held a bowl in his hands filled with torn pieces of bread. There were over a dozen ducks, some in the water, others around the pond, and they gathered near him. He tossed some bread to the ones around his feet and out into the water to the ducks that had swam to the edge of the pond where we stood.

His house had been just as well-kept inside as out. He told me he had put a lot of work into it, that the place had been pretty run-down when he bought it at a bank foreclosure auction. He showed me earlier some of the molding and baseboards he had replaced, carefully matching the original woodwork. He had stripped and refinished most of the wood floors until they shone like glass. He had even retouched the brickwork around the fireplace. Most of his free time was spent working on the place, he said. Between that and taking care of his mother.

"How is your mother?" I asked, trying to break up the silence.

"The same," he responded. "Doesn't get better; doesn't get worse."

I looked around Martin's yard. There were no houses visible on either side of his. He had found a pretty secluded spot for himself and his mom.

"It's good that she has you to take care of her."

"I just hope I outlive her."

He said it so casually, so naturally. Yet it was frightening to think our lives could end so abruptly.

"I've been thinking," I said. "And the more I think, the more I believe it's Oliver we have to watch out for."

He looked at me but said nothing. The ducks quacked around his feet and he scattered a few more pieces of bread.

"I know I'm not the one," I continued, "and I hope you can believe that too. I have no doubt it's not you. I just want you to be very careful. We both have to." I pondered whether to tell him about Woody, but I just wasn't sure that was real or not. I wouldn't be able to explain to him why it might not be. I wasn't ready for that yet.

"Be alert," I said to him.

"Whatever happens, happens. There's nothing we can do to stop it."

There was no emotion in him. I looked at his face and could see he really wasn't worried.

"You don't care, do you?" I asked.

He was silent, tossing pieces of bread, then stopped and looked up at me.

"You know what I keep thinking about?" he said. "That day we played Relievo, when Oliver sent Jason up into that refrigerator to hide." He gripped the bowl in his hands tight. "I was worried about him being able to breathe in there. And I was going to say something, but I figured that Oliver and you guys knew better, that it must be all right, cause Oliver knew everything and if it wasn't all right, one of you would have said so, so I kept quiet and didn't bother saying anything, because you guys always knew better than me, so I didn't say anything and I keep thinking about that all these years, that maybe I could have done something." He lost his grip on the bowl and it fell from his hands, spilling bread crumbs onto the ground. His red face stared down as the ducks swarmed around his feet.

"So now I stay out here, where no one else is around, and I take care of my mother and my house and my ducks and that's pretty much all there is and that's probably more than I deserve."

I think that was the longest I had heard Martin speak uninterrupted in my life. I wondered how long he had been waiting to say it.

"You can't torment yourself, Martin. And you can't hide. Not even here anymore."

"Hiding is over. I'm just tired of hiding."

"You can't give up," I continued. "Don't you think about your loved ones? What about your mother? Who'll take care of her if you're gone? Who will feed your chickens?"

"They're ducks, dammit! They're not chickens, they're ducks!"

I thought about when we were kids, when we were in the club. Everything was so easy and carefree then. We had nothing to worry about. Everything had changed now. Everything had gone wrong.

I looked behind Martin, up at the back of his house. A face appeared in a second-floor window. It was an old face with thinning gray hair and round, wire-rimmed glasses. I looked at Martin, then back up at the face in the window, then back again at Martin. The resemblance was uncanny.

Martin was turning into his mother.

"Don't give up," I repeated. "You have to keep hope going. I still do. I hope to still publish a book (I do, maybe even this one). Heck, I even still have hopes Meg and I can be together again someday."

He looked bewildered.

"What is wrong with you?" he asked.

"Huh?"

"You're still so obsessed with her you don't even realize it."

"What are you talking about, Martin?"

"Meg. You've had this big lifelong crush on her, but the two of you never even dated." He looked angry with me. "Christ, Dale got so tired of you waiting that he went out with her, took her to the prom. We all went to their fucking wedding! Don't you even remember?"

I staggered backward, away from him, my mind going numb, and then I turned and ran back round to the front of his house and my car.

"No!" I screamed when I got behind the wheel. It couldn't be. But it was, of course. It was Dale, not me. Hell, I'd just spoken to Meg the other day when I called from the phone booth to try and tell her what happened to Dale.

I sped off wildly down the road, my nerves shaking. All those years. But it was true, wasn't it? God, what happened to me? I imagined it. A whole relationship, all those times together, those experiences and memories never existed. She never read my stories in the chairs in her front yard overlooking the lake on a warm summer day. Never held my hand, never pressed her lips against mine.

It had felt like it really happened.

But when?

When did I start to think Meg and I had been together? Was it when the tumor started? Or did it go all the way back to those years in high school?

How could my imagination play such a trick on me? Or was it just trying to give me what I really wanted? God, I was so scared. I didn't know what to believe in anymore. I didn't know what to do.

No. I did know what to do. Time was running out. There was something I had to accomplish. I sat at my desk in my room at the inn and inserted a fresh sheet of paper into the typewriter. My view through the window showed me a good portion of the lake and the town. There was my landscape; now it was time to create. There was only one thing missing. I glanced over my shoulder at the bed. The Joker sat on the end of it.

"Where do I go from here?" I asked.

"Wherever you want the story to go," he answered.

I began to type.

The pages kept flowing as the images of everyday life in Malton dripped onto the white emptiness. My hands sometimes felt like they couldn't keep up with my thoughts. It was as if I were possessed by a demon that had cut open my skull and spilt out all the memories that filtered down through my mind over the years.

There was so much to tell and so little time.

I had never been capable of writing at the clip I proceeded at now. I poured out everything I could onto the pages. I didn't want to stop, I didn't think I was capable of stopping. As the day progressed, I felt I wouldn't even have to take a break to eat, thought that feeding off the creativity of my writing would be nourishment enough.

But I did take a break.

I walked into town to Loon Tavern to grab some lunch. My mind was constantly molding and shaping thoughts that continually sprouted in my head.

After eating, I went back to the inn and kept on writing. I was on a mission. A mission to get my story out while I still could. The pages kept mounting.

Before I knew it, the past caught up with the present.

Here we were, gathered at the Tower House Inn.

That was when the story came full circle. That was what this was all about wasn't it. The story had to be finished. The story that had begun those many years ago.

But how was it to finish? That was the question.

There was a killer among us. It could be anyone. Oliver? Woody? Martin? Maybe even me.

I dropped my hands into my lap and leaned back into my chair. My fingers throbbed with a dull aching pain. I stared at the pile of pages I already had and the uncompleted one I still had in the typewriter carriage.

I couldn't write anymore. I was spent.

Besides, I was at a crossroads.

I just wasn't sure what was going to happen next. I thought that maybe, just maybe, if I wrote what I wanted to happen, that it would. As if I had the power to change the story at will. It was a bizarre sensation. I felt like I was in charge. I was the one telling the tale.

The story had now become a puzzle. But the problem was there were still too many pieces missing.

Missing?

Lonny's toupee was missing. That's what the story needed next. What had happened to Lonny's toupee?

THE SLAUGHTER OF THE LAMB

Following the last day of Junior High School, Jason Nightingale's family moved out of Malton.

Oliver watched the moving van drive past his house with glee. He looked at it out his bedroom window with a smile on his face, his first smile in quite some time. That family had caused enough trouble in his life, he thought. Good riddance to them.

Now that the inquest was long behind them, life had returned to normal. He no longer wanted to think about Jason Nightingale, but it was hard with the family still living right around the corner. They were still a constant reminder, and Oliver wanted to forget. Forget everything. It was bad enough seeing the blackened carcass of a tree in his backyard to remind him of what had happened to his clubhouse, but to see Jason's parents, little sister in tow, driving down the road nearly every day really sickened him. Why would they even want to stay around here? Wouldn't everything be a constant reminder, especially living right down the street from the Tin Man's house?

Then one day, Oliver saw a "For Sale" sign sticking in the ground in their front yard. About time, he thought.

So seeing the moving van roll past his house made Oliver happy.

He had other reasons to be happy. Junior high was finally over. Next school year, he'd be in high school. *That will be cool,* he thought.

Well, freshmen year will probably be a bit tough, but once he got through that first year, everything else would be smooth. He had a brother who was a senior, and one who was a junior, and he was sure they'd pick on him a little bit. That was to be expected. But he could take it. He wouldn't allow himself to be intimidated by them, or anyone else in school. He was tougher than that.

Besides, being on the sports teams in high school would help. Upperclassmen respected that.

Of course, he also couldn't wait to make new friends. That was another thing Jason Nightingale had ruined. After the inquest into his death was over, so was the Jokers Club. Things were just never the same among the six of them. Sure Lonny and he were still tight. Lonny was very loyal, and Oliver could always count on him. But the others kind of drifted off.

He didn't mind not hanging out with Martin or Woody. After all, Martin was such a wimp. It was kind of embarrassing sometimes to be around him. Oliver couldn't really believe he had ever hung out with him now that he looked back.

And Woody had become really weird. It kind of freaked Oliver out. He remembered an incident with Woody in the cafeteria at school one day. Oliver had just gotten his food tray, some dark-colored mystery meat as the featured entrée, and he was looking for the seat Lonny usually saved for him. He passed a table that Woody was sitting alone at. Woody was playing with his food, pushing it around on his tray with his fork.

"You're supposed to eat it," Oliver quipped, "not torture it."

Woody just glared at him, upper lip turning into a snarl. After a few seconds, he flipped his tray in the air, meat, string beans and mashed potatoes scattering all over the table and floor.

Oliver watched, dumbfounded, as Woody got up and stomped off. After that, Oliver steered clear of him, both at school and in the neighborhood. In fact, Oliver didn't see much of Woody around Maple Street. It seemed like he didn't leave the house much.

But Oliver did miss hanging out with Dale. Carpenter was a cool kid. Dale and Geoff were still pretty close friends and seemed to spend their time together, just the two of them. At first, Oliver was jealous. He didn't like being excluded, and that was how it felt. He'd much rather hang out with Dale than Lonny. But Dale and Geoff didn't seem to care to include Oliver anymore. Geoff probably had a lot to do with that. Oliver always felt Geoff judged him too much. But Geoff didn't know what it was like growing up without a mother and with a bastard for a father. Geoff was an only child, a golden boy, who didn't have to grow up in the shadow of older brothers whom he always had to try to live up to even though they constantly picked on him.

Plus, Geoff spent too much of his time with his head up his ass. Oliver got sick of listening to Geoff read his stupid horror stories. Hell, they weren't even scary, and Oliver could always figure out the endings. They were pretty simple. How the hell did he ever think he'd get to be a famous writer? It was all a stupid dream. That was Geoff's problem. He was always dreaming. He should stick to reality for a change. Maybe high school would smarten him up.

But the real reason Geoff and Dale didn't hang with him anymore was Jason. Jason had ruined the club and now Oliver was glad to see the moving van drive down Maple Street, stop, and turn onto Autumn Avenue where it would continue out of town and out of his life.

Maybe some new kid would move into the house on Shadow Drive. Maybe someone a lot hipper than that shit Jason Nightingale.

If not, there was always high school.

But in the meantime, there was a reason to celebrate and maybe one last chance to win Dale over. Junior high was over. Oliver had convinced his oldest brother to buy a case of beer for them to celebrate. Both Dale and Geoff (though reluctantly of course) had agreed to head out with Lonny and him to the woods near old man Callahan's farm.

Oliver's brothers gave them a ride out that way in the back of their pick-up. After being dropped off the four of them hoofed through the woods, taking turns carrying the beer till they reached the clearing where they used to hang out sometimes. The clearing had become a favorite spot for a few kids to congregate. It was secluded enough where you could build a campfire without betting noticed, but was also near enough to Autumn Avenue that you could thumb a ride back into town late at night.

A fallen tree served as a bench and they sat around drinking the beer and talking, mostly about what high school would be like and the anticipation of someday getting their driver's licenses so they wouldn't have to worry about bumming rides off people or thumbing home from places like this.

Lonny had gathered some small branches and twigs and built a tiny fire in the middle of the clearing. The flames drove away what little chill there was in the night air and lit up the immediate area. Oliver kept the beer away from the fire.

The beer was already getting warm so Oliver drank as fast as he could. He had snuck beers from his dad's fridge in the past, often at the urging of his brothers, so he was kind of used to the taste and the effects. The others were drinking a little slower, and he couldn't wait to see the effect on them, especially Geoff.

"This is like a rite of passage," Dale said. "The next phase of our life."

"A better phase," Oliver said. "No more stupid junior high."

"Now it'll be the big time for us," Lonny added, swilling his beer.

"Not so much as freshman," Geoff said, still working on his first beer, though Oliver was already on his third.

"Maybe for you, Thorn," Oliver said. "When they see me on the football field, they'll treat me a little different than you."

Lonny chuckled.

"But that's all right," Oliver continued. "You keep writing your stories, I'm sure that'll impress a lot of people." Geoff just stared at him. "Maybe you can become some English teacher's pet."

"If you're lucky, it'll be Mrs. Stern," Dale said. "I hear she has a nice rack."

"That'd be too much for Thorn to handle," Oliver replied, enjoying the setup Dale had just given him. He stared at the fire, knowing Geoff's eyes were on him, loathing him right now. Good, Oliver thought. Let him stew in that for a while.

They were all silent for a moment, except for the occasional gulping of beer and the crackling of the fire.

Dale had been the first to hear something.

"Someone's coming," he said.

Everyone stopped moving and listened closely.

A twig snapped in the fire.

"It's just the fire," Oliver said.

"No," Dale said. "I heard someone moving around, out there." He pointed to the field beyond the edge of the trees.

Oliver waited to see if anyone was approaching, maybe some other kids out drinking, maybe old man Callahan. Maybe Hooper and his men. There was nothing they could do but sit and wait; there was really no place to go.

Then Oliver did hear something, a rustling, like footsteps in the grass.

"Go take a look," he told Lonny.

Lonny put his beer can down and walked toward the edge of the clearing, disappearing into the darkness.

Oliver looked at Dale and Geoff beside him on the log. Dale looked curious, but Oliver relished the nervous look on Geoff's face. Oliver wasn't scared, in fact he felt a little rush of excitement as he began to wonder what could be the origin of the sound in the dark.

"Maybe it's one of your monsters, Geoff," Oliver said. "Maybe the thing that crawls up out of the well," remembering one of Geoff's better tales.

Lonny cried out.

Not a cry of fear, or pain, but a cry of wonderment.

It was followed by a loud thrashing noise and more yelling from Lonny. It sounded like a struggle was going on.

Oliver stood up from the log, clenching an unopened beer can in his right hand, thinking he could hurl it as a weapon.

No one else moved and suddenly the thrashing and yelling stopped. The sound of movement in the grass came toward the clearing. Oliver gripped the beer can tighter, getting ready for whatever was coming. Dale and Geoff remained seated on the log.

"Look what I got," Lonny said, bursting through the darkness into the clearing.

There was a shape in his arms, squirming around, crying out. Oliver had to stare for a moment before realizing it was a lamb.

"It must have got loose from old man Callahan's farm," Lonny said, having a hard time holding onto the animal.

"What the hell you planning to do with it?" Dale asked, standing up and moving closer.

"Maybe he wants to fuck it," Oliver said laughing.

It squirmed and kicked in his arms, but Lonny held tight.

"I don't know why I grabbed it. Just seemed like the thing to do."

"Well, why don't you just let it go," Geoff said.

"What do you think?" Lonny said, looking at Oliver.

Oliver did think. He stood there silently, staring but not seeing, the mind behind his dark eyes working, the gears turning. He had an idea and his mouth widened in a grin. Finally he spoke.

"Let's eat it."

"What?" Geoff said.

"Kill it and cook it. Right here on the fire."

"You're not serious?" Geoff said. But Oliver was, and the look on the faces of the others told him they all knew he was.

"I don't know," Dale said, shaking his head.

"Yeah," Lonny said. "Let's do it."

"Who's going to kill it?" Geoff asked, but it was a foolish question.

Oliver stepped forward, his hand grabbing onto the hunting knife he almost always had attached to his belt.

As if the lamb knew what was coming, it jumped out of Lonny's arms.

"Get it!" Oliver screamed.

Dale and Geoff just moved out of the way as the lamb ran in a circle, confused as to how to get away. Lonny dove and grabbed the animal by the wool on its backside. He lay on the ground gripping two fistfuls of white, the animal dragging him a bit as its legs dug at the ground trying to escape.

"Don't let go," Oliver said and grabbed a thick branch from the pile Lonny had gathered for the fire. He stepped in front of the lamb and raised the branch over his head.

The beast struggled in Lonny's arms and as Oliver held the branch high in the air, he looked down into the wild panic in the lamb's eyes and thought about how helpless the creature looked. Innocent and helpless, just like he felt the times his old man would yank off his belt and give him a strapping, usually with the buckle end stinging into his arms and legs and back as he cowered beneath the blows wishing they would stop, wishing he could turn the tables on the bastard and just grab the belt out of his hands and give him a kick-ass whooping. Then he would see how it felt, how humiliating it was. Never mind the pain. Oliver could take the pain. He was tough. It was the degradation that really sickened him. How the beatings made him feel like a helpless animal.

Like this little lamb.

The helpless lamb's eyes looked away as Oliver swung the branch down onto its head, again and again. His eyes widened, the muscles in his face grew tight in a mad grin as he watched the blood fly from the lamb's head as the branch struck it over and over. His own blood was pulsing through his body with exhilaration as he realized this must be how his dad felt when beating him. It was a mad rush that made him feel good, made him feel strong.

Finally there was a loud crack as both the lamb's skull and the branch gave way at the same time.

Lonny let the animal go and got up on his knees. The lamb's legs kicked a couple more times then stopped. Oliver stood there with the broken end of the branch still in his hands. He looked at the dead carcass, then up at the boys, the grin never leaving his face. He tossed the broken branch aside.

"It's dinnertime!"

He withdrew his knife. Everyone just watched in amazement as he grabbed the top of the lamb's head in his left hand, holding it up, and drew the blade across its throat, a wave of blood gushing out. He flipped his knife over to the serrated side and began sawing at the neck till he hit bone and continued. It was tough cutting through the spine, but once the blade fractured and splintered the bone, the head tilted back further and he felt the separation. The rest was easy, slicing through the muscle and skin in the back of the neck; he felt it give way. The body dropped to the ground and the head hung free in his hand.

He held the trophy in his outstretched hand, turning it so he could look into its dead eyes, so it could see who the real master was.

Oliver looked at the others. Dale and Geoff looked stunned, the latter's face pale. Lonny looked on with glee.

Oliver set the head down on the log and then proceeded to the lamb's body. He gutted it and skinned it, tossing its inner organs into the fire where the flames engulfed them.

He didn't care that blood was getting all over his clothes and hands. It actually felt good. His brothers would appreciate this if they saw what he was doing. They would think he was a man, not just some teen boy.

He knew what he wanted to do, how to finish the kill, to make it complete. He wanted to taste its flesh.

With Lonny's help, he drove some sticks into the ground on either side of the fire, and then with his knife he cut another stick to make a spit and impaled the carcass of the lamb on it. He hung it over the fire on the two upright branches.

They went back to drinking and watched the meat cooking, taking turns to turn the spit over. Oliver got an idea and stuck another branch deep into the ground. He picked up the lamb's head, looking into its dead eyes once again, and then rammed the head on the top of the stick.

"I want him to be able to watch himself cook," he said.

He and Lonny laughed. Oliver grabbed another beer, popping open the top, and stood beside the head, prying open its mouth and pouring the beer into it, the warm suds washing over the dead tongue, down its throat and draining out the bottom of its torn neck.

Oliver turned to see the bewildered looks on Dale and Geoff's faces and knew that any chance of renewed friendship with these two was long gone. Only Lonny seemed to appreciate the moment.

Fuck it, he thought. Who needs them? I'm Oliver Rench, king of the lambs. He chuckled to himself.

After the lamb cooked for a while, Oliver cut a few strips of meat off and they all tried it. It wasn't very good, but Oliver quickly washed it down with warm beer. They never got to eat any more because as it cooked, the branch cracked and the body went crashing into the fire. All they could do was watch the carcass burn, its skin sizzling, juices bubbling out of it as it blackened in the flames.

After finishing the beers, they all pissed on the burning embers to help put out the fire. Then Lonny stomped out the remaining smoldering embers, and they began walking through the woods toward Autumn Avenue. Oliver figured they were in for a long hike home, because he didn't think they would get a ride with his shirt all covered in blood.

Both he and Lonny smelled like sheep. As the four of them ventured through the woods, Dale and Geoff in the lead, Oliver began bleating like a lamb. Lonny laughed and began doing the same. It seemed to annoy Geoff especially, so Oliver kept it up.

It would become something he'd do every now and then when he'd pass Geoff in the hallways in high school or pass his locker.

"Baaaaaaaa."

He got quite a kick out of it because it seemed to torment Geoff.

When they finally left the woods and began the long trek down Autumn Avenue, Oliver thought of something cool.

He decided he would go back the next day and get the lamb's head. He could boil the skin off, clean it all up and keep the skull for a souvenir.

It would be a symbol of his first kill.

Unless you counted Jason Nightingale.

CHAPTER SEVEN

My feet would not stop. They took me down the long lonely dirt road on the east side of the lake, down the road I hoped I remembered from the day we tossed the eggs at Carrothead's house. I needed to find him and find out what he saw at the ballpark. He must have seen something.

When I left the inn, I originally walked down to the boardwalk, expecting him to be there. When I saw no sign of him, I headed to the ballpark, figuring maybe he had been hanging out there too. That place was as empty and quiet as the cemetery beside it. It was then that I decided to go right to his house and find him. I thought about going back to the inn and getting my rental car, but decided I liked having my feet on the ground, breathing in the air, feeling the breeze around my face. This could be the last time I walk around this town, feel its pulse beneath my feet. I wanted to enjoy every opportunity.

Now I found myself walking down the dirt road, not even sure if it was the right one. A couple of other dirt roads had sprung up on this side of the lake since I had last been here, and I passed a few newly built houses. The place had changed, and I wasn't sure if I could find his home again. Maybe I should turn back? No, I had come this far. There was no sense stopping now.

I came to another dirt road on the left and stopped. I stared down it, and then up the road I was on. Maybe this was it. Maybe if I stared at the road hard enough I could see the tire tracks our bicycles made when we were kids. Maybe if I waited long enough he would come shuffling down the road. If I had his other walkie-talkie I could try and contact him, ask for directions.

I closed my eyes and tried to remember that long ago ride, tried to find something familiar about the route that would help me now. The memory was too distant. I took the left fork and hoped for the best. It soon began to look less like a road and more like a trail through the woods. It eventually led me to the edge of the lake. There I stood, not knowing what to do next. My legs were tired, my feet hot.

As I stared out at the still water, a tingling sensation began stirring in the back of my head. My ears were ringing and I heard a jingling noise.

"Beautiful, isn't it?"

"Yes," I answered, staring at the lake, not even bothering to turn and look at the Joker behind me. "This is a beautiful place."

"But you never know what horrible thing might be lurking beneath the surface."

"That's right," I said, still staring at the lake. "Like the prehistoric fish Professor Bonz is trying to catch."

"Or like the carnivorous fish that eats the fishermen in that story I wrote."

I did turn around.

"You wrote?" I said. "I wrote that story."

"But you got all your ideas from me," the Joker said, smiling. "Don't you remember? I would whisper them into your ear."

"No. That's not true. They were my stories. They were always my stories. I didn't need you. I still don't. I can clean out that attic room anytime I want."

"Then why haven't you yet?"

"I'm afraid."

"What are you afraid of? Are you afraid of dying?" He took a step closer. "Or are you afraid of living?"

"I'm afraid of letting go."

"Of what? Me?"

I studied the lines of his curious painted face. He seemed so real. "I'm not sure."

"You weren't afraid of letting go that winter night on the lake."

I turned away from him and squeezed my eyes shut.

"No," I said. "I don't ever think about that. Not ever."

But without even opening my eyes I could see the frozen lake that March night. I could feel the icy chill around my body as I stepped onto the smooth hard surface. It was late, well after 2 am. I had just gotten off duty from tending bar that night. But I had been serving myself almost as much as the customers. If I had been caught, I could have lost my job, but I didn't care. I had received something in the mail earlier that day. It was in response to a writing contest I had entered several months earlier. One of my stories (about a telepathic rat) had made it to the final round of entries. I thought my moment was finally about to arrive.

But when the mail came that day, I almost didn't even have to open it. I held the manila envelope in my hand and turned it over and over. Finally I did unseal it and slipped out the copy of my story and an attached rejection form letter.

I stared at it in wonder, wanting to cry but only able to sigh. It seemed hopeless. All the trying just didn't seem worthwhile. Then, looking at the form letter, I became angry. They couldn't even have jotted a personal note. I wasn't even worthy of that.

After college, I had wanted to concentrate on my writing, while fellow classmates began careers in their chosen fields. I wanted to give myself at least a year. Write during the day and tend bar a few nights during the week. But the year was long up, and nothing had come of it, not even this stupid magazine contest. Now it was my time to start thinking about a career, making something of my education. It wasn't what I wanted to do, but what I had to do.

So I began sneaking drinks at the bar that night. After awhile I didn't even worry about being inconspicuous. I didn't care anymore. My job didn't matter. With my writing career fizzling, nothing seemed to matter.

After leaving the bar and heading back to my apartment, the frozen lake seemed to beckon me. I don't know what I thought when I stepped onto that frozen surface. At first it seemed like a neat idea to walk all the way across, something you talk about as kids.

When I got to the middle, mist swirling around me, I could hear the slow creaking as the ice groaned beneath my feet. I stood there, looking back at the town and its dwindling lights in the night, and I could almost feel the ice swaying underneath in arthritic strains.

I waited.

Part of me wanted to sprint as fast as I could for the shore, hoping the ice would hold long enough till I reached the edge. Another part wanted the whole thing to give way beneath my feet, swallow me up in the cold dark waters where I would sink to the unending depths. The hole that marked my departure would freeze over and no one would ever know where I went. And no one would ever miss me.

Of course the ice didn't open up. I suppose if I really wanted to I could have jumped up and down on that frigid surface. But instead, I only waited for something to happen, and as usual nothing did. Wasn't that always the way. That I always waited for things to happen instead of making them happen?

But I could make things happen. Wasn't that what I was really doing back here in Malton, making things happen? The work I was doing on my book was the most productive writing I had ever done. Wasn't that why I really came back? Not to find Meg or see my friends, not to reminisce about the Jokers Club, but to see if I could recapture the creativity I once had, to make things happen. Wasn't that what writing was all about? Making things happen.

That's what I had to do. I had to take action. When I got back to New York, I'd call Dr. Cutler and rip down the walls of that attic room. Let the sun burn bright inside and remove all the blackness. Then only time would tell whether it's really me that's in control.

But time, there was the true villain. I still needed just a little more time. I needed to end this tale.

I turned around. The Joker was nowhere in sight. But I knew he was lurking, not too far away.

Right now I felt as if I were wasting time. I had accomplished nothing in trying to find Carrothead's house. Now here I was, lost out in the woods alone.

Off beyond the thickness of the trees was a noise: a faint distant sound that reminded me of either the soft rustling of leaves or the crisp crackling of static. Either way, it meant I was not alone.

Someone was nearby.

How foolish of me. I had wandered out in the middle of nowhere, making myself an easy target for whoever was stalking the Jokers Club. I had actually felt a sense of security when Chief Hooper said he would be keeping an eye on us, but look how easily I had slipped away. Maybe before, not caring what happened to me, gave me a sense of invulnerability. But now that I found a reason to keep on living, my time might be up.

I didn't move. I stood and listened, trying to pinpoint the direction of the noise. I heard it again. This time it sounded like a combination of radio static and footsteps in the crunchy underbrush. And it was coming toward me.

I needed to move, but which way to go? I had gotten lost out here in the daylight, now the sun was going down. How could I find my way in the dark?

Quietly, with light steps, I made my way along the edge of the lake. But no matter how softly I treaded, each footstep crunched a dry leaf or snapped a dead twig.

I abandoned that tactic and began sprinting like mad, thrashing through the woods, pushing aside low branches that lashed out at my face, stumbling through the leaves and undergrowth, tripping over roots. I could no longer hear the person coming toward me. I was making too much noise to hear anything else; speed was my main concern. I tried to take the most direct route through the woods possible but occasionally had to veer around thick stands of trees. Eventually I had to hit a road or something.

Through a gap in the vegetation ahead, I caught a glimpse of blue and headed for it. When I burst into a clearing, my chest chugging, sweat coating my body, I saw a small rundown shack of a house. I stared at it for a second while trying to catch the breaths my lungs kept spitting out. I only had to step back in time for a brief moment to realize where I was.

I had found Carrothead's home.

This was only the second time I had ever seen it, but it looked exactly as it had back then: faded blue paint peeling in several places, front edge of the roof that sagged in the middle, tiny windows one could barely squeeze through, weeds crawling up around the foundation, suffocating it.

This was it.

Now that I had found it, I wasn't quite sure what to do next. Behind me the woods were still. Maybe I had only heard the wind rustling the leaves or a squirrel scurrying around for acorns.

I approached the house. Having come all this way, there was no use wasting any more time. I had done plenty of that already. Standing in front of the wooden door, I raised my fist and paused, knuckles poised, drew in a deep breath, then rapped three times.

No answer.

With my hands on my hips, I looked around, trying to glance into the dusty windows. I knocked again, louder. Still nothing.

There must not be anyone home, I thought. Could it be Carrothead lived alone? Maybe there was no mother. If he were hanging out down by the boardwalk, maybe the house was empty. Maybe I could get inside and snoop around? Could I be so lucky as to find the door unlocked? I doubt it. I grasped the doorknob (*Don't open it*) and turned.

The door opened a crack and I stopped. This is crazy, I thought, looking around at the dirt road behind me. If Hooper caught me, he'd have it in for me. But there was no one around.

I pushed the door open slowly but did not enter. The door gave way to darkness, like the entrance to a cave. I could see nothing inside. The only way would be to step across that threshold. I stepped forward, absorbed into the blackness, and waited for my eyes to adjust.

When things became clearer, I found myself in a long room that seemed to be a combined kitchen, dining area and living room with no separations to distinguish each. On the far right end was the kitchen. Dirty dishes rose up out of the chipped porcelain sink and spilt over onto the counter in a trail like some spreading infectious disease. A huge pot sat on the front burner of the olive-colored stove, a large, dried red stain running down the side of the pan and over the lip of the appliance where its journey halted halfway down the front of the oven door. Nearby on the cracked linoleum floor was a tiny table with two padded chairs at either end. The vinyl on the chairs was split in several places revealing yellowed stuffing beneath. Crumb-covered plates were abandoned on each side of the table, with silverware scattered nearby. The only sound was the humming of the refrigerator and the buzz of a fly on one of the dishes.

I looked at the living room around me, its walls paneled in dark pine, warped and pulling away from the walls at some of the seams, and I took a deep breath. I could almost taste the soft layer of dust that coated the furniture. I managed to suppress a cough. Immediately in front of me, a pine coffee table squatted before a green couch. Spots on the legs of the table were worn down to the bare wood, like a pair of scuffed knees. The surface of the table could barely be seen beneath piles of magazines.

Beside the couch, next to an end table that held a lamp absent its lampshade, were stacks of newspapers. I looked around and saw more newspapers on the other side of the room, some neatly piled, others scattered haphazardly around the floor and furniture. I went over to the nearest stack and picked up a yellowed paper with curled edges. I had to squint in the darkness before seeing the edition was several years old. I glanced over some of the other piles, noting more recent dates and even older ones.

I dropped the paper on the floor, not concerned with where it fell, and walked over to the wall at the end of the room. On the wall, above a tall bookcase, hung several enlarged framed photographs. It took close examination in the dark interior of the house to realize I was looking at pictures of a young Carrothead. A young, *normal* Carrothead. There were photos of him in baseball, football and basketball uniforms. He was handsome, with a laughing smile and an athletic body. He looked like a different person, yet there was no mistaking it was him.

I looked down at the bookcase before me and saw the shelves were covered with trophies from all three sports. I reached out and touched one, running my fingers along the smooth, shiny, gold-painted baseball figure. Something struck me as unusual and in a moment I realized what it was. This trophy, and all the others, were completely devoid of dust. The top of the bookcase and all the shelves held a thin coat, but the trophies were spotless.

I looked down at one of the lower shelves and saw a large scrapbook. I picked it up and began flipping through. The pages were filled with newspaper clippings from Carrothead's sports career, starting with youth leagues and going all the way through to his high school years. The book ended with several empty pages, pages that never got filled by a sports career that abruptly ended, cut short by – by what? Was the rope-swing story true?

I looked at the last newspaper photo of him, wearing a basketball net around his neck and holding his index finger high in the air. I closed the book with a thud and held it tight to my chest.

My god, what had we done?

All those years, all the teasing and torment. How could we? I felt ashamed. Deservedly so.

I gently placed the book back on the shelf and turned, a sick feeling in the pit of my stomach. I just wanted to leave this place, go home. What was I trying to accomplish here? Did I find the answers I was searching for?

I looked to the right of the green couch, at a hallway that obviously led to the back bedrooms.

No.

I might as well finish what I started. I had come this far.

It was a short hallway that ended with a small window looking out to the backyard of the house. To my right and left were two partially opened doors. Two bedrooms. I pondered for a moment then, for no particular reason, chose the one on the right and pushed the door open.

The room was pitch black. I imagined the sun must have set by now, for no natural light existed in here. I stood in the doorway scanning the dark silhouettes of shapeless furniture, like huddle figures, trying to see something, anything. It was no use. I needed light.

Still staring into the far depths of the corners, I slowly reached my left hand out, trying to find a light switch on the wall beside the door, when my fingers touched someone's hair.

I froze, fingers still entangled in the soft locks, my heart thudding in my chest. I turned my head slowly as I withdrew my trembling left hand, feeling the fibers of the hair slip from my fingertips. I met a pair of dark eyes that seemed to look right through me. My hands gathered in front of me in a protective pose, as if ready to ward off an advance. My feet would not move.

As I stared at the unmoving face in front of me, the darkness dissipated and I could see a crooked grin.

It was a carved pumpkin sitting on a tall bureau up against the wall. I almost laughed when I realized what I had touched.

It was wearing Lonny's toupee.

He *had* been there.

Here was proof. But proof of what? I wasn't sure. I only knew I had to let Hooper know. But how? I surely couldn't tell him I snuck in here and found it. He'd never believe me. He'd think I planted it.

I stood there in the darkness, trying to think of what to do next, when I noticed deep breathing coming from behind me.

For the second time inside that house, I froze. Everything was silent except for that sound of inhaling and exhaling, so clear I could practically feel it on the back of my neck.

Slowly I turned around, sure of whom I'd see.

Nobody was there. Only the breathing.

I thought maybe Jason followed me in here and the breathing would soon turn to a ghostly laughter. But then I noticed the sound came from behind the partially opened door on the other side of the hallway.

I walked toward it, moved the door open just a little, and peeked in.

Up against the back wall, in the middle of a queen-sized bed, lay an enormous sleeping woman. Her body covered the bed nearly from side to side. Her bloated form swelled from her chest up into her face so you couldn't even tell where her neck ended and her chin began. Great sucking sounds of air were drawn deep into her cavernous nostrils and exited just as loudly, her whole body rising and falling in rhythm.

I watched her hypnotically, till I was jolted out of my trance by a sudden burst of static.

It came from a walkie-talkie on a bedside table.

"I coming home, Ma!" came Carrothead's screeching voice.

The old lady stirred but did not waken.

I started to back out of the doorway when the static buzzed again.

"Can you hear me, Ma? I coming up the driveway!"

Oh shit.

I backed into the hallway, looking around, wondering where to go. I didn't see a back door. I stepped into Carrothead's room and shut myself in just as I heard the front door bang open.

I'm trapped.

I leaned against the wall and looked across the room at the window on the opposite end.

I heard footsteps shuffling and I bounded across the space, momentarily thinking about grabbing Lonny's toupee and shoving it in my pocket but then decided against it.

As I quickly made my way across the spongy carpet, I stumbled over something, muffling a cry of surprise as I nearly fell against the window.

The glass opening looked tiny as I threw up the sash, doubting I'd ever be able to get past it, but somehow, sheer panic forced my body through the cavity just as I heard the door opening behind me.

I dropped to the ground and pressed my body up against the rough clapboards. Carrothead must have heard me banging around because I could hear him cross to the window, quicker than I ever imagined he could move, and as I tried to make myself as much a part of the side of the house as possible, I could see his head peer out from the edge of the window.

I dared not move as his face turned from side to side, scanning the shadows beyond the house. I felt a small drop of drool land on my cheek, but I suppressed an urge to wipe it away in disgust. Soon, his head popped back into the room and the window slammed shut. I waited a second longer and then sprinted away, rubbing my cheek as I went. I ran from that house like I did those many years ago, half expecting his steel-like arms to wrap around me and squeeze the air from my lungs.

When I was back at my room at the inn, I sat on the edge of my bed, thinking, wondering what it all meant, wondering what to do. There was no way to explain to Hooper my discovery of Lonny's toupee. The typewriter sat cold and silent on the desk, a machine waiting for its engine to be revved up again. Maybe I could write a solution for my dilemma, explain away Carrothead's possession of the toupee.

I fell back against the mattress, hoping its comfort would soften my frustration. My eyes traversed the tin pattern above me until my lids became heavy. I closed them for only a second.

I dreamt.

In the dream, I was running through the ravine. It was nighttime, the moon was obscured by black clouds. I picked my way through the ravine, being careful but trying to be quick.

Something was chasing me.

I could not see what it was. All I saw behind me was a shadowy figure with a misshapen head.

I veered around bushes, ducked beneath limbs, stumbled over exposed roots, all the time glancing behind me to see the thing gaining, moving slowly, methodically, but gaining ever so slightly.

I bolted out of the ravine to the yards behind the houses on Elm Street. I stopped, for just a moment, turning around and looking back into the darkened ravine. I didn't see the thing emerge from the misty blackness. Maybe it had stopped. There came a thrashing from the branches and I realized it was still coming.

I sprinted around to the front of one of the houses and ran to the door. It was Chief Hooper's home. I pounded on the door with my fists, yelling and screaming for him to open it. After a moment, the shade on the window beside me lifted. I saw Hooper looking out at me, his fat face grinning, food particles embedded in his teeth. I screamed for him to let me in. He laughed and slowly pulled the shade down.

I looked left and saw the shape coming across the lawn toward me. I turned and ran across the street screaming the whole way, hoping someone would come help me, but all the houses were dark and quiet.

I ran toward the Pines, mounting the hill, feet digging into the ground. The climbing was slow, as if my legs were weighted. I glanced over my shoulder and saw it right behind me, climbing up the hill. I looked away, continued moving up, thinking any second it would reach and grab me by the ankles and drag me back down.

I scrambled to the top, out of breath. I was hunched over in a clearing amongst the pine trees, leaning up against the big boulder at the top. I tried to suck in air but not much came. I couldn't run any more. I would make a stand here.

The thing came upon me, standing over me. I looked at it. A cloud moved away from the moon and light streaked down between the trees and shone on the thing's head. It had the dead, rotting head of a lamb on its shoulders. Flies crawled all over it; maggots weaved their way throughout its molted fur.

I stared in fright, heart racing. But then I mustered the courage to do something. If I was going to die, I had to see.

I reached up and pulled off the lamb's head.

I screamed in horror.

The face beneath the lamb's head was my own.

I awoke.

I lay in my bed, staring at the dark ceiling above me. My hands gripped tight to the sides of the mattress. My breathing was hard; sweat dampened my flesh. It was hot in the room. I needed air, needed to open the window. I looked to my right and through the darkness could see the window was open. I sat up in bed.

I heard a creak to my left.

In the shadows I could see the closet door was open about six inches.

Strange. I didn't recall using the closet at all since I'd arrived. All my clothes were in the bureau and I was sure I'd placed my jacket over the back of the desk chair. I had hung nothing in the closet, and I didn't recall the door being open. Not that I'd really paid much attention to it till now. Its gaping opening stared back at me like a sinister grin.

Was that where the creaking had come from?

I had a strong urge to either run over there and fling the door open the rest of the way, *(Don't open it; Don't open it)* or to slam it shut and hold it tight. But I didn't do either.

I stared at it, almost daring it to move. It didn't. Through the dark crack, I thought I could see the outline of a jacket. I must have hung it in there without realizing it.

I looked over to the desk. There was my jacket hung over the chair.

I didn't want to look back at the closet, wanted to only crawl into the bed and pull the covers up over my head. But I did look back.

The door pushed open.

I sat frozen on the bed.

A figure walked slowly out.

I couldn't move. My mouth opened but nothing came out, not a single breath.

The figure approached, slowly, not at all in a threatening manner. I finally found control over my muscles and stood up. Light coming through the window from a street lamp outside fell on the floor and cut a path through the fog between us. The figure stepped into that light and I saw its face.

It was Woody.

He stopped a couple of feet before me and looked at me, but it was almost like he couldn't see me. His eyes were glassy and distant. He looked thin, thinner than when I had seen him at the asylum. His skin was practically stretched over his bones. His clothes were filthy, covered with remnants of dead leaves and pine needles, as if he had been sleeping in the woods.

"Woody?" I said, my voice a hoarse whisper. I was scared, but I didn't know what to do. Even though I was afraid, I didn't really feel threatened by him.

He reached a hand out, an empty hand, but the effort seemed too hard and it dropped back to his side.

"Are you okay?" I asked.

He did not respond, just stared at me, his jaw slack, eyes unblinking.

Then it looked as if he were about to speak. His mouth opened slowly, wide. No words came out but a long brown worm did.

I was about to scream but my own voice was driven mute from shock. His body pitched forward, and I reached my arms out to catch it. It was light and lifeless. I held tight to him, so tight that my hands sunk into his back, right through his flesh.

Once again my mouth opened to scream, but once again the words and voice were lost. His legs buckled and I tried to maintain my hold. His flesh began peeling away from his bones. The front of his body split wide open and intestines and stomach spilled out onto the floor. I looked at his face and saw his lips peel back from his teeth, an eyeball slide from its socket. I tried to adjust my grip, tried to hold him together, but I couldn't. He was decomposing right in front of me.

I let go and his whole body collapsed to the floor, bones poking up through tatters of flesh, innards lying in an oozing pile. An eyeball still looked at me, the teeth in his skull opening and closing as if trying to speak to me.

I stumbled backwards onto the bed and sat there, shaking, my face in my hands, crying in heaving sobs.

God, what's happening here?

I took my hands away and looked to the floor.

There was nothing there. Never had been. I knew now that Woody was not here.

I gulped deep breaths of air as my breathing slowed to normal. My body was covered in sweat, my head ringing.

What time was it?

I looked to the small clock on the nightstand beside the bed but it was no use. It wasn't working.

A faint sound came from beyond the open window and I went to it and paused.

It was a soft, stuttering, pinging sound. I knew where it came from. It was the sound of Mr. Under carving a name onto a headstone. (Lonny's?) Each stroke felt like a chisel of ice chipping into my spine.

It reminded me of something I had to do.

I grabbed a pen and piece of stationery from the bedside table, sat at the desk and quickly, with just a slight pause to refresh my memory, scribbled a few lines. I then threw on some clothes and left the room.

Once outside I walked at a quick pace, as if I were in a race with time. As if the sands were running out of an hourglass and smothering me.

As I walked along the boardwalk toward the center of town, I looked up at the sky. A fat, swollen yellow moon hung over the lake, seemingly ready to burst. Beneath it, sitting in his rowboat in the middle of the water, was Professor Bonz. I smiled.

I crossed the boulevard and Main Street to the opposite sidewalk. I walked past the closed shops until I got to Mr. Under's place.

A bell rang over the door as I opened it. I walked to the counter and looked over at Mr. Under who sat at his work table. A wide smile broke over his face when he looked up and saw me.

"Are you next?" he asked.

There was an ominous familiarity about the question.

"I hope not," was all I could think to reply.

He got up from his chair and approached the counter, leaning his angular frame forward in an almost leering manner, smile never leaving his face.

"I've been following the events up at the Tower House," he said.

"They haven't been very pleasant."

"There's a lot in life that isn't very pleasant."

There was a chalky smell of dust in the air. I looked around the small shop. Even though he had stopped working, I could still hear a pinging in my head.

"You're working late," I commented.

"Business has been good." His smile would not subside.

"And that makes you happy?" I queried.

"It keeps me busy. I like being busy."

"Then I can help you out." I removed the piece of paper from my pocket. "I have something for you." I handed it to him.

"Something – for me?" He took it in his hands with childlike glee. "What is it?"

"My epitaph."

He looked at me queerly, smile fading this time, and unfolded the paper. As his eyes moved over the words, I envisioned them as I had written them. My full name on the top, with my birth date beneath it. Then a few lines below that, six short words.

He looked up at me. "The second date is missing."

"I'll leave that for you to fill in later."

He glanced back down at the paper and read out loud the last line: *He was a teller of tales.*

He looked up at me and his smile returned. "I like tales. How about telling me a tale?"

I thought about the stack of pages sitting on the desk in my room at the inn.

"I can't," I replied. "I haven't finished it yet."

I stepped onto the sidewalk. The realization that I hadn't really seen Woody made what I had to do – fast — clear to me. I looked up and down the street. It was quiet. Then I noticed a figure standing in the gazebo. It gave me a chill. Not again, I thought.

The figure waved to me.

It was Carrothead.

"Hullo," he called as he continued waving.

I thought about going over and talking to him, find out what he saw at the ballpark, ask him about the toupee. But then I thought it best to avoid him. There was something else I wanted to do.

I walked down the sidewalk, ignoring him. He continued to call out to me.

As I passed the Loon Tavern, I paused and glanced in the window. I scanned the inside of the bar. Nick the barber was in there, sitting by himself at a table, dark spots covering the front of his smock. He was probably waiting for Mr. Under to join him.

Then I noticed Oliver sitting at the bar talking to a woman. When the woman turned her head, I noticed it was Mary. I felt a twinge of jealousy, but I couldn't bother with that now. I had something to do. Now was my chance if I hurried.

I crossed the street and headed toward the direction of the inn. Behind me, Carrothead was still calling out to me, becoming fainter until, by the time I reached the inn, I could either no longer hear him or he had given up on me.

When I entered the inn, I greeted Bob Wolfe behind the counter and headed up the stairs. I could feel his suspicious eyes on me the whole way up the first flight. And I don't know how it was possible, but when I passed by the moose head, those eyes followed me too.

All the rooms were dark on the second floor. Professor Bonz was still out on the water. Mary was at the bar with Oliver.

I continued up to the third floor and went straight to the stairway that led to the tower room and headed up to the door at the top. When I opened it and walked inside, I had the strange sensation I was stepping into a trap.

This was too easy.

I looked around the room, trying to decide where to start first. It was dark, so I went to the window and lifted the shade to let in what light was thrown from the moon and the street lamps outside. I didn't want to turn the light on inside. It would be like a beacon in a lighthouse tower from the outside.

I decided to start with the dresser. I wasn't sure exactly what I was looking for. A weapon is what I was hoping to find, maybe the same hunting knife Oliver used to always carry with him as a kid, but anything would do. Anything that could resemble some kind of evidence. Something to make me believe Carrothead innocently took Lonny's toupee.

Knowing now that I had not been seeing Woody around made one thing clear. From the beginning it had seemed Woody was the obvious choice as the killer because he had been in a mental asylum. That coupled with his mysterious disappearance. But Woody was not at Acorn Estates because he was crazy. He was there because of a physical condition brought on by a psychological problem.

Oliver on the other hand, I truly believed had a sick, twisted mind. I think it had been like that since his childhood.

There was nothing in the drawers and I quickly moved on to the closet. I was trying to proceed as fast as I could. I did not like being here. The closet yielded nothing, and I checked the desk and under the bed and mattress. Nothing. This whole idea was futile. I felt like an idiot. Did I think I was some kind of detective? Even Hooper wasn't this stupid.

I stood in the middle of the room, staring at the window and the night beyond it, frustrated. I had wanted to find something – anything – that I could bring to Hooper and stop Oliver.

Then, for the second time that day, I was frozen by the sound of breathing behind me.

I prayed to God it was my own I was hearing but realized I was holding my breath. I felt like I was in a state of suspended animation. I turned in the slowest motion possible. Standing in the dark behind me was Oliver.

"Looking for something?" he said.

I glanced down at his hand and saw moonlight gleam off the blade of a knife. I looked back up at his eyes, trying to think of some reasonable excuse for my presence, but there was no reasoning in those eyes.

"You know," he said, a little smirk on his face. "I felt all along it would come down to this. Me and you."

I took one step back. "I guess I did too."

"You're a loser, Thorn." He stepped forward. "Just like all the others. You're all a bunch of pathetic losers."

I took another step back, looking over his shoulder at the door to the stairway behind him. There was no way to get to it without going through him first.

"What makes you so above us all?" I asked, almost spitting the question out.

"Because I have strength and power." His face grimaced. "I'm a survivor." He took a step forward.

The room was dark and the shadows seemed to cling to him, dripping from him. The only thing that stood out was the gleaming blade and his contorted face. He moved forward.

Then he stopped. He tipped his head back and started laughing hysterically.

"You know what this reminds me of?" he asked. He didn't wait for an answer. "You and me, here in this room? It reminds me of when I used to put two praying mantises in a jar so they would fight to the death. Do you remember that?"

I nodded.

"Well, that's what we are. A couple of praying mantises in a jar." His face grew serious. "And I'm going to bite your head off."

He lunged at me.

The reality of that blade coming at me brought on a tremendous wave of fear. I jumped back, out of the way. He then swung his arm, swiping at me. I ducked, then bounced back up and grabbed onto his wrist. All I could think of was keeping that blade away from my body. He tried to push me away, but I locked my right arm around his neck. Our faces were inches apart. I glared into his vacant eyes a saw his wild grin. I realized I had seen this face before. It was the same face he wore the night he beat the lamb to death.

He was much stronger than I and soon spun me around and flung me to the floor. When my hold was broken, I felt instant panic knowing that knife hand was free and coming after me.

He jumped down on me but I brought my feet up and kicked him in the gut. I think he lost his wind for a second, and I rose and turned toward the door.

I couldn't move fast enough, and suddenly his arms wrapped around me, the hand with the knife holding the blade inches from my face. I had a magnified view of the blade and could almost feel the searing pain that would result if it pierced my flesh.

I pushed backwards, driving with my feet, with all the adrenalin my extreme fear pumped through my body. We crashed into a wall and his gripped relaxed. I spun around and smashed a fist into the side of his face. He was momentarily stunned, but then the arm with the knife came flailing up.

I felt a jolt of pain as the knife brushed my side.

I quickly grabbed onto his knife arm with both hands, just below his wrist. The most important thing on my mind was to hang on to that arm. Keep that knife at bay.

With his free hand, Oliver smashed a fist into my face, once then twice, then again. He literally beat me to the ground and I lay on the floor at his feet.

"Come on, Thorn, you bastard!" he screamed. "Get up!"

I looked up at him, fear and loathing churning in my mind. Then with suddenness that caught him completely by surprise, I sprang up and threw myself into his chest, pushing him backwards into the window.

There was a crash of glass.

His body was off balance and falling backwards through the pane. His free hand reached out to me. I extended my hand to grab it, but at the last moment before our fingers touched, I pulled mine back.

He fell backwards out the window.

I leaned out and watched him fall.

His arms were gesticulating wildly, the right hand still gripping the knife. His face held an expression I had never seen on him before. One of utterly mad fright. He screamed all the way down, until his back struck the porch roof.

There was a loud crack, but I wasn't sure if it was his spine snapping or one of the wooden porch beams. Maybe it was a combination of both. His body bounced off the shingles, as if they were made of rubber, and flipped over so I could no longer see his tortured face.

He landed stomach first on the spikes of the wrought-iron fence. I saw the pointed ends pop out through his back.

Oh my God!

I turned and raced out of the room and down the stairs to the third floor hall. I almost barreled over Mary who stood in the middle of the landing.

"What have you done, Geoff?" she screamed, her face horrified. "Christ! What have you done?"

I ran past her without a word, racing down the stairs, taking them three and four at a time. It felt as if I were going down a dozen flights of stairs. I passed by the moose head on the first floor landing. It turned to look at me.

"Christ, Geoffrey!" it said. "What have you done?"

I didn't think I'd ever reach the bottom. When I did, I burst out the front door.

Oliver's body hung over the fence, the bloody spikes protruding from his back. His hand still held the knife, but then his fingers slowly uncurled and it clattered to the stone walkway with a reverberating rattle.

I went over, kneeling in front of him, wondering what to do but knowing there was nothing I could do. His head hung down so I couldn't see his face, but I was sure he was dead.

Then his head lifted and an arm shot out and grabbed me by the front of my shirt. I was horrified.

His wild eyes looked into mine.

"You think it's over?" he cried, spitting up blood through clenched teeth. "It's far from over!"

Then his hand relaxed and his head dropped back down. This time I was sure he was dead. I sat back on my heels. My whole body felt sapped of life. There was a rush of footsteps and I looked to my right as Mary ran out of the inn. Her eyes were wide, looking back and forth between me and Oliver's body.

"Oh God!" she cried. "Why did you do this?" Her voice was almost angry. "Why did you have to do this?"

I tried to say something, tried to explain that I was only defending myself. But I couldn't find my voice.

Then Bob Wolfe came onto the porch, his hunting rifle in hand, and he pointed it right at my head.

"Don't you dare make a move," he said.

I didn't. Because I had no doubt he would gladly pull the trigger.

THE JOKER IN THE ATTIC

It was early June, a time when kids were anticipating the end of the school year, the beginning of summer vacation, when a kid could really be a kid. It was magical time when the days and nights of summer would soon be turned over to the children. The world of summer would become their playground.

Memorial Day had brought forth the onslaught of the tourist season. Retired folks were the first wave to arrive. The end of the school year would bring the second wave – the families. The cottages on the far side of the lake were gradually springing to life, the inns were swelling to full capacity, and the summer businesses were in full bloom.

Another rite of summer was beginning for twelve-year-old Geoffrey Thorn. It was the haircut his mother always made him get at the first hint of hot weather: the traditional trimming of his brown curly locks. It was as if she was worried he would collapse from heatstroke if he didn't get the haircut. Maybe she thought his thick hair made him sweat too much.

But what was really sweating were his palms as he approached the barber chair like a death row inmate on his final walk. No longer could he enjoy the anxious but somehow comforting waiting period, flipping through thumb-worn comics and magazines while the other customers one by one stepped up to the dreaded chair and put themselves completely in the hands of Nick the barber. As the last customer stepped out of the shop, seemingly pleased, all moisture evaporated in Geoff's constricted throat. The slow shuffle across the tiled floor did nothing to prolong the inevitable. When he climbed up into the vinyl seat, his body stiffened as his nerves began to freeze up on him.

It was more than just the haircuts that made him nervous. That was bad enough, that feeling of helplessness while someone did something to you that you had no control over. It was Nick himself that Geoff had grown to fear. Nick simply did not inspire trust and confidence. The lenses in his black horned-rim glasses were thick. What did the world look like through those spectacles? How distorted did things appear? His breath spewed forth the smell of mints with every exhale, but Geoff swore he could discern, hidden beneath that minty odor, the barest hint of alcohol. Was he drunk? His hands seemed to shake from time to time, spasms shooting through his knobby fingers.

Geoffrey noticed that Nick's white barber's smock never failed to contain a small red spot, large enough for him to notice, but insignificant enough for everyone else to dismiss. How many backs of necks had he gouged open with the points of his scissors? How many times had he accidentally clipped the tip of someone's ear? Geoff thought Nick probably had a drawer full of ear tips. He could string them on a piece of fishing line and wear them like hunter's trophies.

Geoff wrote a story inspired by Nick. It was about a senior citizen vampire whose teeth were no good, so he opened a barber shop that only operated at night. Whenever a customer was unlucky enough to be the last one of the night, the barber would dig his scissors into the person's jugular and suck out his blood. Whenever he went to get a haircut, he couldn't help but think about the story.

As Nick stood beside the chair, Geoff could see, out of the corner of his eye, the tear-shaped red stain on the left breast of his smock. Nick placed the barber's apron over Geoff's body and began to tie it in the back of his neck. It felt like a noose on his throat, too tight as always. He couldn't get any air. He gasped for breath, imagining his face turning blue, then purple. It felt like a tourniquet, forcing his jugular to bulge outward.

"The usual?" Nick said, flashing a grin of rotting teeth.

The steel scissors clicked in his knotted fingers as he snapped them open and closed rapidly. Geoff winced, squeezing his eyes shut as he saw the blurring blades approach his head.

When Geoff stepped out of the barber shop twenty minutes later, glad once again to breathe, daylight was starting to fade. He hadn't realized how late it had gotten. His mother let him walk to the barbershop as long as he made it back before dark. Now it was going to be close.

And he wanted to get home before dark. Darkness scared him now. Darkness reminded him of that night behind the Tin Man's house. Darkness reminded him of Jason Nightingale.

A pinging sounded to his left. Mr. Under was up working late, carving out another dead person's name on a gravestone. Just like Jason's. Whose turn was it now?

A clicking sounded behind him, startling him, and he turned to see Nick locking the door to the barber shop. Nick smiled at Geoff.

"Need a ride, sonny?" Dirty, rotten teeth smiled at him.

"All set," Geoff said, looking at the red spot on the barber's smock and quickly crossing the street to the boardwalk. He looked behind him when he reached the wooden planks and saw the barber still standing outside his shop, staring at him. It looked like great big splotches of red coated the front of his smock. The old man waved. Geoff turned away.

Out on the middle of the lake an empty rowboat drifted aimlessly.

Carrothead was up ahead on the boardwalk and Geoff didn't want an encounter with him, so he kept his head down and quickened his steps, hoping to just walk right by without contact.

As he passed him, Carrothead reached out and grabbed his arm. Geoff spun around.

"Hey!" Carrothead yelled. Geoff stared up at him, wishing he would just leave him alone. He wanted everybody to leave him alone.

"Someone's looking for you," Carrothead said and held out his walkie-talkie.

"What are you talking about?" Geoff stared at the device that emanated only static.

"Go on," Carrothead said, extending his arm. "He wants to talk to you."

"Who?" Geoff leaned away, as if the walkie-talkie were diseased, just like Carrothead's brain.

"You know who." Carrothead laughed in a deep throaty rumble.

Was it him? Geoff wondered. Could it be Jason? Was that who he was talking about? But it couldn't be. Jason couldn't talk. Jason had torn into his own throat with his fingernails because he couldn't get any air, so his throat wouldn't work. He couldn't say anything and never would, because now he was buried underground in a box that must have felt very much like that refrigerator. A small, confined space with no air and no way out.

No way out, that is, unless someone had opened the door.

That's all it would have taken, someone opening the door. And if Geoff had thought to do it sooner than he did, Jason would have been okay. Sure he would have been steamed and probably would have told on them, but that would have been better than this. Any punishment would have been better than feeling miserable during the day and frightened during the night.

The night.

It was getting darker and Geoff had to get out of the night. He looked at Carrothead's drooling grin.

"I don't want to talk to anybody," Geoff said and turned to run up Autumn Avenue. This time he didn't look back, but could feel Carrothead's eyes on him. In the distance, he could still hear the pinging from Mr. Under's shop.

Geoff slowed as he passed the Peas sisters' house; two of them were sitting in rockers on their front porch. At least a dozen cats were sprawled over the porch steps, railing and floor.

"Geoffrey!" one of the sisters called out.

He turned to look. The cats stirred, rising up onto their haunches and stretching.

"Come here, Geoffrey," she called again. "We have milk and cookies!" The other sister erupted with bellowing laughter, her great fat body shaking, the wooden planks of the porch screeching under the strain.

Geoff didn't answer them, but he kept looking over his shoulder.

"Hurry home, Geoffrey," the first sister continued. "It's getting dark!" Then she joined her sister in laughing, and the cats began hissing at him. Several of the cats jumped down from the porch and sprinted across the lawn after him.

Geoff started running again, faster than before till the house was out of sight, but he could still hear the faint sound of the Peas sisters' laughter. Looking behind him, several of the furry little creatures were still on his heels, hissing and screeching as they gained on him.

Geoff cut right between a pair of houses, figuring he'd take a shortcut through a few backyards to get to Maple Street. At one point, passing a row of elms, he stopped, crouching behind one to catch his breath. He peeked around the corner of the tree trunk. The dark yard before him was quiet. All he saw was an empty sandbox with an overturned plastic bucket and a discarded shovel; beside it was an abandoned, rusty swing set. There was no sign of the cats. Maybe they had lost his scent and given up the chase.

Geoff crept across the yard at a slower, but still steady, pace. He didn't like how quiet the night had become. That was usually an ominous sign. At least that was how it was in most of the stories he wrote.

Up ahead was a stone well.

He tried to figure out whose yard he was in. The house didn't look familiar. Maple Street should have been just over the crest ahead.

A moaning sound drifted toward him. He stopped and looked around. Was someone hurt?

It sounded like it was coming from ... the well.

He approached slowly, still confused as to why he'd never noticed this well before. It was just sitting there, in the middle of an overgrown lawn, the crumbling rocks barely holding together to form the circular walls. When he got to it, he laid both hands onto the edge of its cold stones and leaned forward to peer down into its emptiness.

A moan emanated from below, faint.

"Hello?" Geoff called, looking into the black hole for some movement. "Is someone down there?" His voice echoed into the cavernous pit.

He heard a scraping sound as something stirred below. Had someone fallen down the well? There was definitely something moving down there. Maybe one of the Peas sisters' cats fell in.

The scraping and scratching sounds got louder.

Something was climbing up the wall of the well.

"Help," came a hoarse voice. Someone *was* down there.

"Hello," Geoff called again.

"Geoffrey?" answered the voice.

Geoff's heart froze. Whatever it was, it knew his name. He tried to back away, but his hands gripped the stones so tight his fingers were locked into place.

Clouds drifted away from the moon and it helped shed a little light down a few feet along the rim of the well. Geoffrey could hear heavy breathing as whomever it was struggled to climb up the rocks. There was a shape emerging from the dark center of the well.

Geoff watched the line on the stones where the moonlight stopped and the darkness began. A hand, then another, reached up over that edge.

The tips of the fingers were bloody, probably from gripping the stones hand over hand during the climb.

A face broke through the dark surface, like rising out of a lake, and Geoff saw Jason's bulging eyes, pale face and blackened tongue.

"Help me, Geoff." The words lolled out of its constricted throat as a hand extended toward him.

The shock broke Geoff's grip and he backed away from the well. "No!"

Geoff turned and ran, looking back over his shoulder to see Jason clambering over the side of the stone structure. He kept running and didn't stop till he reached his house. He burst through the door out of breath, locking it, and the night, behind him.

"What's all the commotion?" his mother asked from the living room.

"Nothing," Geoff mumbled and began to head upstairs.

"Wait, let me see your haircut."

Geoff stopped halfway up and turned to face his mother who had gotten off the couch and came to the bottom of the stairs.

"Very nice," she said. "Nick always does a good job."

Are you kidding? Geoff thought. The man's a butcher.

"Now go do any homework you might have."

Geoff turned and bounded the rest of the way up the stairs. Once in his room he shut his door and went to his desk. But no, it wasn't homework he was going to do. He had finished that in school. But there was something else he had to do. No, wanted to do. No, needed to do.

He opened up one of the desk drawers and looked at the pile of typed pages inside. There were his stories. Tales of horror he had written over the past couple years. Many times after school he would sit in the clubhouse alone with a pen and a notebook and scribble out a tale. Then he convinced his parents to get him a typewriter at the used office supply store downtown, and he would type up his tales in his room at night.

And this was his stack of stories about all the horrible things his imagination could conjure up: Oscar the telepathic rat, the haunted well, the moose head that seeks revenge on the hunter, the ghostly baseball team, the prehistoric fish in the lake, the carnivorous caterpillar and many others.

Geoff looked above his desk at a shelf that held all the monster models he had made from the kits his parents got him for birthdays, Christmas, and sometimes just because they knew he liked them. The bookcase on the left held the horror novels and anthologies that inspired him over the years. On top of the bookcase were a collection of rubber dinosaurs. Posters from horror movies were tacked to the walls of his bedroom.

And before him on the desk was his typewriter.

He blew dust off it. The ribbon was probably dry. It had been a while since a tale of terror had been typed with these keys. Not since that night at the Tin Man's house. He grabbed a blank sheet of paper from another drawer and rolled it into the machine, then took a deep breath.

No, it had been awhile. He loved writing horror stories, loved letting his imagination loose where it would reach its tentacles out into the world and gather up the dark twisted things that existed out there in the night.

The night and the dark.

Now he knew there were horrible things out there for real. He had seen real horror in the Tin Man's back yard when he climbed that mound of metal and opened that damn door. He had stared into the face of horror, into those panicked glassy eyes and into that dark mouth opened in a silent scream with its black tongue hanging out.

And those twisted hands with the bloody fingernails had tried to reach out and grab him. Tried to pull him into that dark refrigerator where the door would shut and he would not be able to escape the grip of those dead fingernails with pieces of flesh beneath the tips. Those fingers would dig into his skin and hold him as the air was sucked out of that confined space.

Geoff let out a breath and looked at the blank piece of paper. He brought his hands up and rested his fingertips on the keys.

If I can only write something, he thought. Some monster tale that would remind him of how much fun it was to write these stories. That's what it was all about: fun. Monsters were fun; everyone liked monsters. That's why people young and old celebrated them every Halloween. Who didn't like a monster?

Unless of course, Geoff thought, the monster was me. A monster that would let a little boy die in a dark confined space where he would try to rip his own throat out just to get some air. No one likes that kind of monster.

Geoff withdrew his fingers from the keys, lay his hands on the desktop and put his head down on top of them.

"I can't do it."

"What's the matter?" The voice came from behind him.

Geoff lifted his head and looked back. The Joker stood in the middle of his room, though it wasn't his bedroom anymore. It was now that attic room in the corner of his brain where his stories came from and the Joker inhabited.

"I'm afraid," Geoff said.

"Afraid of what?" The Joker approached his desk.

"Afraid of writing."

"Don't be such a fraidy-cat."

"Everything scares me now."

"They're just stories," the Joker said. "They can't hurt anybody."

"But they're not fun anymore. Nothing is fun anymore. Not since …" He looked at the Joker. "Well, you know."

"But you can't stop," the Joker said, his face a bit sad and rejected. "We need each other."

"What do you mean?" Geoff asked.

"We depend on each other, feed off each other. We're together in this, till the end. We can't exist without each other." The Joker took a step closer and placed a white-gloved hand on Geoffrey's shoulder. It felt surprisingly reassuring.

"Geoffrey!" A distant voice came from somewhere outside.

Geoff stood up, went to the open window and looked out. There was a figure down below in the back yard.

It was Jason.

"Geoffrey," he called out again.

He could see the lifeless eyes, the black tongue when he opened his mouth and the red scratches on his neck.

"Come on out, Geoffrey," Jason said. "Come out and play Relievo!"

"No," Geoff yelled down. "I'm not coming out. It's dark."

"It's not dark where I am," Jason said. "Come on out, you'll see."

"Don't," said the Joker from over Geoff's right shoulder. "It's a trick."

"Go away," Geoff yelled back down. "We don't want to come out."

"Then let me come in," Jason called back.

Geoff stood silent for a moment, turning to look at the Joker who shook his head slowly from side to side.

"Sorry," Geoff yelled out the window. "I just can't."

"Sure you can," Jason said. "Just open the door. It's as simple as that."

"No," Geoff said, trying to remember if he had locked the door tonight when he came home. He sure hoped he did.

"I have cigars!" Jason yelled up and then began laughing.

Geoff backed away from the window. He wiped sweat off his brow with the back of his hand. It was hot in his room. But summer was just starting. It shouldn't be this hot already. He could feel heat rising behind him and turned to see the walls engulfed in flames. Fire crept along the floor eating up the carpet and swarming up his desk.

No! he thought. Not my stories.

The typewriter began to melt, caving in on itself, the letters on the keys running together and flowing out, forming twisted words.

Flames leapt onto the bookcase and the shelf above the desk, grabbing onto the legs of Geoff's monster models, liquefying the plastic as the creatures writhed in their own melting horror.

The bookcase became a conflagration as the pages of the books fed the fire that rose up shelf by shelf till it reached the top where the rubber dinosaurs sunk into a pool like timeless beasts in a black tar pit.

Geoff heard laughter and turned to see the Joker, his suit in flames, thrashing in a crazed St. Vitus dance. The Joker stretched a flaming gloved hand out toward him.

"Come on, Geoff," the Joker said. "Dance with me!"

Geoff backed away as smoke swirled around him. He began to cough and covered his nose and mouth with a cupped hand. He looked around for a way out, but flames were everywhere and the Joker danced circles around him.

There was the window, but Jason was out there. He couldn't go out that way. He wouldn't.

He dropped to his knees as the smoke thickened and it began getting harder to breathe. His clothes were soaked with sweat as the temperature rose. Through the smoke he saw a door and began crawling toward it. *Strange, though,* he thought. There was no door in the attic room. Where had that come from?

He got to it and reached up to grab the doorknob. It was hot and burned his hand, but he managed to turn it and pull it open enough to crawl through and close it behind him.

He found himself in a dark and small space, the walls close around him; it must be a closet. He curled up in a corner, bringing his knees to his chest and wrapping one arm around them, keeping the other arm up to his mouth to ward off the smoke that seeped through the underside of the door.

His lungs burned and his throat thickened as smoke choked him. Everything was dark and his eyes stung and watered.

Is this what it's like to suffocate? he thought. Is this how Jason felt, not being able to breathe? Yes, it must be. Geoff had the urge to claw at his own throat but knew how useless it would be.

Just die, Geoff thought. You deserve it. It was as much your fault as anyone else's. Just close your eyes and let the darkness take you.

There was a knock on the door.

No, Geoff thought. *(Don't open it).* The door must remain closed.

But there was light as the door slid slowly open.

The Joker stood in the doorway. Smoke flowed out of the closet and Geoff could breathe once again. The Joker was blackened from burns, his clothes melted onto his scorched flesh, his face torched, his jester cap singed. But his teeth were white as he smiled in the doorway and extended one blackened hand.

"You didn't think I would leave you did you?" the Joker said.

Geoff coughed and spat out thick black phlegm.

"I was afraid."

"Don't be afraid," the Joker said. "I will never leave you."

"Never?"

"Like I said. We need each other. Where would I be without you? And you me?"

"I don't know," Geoff said, reaching up and taking the Joker's hand.

"Let's hope you never have to find out."

CHAPTER EIGHT

I spent the night in the Malton town jail. It wasn't very pleasant. The cell was cold, the bed hard. They took my shoes because I had the option of taking out the laces or giving them the whole pair. I didn't want to bother with the trouble of taking out the laces when I knew I'd only have to re-lace them later.

When I first woke up in the cell, I was disoriented. I had no idea where I was, or why. Then the night's events came back to me.

I remembered sitting in the back of a police cruiser, my hands cuffed behind me, and watching them pull Oliver's body off the spiked fence and load him into a plastic bag just like the others.

My wound was superficial, just a scratch. It only took a couple stitches to close. Only a dull, throbbing pain remained. My face was bruised a bit. At the police station, I went over the story half a dozen times with Hooper, stressing the fact I was defending myself from Oliver. I wasn't sure if he believed me.

When they put me in a cell, I had no idea what was going to happen to me.

And now as I sat on my bunk, my feet resting on the stone floor that sent cold chills up through my socks, I began to think I might never get out of here. Hooper had hated our club back when we were kids. We had caused nothing but aggravation for him. He seemed to have carried that hatred with him into the present. And now he had the perfect opportunity to get revenge by putting one of us away for a heinous crime. I didn't think I stood a chance.

They gave me my shoes back and I was brought into Hooper's office. It reminded me of the time the whole club was brought in here after the Halloween incident with the "Colonel's" mummified corpse. He had tried hard to pin that on us. I imagined he would try even harder to pin this on me.

He sat at his desk across from me and took a bite from a hunk of pepperoni, staring back at me in silence. He made me re-tell my whole story from the moment he dismissed the three of us from the Little League field to how I happened to go up into Oliver's room. Then he gave me a reverse angle of the whole scene as told to him from Mary Torr, who had been with Oliver from the moment I dropped him off at the inn to Oliver's arrival at the room. How he had been going up to his room with Mary Torr when he heard someone moving around and told her to go to her room and wait for him there.

All thoughts left my mind about the fact that I was suspected of murder. All I could think of was Mary Torr. She was going up to his room with him? It was unbelievable. I was enraged and jealous at the same time. Did she realize what kind of man he was? That he was married? Was he that charming with women? What was she thinking?

"Prints were done on the knife," the chief said, interrupting my thoughts. "Only Mr. Rench's were on it."

I regained my perspective on where I was and why.

"I'm willing to accept the self-defense theory," he finished.

"Are you checking the knife?" I asked, "to see if it matches Dale and Lonny's wounds?"

"In time," he said. "Mr. Rench committed the murders as far as I'm concerned. That will be the conclusion in my report to the county attorney's office."

"Just like that?"

"I'm happy with the results."

"But, you are going to check his knife out?"

"Not your concern. I'm letting you go. Be happy with that." The stench of pepperoni hung in front of my face. "We'll be in touch with you if we need anything further."

He didn't really care. For all I knew, he could still think I did it, but he had a possible suspect, dead, and that was enough to satisfy him. No need for a long messy trial. No need for any more attention on the town.

"I want you to leave town now," he said. "I'd rather you didn't come back."

I was stunned.

"You're not going to check this out more?" I was almost angry that he was willing to accept the conclusion I had come to myself. He was willing to accept anything as long as it made a neat finish to the whole sordid mess. I was ready to argue against my own defense.

"It's over!" he yelled. "You can leave town. And you're not welcome back."

I sat there looking at him, knowing he didn't care anything about justice. He just wanted his town back to its routine.

"Get your things at the inn and leave." Pieces of pepperoni flew from his mouth onto his desk.

I stood up from my chair. I was almost waiting for him to pull some trick. This was all too easy.

"You can get your valuables from the sergeant at the desk."

"We'll be keeping an eye on you," Hooper said. "Making sure you really leave."

I looked back at him. There was no reason to stay here anyway, I thought. There was nothing left for me here.

When I got to the inn, I got in my car and drove over toward the west side of town. I wanted to see Martin before I left. I pulled into his driveway, killing the engine, and strode to the front door wondering what he was thinking of me and what I had done.

I rang the doorbell.

I stood there, hearing the noisy quacking of ducks in the back yard, and then heard a faint voice coming from somewhere deep within the house.

"Martin?" An old woman's voice. "Are you there, Martin?" It was Mrs. Peak.

I hesitated, and then rang the bell again.

"Martin, there's someone at the door!"

I felt uncomfortable.

I turned to go when the continual noise of the ducks made me realize Martin might be out back feeding them. I walked around the side of the house to the back. I didn't see Martin. The quacking was loud and grating. They were running all around the edge of the pond. None of them were in the pond itself. As I approached I could see why.

Martin's body floated face-down in the middle of the water.

My knees almost buckled.

Swirls of red permeated the area around his body.

The ducks danced around my feet, their quacking growing louder, penetrating my eardrums like an alarm clock buzzer that refused to shut off.

"SHUT THE FUCK UP!" I screamed at the ducks.

The noise hindered my thoughts. I needed to think. What was happening here? It was supposed to be over! But what did Oliver say before he died? *It's far from over.* That was it. Maybe he had gotten here before I killed him. Murdered Martin and saved me for last. But no. What was it Hooper had said? Mary Torr had been with Oliver from the moment Martin and I had dropped him off at the inn.

I turned and ran.

It wasn't Oliver!

I got around to the front of the house and headed for the car. As I got in, I could still hear the voice calling out from upstairs in the house.

"Martin! Where are you? Why don't you answer?"

I got in the car and drove away.

If Mary was with him, then Oliver couldn't have gotten to Martin. I killed Oliver and it wasn't even him. Oh Christ!

The pain started in the little attic room. The walls were bulging. The horror was trying to get out. I might have been the last one to see Martin alive. Just like I was the last to see Dale and Lonny. Why was it always me? But no. I wasn't the last to see them. Of course not. The killer was the last to see them, not me. Right?

My head was pounding by the time I got to the inn.

I didn't see anyone around as I went up to my room. The room itself was a mess. Hooper and his men must have gone through it last night. The bureau drawers were open and clothes were strewn everywhere. I grabbed my suitcase and started throwing everything into it. I didn't care about neatness. I just wanted to get the hell out of there.

When everything was packed, I looked at the manuscript on the desk and the blank piece of paper in the carriage of the typewriter. Maybe I needed to write a quick fix to this story. Give it a neat tidy ending. The left side of my head pounded as my fingers tapped against the keys. After a few minutes, I pulled the piece of paper out and placed it on top of the others. I didn't like the way this story was turning out. This wasn't the way I wanted to write it. I tossed the manuscript into the suitcase.

As a came upon the first floor landing, the moose head's eyes rolled to look at me. I tried to ignore them as I passed and continued down the stairs.

"Leaving so soon?" the moose head said behind me.

As I stepped off the stairs to the lobby, I heard faint voices off beyond the den. They were coming from the dining room. Though I knew the dining room was closed and was going to ignore it, I hesitated before going out the door.

The voices were joined by a jingling sound.

I set my suitcase and typewriter case down and walked to the dining room.

At one of the round tables sat Oliver, Lonny, Dale, Martin, Woody and the Joker. They were playing cards: Blackjack. The Joker was dealing.

I didn't even want to move, didn't even try, but my legs approached the table.

"Hit me," Oliver said, and the Joker dealt him a card face up. "Again." Another card was flipped. "I'm good."

"What's going on?" I asked.

Lonny rapped his knuckles on the table and the Joker flipped up a card. He rapped again and another cared was flipped.

"I'm busted," he said, disgusted.

"What are you doing here?" I asked.

The Joker turned to look at me. "Everyone's here together. Isn't that how you want it to be?" He was smiling.

I walked over to Oliver.

"I'm sorry," I said. It was all I could say.

"Don't think about it," Oliver said, his teeth stained with blood. "I believed it was you. I wanted to get you, before you got me."

I looked around the table.

I'm the only one left. The last of the Jokers Club.

Martin placed his cards down on the table. "I'll stand," he said. His chest was full of puncture wounds. Dale was beside him, holding his cards, his whole front split open.

"I don't like this," I said.

"It's not that bad, Geoff," Lonny said, the slit in his throat moving in tandem with his lips. "It really didn't hurt that much. It felt kind of like a paper cut, only much deeper."

I looked to Woody. The fingers holding his cards were fleshless. Only patches of skin remained over the grayish bone of his skull. He looked at me and his lipless mouth opened.

"It had to come to this," he said. "It was our destiny."

I looked to the Joker who still grinned at me.

He gestured with the deck of cards in his hand. "Do you want to play?"

"No," I said. "I'm tired of games."

I looked the Joker square in his puppet-like eyes.

"Did Jason send you?" I asked.

"Of course not," he said, shaking his head, his bells jingling. "I came here to help you."

"Then help me," I screamed realization dawning on me. "Did I kill anybody?"

"Are you capable of killing somebody?"

I looked at Oliver, who sat at the table with a disgruntled look on his face. *But that wasn't murder*, I thought. That was an accident. Just like Jason's death was an accident. We never meant to kill anybody. Did we?

"I'm confused," I said, turning away from the table. The pounding in my head amplified. It throbbed, and I wished it would stop.

"Why are you confused?" the Joker's voice came from behind.

"I'm not sure of any of the answers."

The pounding grew louder.

"Where can you find the answers?"

"I'm not sure," I said, raising my voice to hear myself over the pounding in my head. "The answers may be in the past."

"Then why don't you go find them."

"I don't know where to start."

The pounding was deafening, and I realized it was not only in my head. It came from outside me. It came from the kitchen. It came from the refrigerator.

(Time to open the door.)

"Start from the beginning," the Joker said.

The Tin Man's house.

When I pulled up to the Tin Man's house, my heart was pounding along with my head. I got out of the car and looked around. The street was empty. I turned and looked at the house, scanning the shade-covered windows for Emeric Rust. The entire place bore no signs of life.

Hearing a whisper of sound, I looked to one of the windows on the right side of the second floor where a shade fluttered. Out of the corner of my eye, I thought I saw a glimpse of a hand pulling away from the edge. I couldn't be sure. But the shade did sway back and forth slightly, though no breeze could be blowing in because the window was shut.

I walked around to the back of the yard.

There stood the junk pile.

I expected this towering mass of twisted metal and aluminum, but it was much smaller than I remembered, barely more than a small stack.

Grass had grown up around the edges of the pile, almost overtaking it. There was even a small tree that had somehow managed to sprout up in the middle and now rose above. I imagined the young sapling as it grew up, weaving its way through the gaps between discarded scraps of metal and tin, striving to reach the sunlight that filtered down through the cracks.

Life had grown from a pile that had held death.

I stood before the junk, as if it were some kind of altar. I heard the jingling behind me and turned to see the Joker.

"I'm here," I said.

"And why are you here?" he asked.

"Because death has been here, and I can smell its scent."

"And what form has it taken?"

"That's what I want to know."

"Well, look there," the Joker said, extending his arm, pointing his index finger, "and see if you can recognize it."

My eyes followed the path of his finger. It pointed to a large, broken piece of glass that stood perched halfway up the mound like a mirror hanging on a bathroom wall. I stepped up to it and looked in.

My reflection stared back at me.

I looked at my bruised, haggard, disoriented face. I almost didn't recognize myself.

Then as I stepped aside, another face appeared in the reflection, just behind mine. It was a face framed in glass. Its eyes were vacuous. I recognized it. It was a face that had peered out of glass at me before. Once behind the window of a locked cell at Acorn Estates. And once from a second floor window at the Tower House Inn.

I spun around.

Mary stood behind me.

My head had become an engine, with a driving, locomotive beat. I shook it to clear it, with no avail.

"I don't get it," I said, confused.

"None of them did," she said. "Until I told them. Torr is my married name. I kept it, even after my divorce." She smiled. "My maiden name is Mary Nightingale."

I saw a little girl's face as she held her mother's hand at Jason's funeral, looking at me with eyes sad and cold.

"I made sure they all knew," she said. "Before I killed them."

I looked down at her hand and saw the hunting knife it held. The blade was much longer than Oliver's.

"I saw you," I said, still in shock. "At Acorn Estates."

She smiled. "That's where I met Woody. It was quite a coincidence, us both ending up there. He had no idea who I was, but I remembered. I befriended him. And after we both got out, we dated. He never had a clue." Her grin was widening. "He confessed to me. Told me about what you all did to my brother. I pretended to sympathize with him. I even got him to arrange this whole reunion. He had no idea what I was planning till it was too late."

"Where is he now?" I asked, afraid of the answer.

"Buried, deep in a forest."

I shuddered.

"He seemed willing to accept it," she continued. "As if it was inevitable."

I felt dizzy.

"The others were more reluctant," she said. "Their eyes begged forgiveness when I finished them off."

I swayed a bit, my balance weakening. I wanted to tell her it wasn't our fault, but I knew I couldn't be convincing. Not even to myself.

She took a step forward. "It had all been going so well," she said, "until you spoiled it. I wanted Oliver the most. Then you went and killed him on me."

I remembered her wild anger at his death.

"I wished you hadn't done that," she said. "That made me very unhappy."

My body wanted to turn and run, but my limbs wouldn't cooperate. My legs were anchored in place. My head was spinning and black dots were bursting before my eyes. I was having another spell and it couldn't have been a more inappropriate moment. I tried to speak, tried to buy myself some time, but that had recently become my enemy.

"Jason wouldn't tell you to do this," I said.

"Jason can't breathe," she answered, still coming forward. "Jason called me a few days after he disappeared. He told me he couldn't breathe. He asked me to help him."

Her voice became rapid, high-pitched.

"I wanted to help him," she continued. "But he forgot to tell me where he was. I could have saved him if he only told me where he was!"

My legs gave way, and I fell to my knees. She came closer and stood before me. Maybe it was better this way, I thought. I might not be around much longer anyway. Maybe it was justice that things end this way.

My body had no will to struggle. My mind was willing to accept it.

She moved forward.

"Now," she said. "This is the only way I can help him."

I saw the blade move before me.

It glistened.

I closed my eyes.

Just like a paper cut, I thought.

There was a loud thunk, and my eyes popped open.

Mary stood before me, and her eyes rolled up in her head. She pitched forward and fell to the ground in front of me.

Behind her was the ancient figure of Emeric Rust.

He stood there, rail thin, clutching the long-handled spade shovel that he had just clubbed her with. His hair like snow, his face a mass of wrinkles, his eyes bugging out. He took a step closer and peered down at me.

"KEEP OUT OF MY YARD!" he yelled.

CODA

Chief Hooper had meant what he said about keeping an eye out for me. His men must have seen me heading toward the old neighborhood, and he went out after me. But he had arrived just a bit too late. If Emeric Rust hadn't stopped Mary, I would have been dead. It had been scary coming so close to the end.

But death might be coming soon enough. I was still standing a little too near it.

Mary was unconscious when they strapped her onto a stretcher and hauled her away. I had no doubt she would soon be heading back to Acorn Estates. I explained everything to the chief but still did not say anything about what had really happened to Jason Nightingale. I kept our oath. I was the last one left and the secret would die with me.

The chief talked with Emeric Rust and then had me come down to the station to file a statement for his report. Afterwards, I was once again told to leave town and it was suggested I not return. I didn't think I would. There was nothing left for me here.

I was the last of the Jokers Club.

I sat in my car outside the station, toying with my keys, hesitating before inserting them into the ignition. I glanced out of the car window at the steeple on the town hall and saw that the clocks were finally working. It was almost eleven o'clock in the morning.

I drove to the inn to retrieve my stuff and then headed down to the used office supply store to return the typewriter. The jingling sound as I opened the door startled me, and I whipped my head around, expecting the Joker to be there. I realized it was only the bell on the door, and I breathed a sigh of relief. The old man came out from a back room, adjusting his glasses. I set the typewriter case on the counter.

"All set?" the old man said, opening the case and examining its contents.

"I think I've done all I can with this," I replied.

He nodded several times, still looking over the machine. He glanced up at me. "Work out okay for you?"

"It worked very well indeed." Yes, it worked just fine. I guess you could say I was quite pleased with it. "Thank you very much."

I paid him the remainder of my bill and turned to go. I heard the bell jingle and looked to see who might be coming in the door. But the door was closed.

I looked to the right side of the store and saw the Joker sitting behind an oak desk with a pile of papers in front of him. My insides felt hollow. No, I thought. I had had enough of this and didn't want to deal with it anymore. I approached and sat down in a chair across from him.

"It's all over," I said. "I thought you'd be gone."

"I'll always be here," he said, lips spread in that stupid grin of his. "Just like I always have been."

"Always?" I questioned, confused.

He nodded. "From the beginning."

"From when I first conjured you up?" I asked, thinking about the little attic room in my mind where I imagined all the horrors that became the seeds for my stories and ideas. That dark room of evil thoughts and death whose only tenant besides the creepy things that lurked there was the Joker. The Joker who whispered those sick tales to my mind.

"Oh, from even well before that," he said. "From the very beginning."

I was confused. "How could that be? I created you back then. You couldn't have existed before then."

"You only created this image you see before you. Where do you think the wellspring of horror in your mind came from?"

"I created it," I cried. "I imagined all those things, those stories. Because I chose to."

The Joker shook his head, bells jingling. "You didn't have any choice. You never did."

The muscles in my face went slack as my jaw opened. I looked at his beady little eyes.

"I know what you are," I said. I thought of all the sick things and horrors that seeped out of my head onto the pages of paper. I never stopped to think why. Never cared where they came from. "Don't you realize what you're doing to me?"

"It's not my fault," the Joker said. "I just want us to be together, just like always."

"But why did you show yourself now, after all this time?"

"I got tired of festering alone."

"What will happen to my imagination when you're gone?" The idea scared me.

He looked up from his reading. He looked serious. "You really don't want to find out."

He glanced back down at the papers in front of him on the desk.

"What are you reading?"

"The ending to the story."

"Where did you get that manuscript?"

"Why, you gave it to me, of course." His lips moved as he read the last page in his hands, and then looked up at me. "So the woman at the inn turns out to be Jason Nightingale's sister. A little contrived isn't it?"

"I told you before, my stories aren't contrived." I felt the need to defend myself.

He looked puzzled. "When did you finish this?"

"At the inn, when I first went back to get my stuff."

"Are you sure? That was before you went to the Tin Man's house."

I was now puzzled. "I'm not sure. I think so."

"How did you know how it was going to end?"

"I'm a writer. I'm supposed to know the ending."

"Even before it happens."

I looked into his quizzical eyes. "Maybe I'm a better writer than I thought I was."

I reached to take the manuscript away from him, not wanting to think anymore about the story right now. Afraid of what I might learn from it.

A hand came down and stopped me. I looked at it and noticed the Joker's hand was no longer gloved and the sleeve was white instead of the black and white striped pattern.

"Why did you change the story, Geoffrey?"

"What do you mean?" I was afraid to look up at his face. "I didn't change anything. This is the way it all happened."

"I see a couple of very big changes," he said.

I pushed away from the desk and stood up, turning away from him, but before I looked away, I could see that he did not have make-up on and wasn't wearing the jester costume. Instead he wore a white doctor's coat. His face was different. It wasn't the Joker sitting behind the oak desk.

There was a full-length mirror on the wall in front of me and I could see my reflection.

"You changed the story for a reason, Geoffrey."

"No. That's the story." The image staring back at me in the mirror was long and thin, skin drawn tight on the cheek and jawbones like dried leather. There were dark bags beneath bloodshot eyes swallowed up in their sockets.

"You changed the story," the doctor continued, "because you wanted to deny the fact that you killed your friends ..."

"No."

"... and that you were the one who opened the refrigerator door that night."

"I can tell the story anyway I want," I said, staring into my emaciated reflection. "I'm a writer."

THE END